THE TIMES
& DILLONS
SUMMER
ANTHOLOGY
1995

Hodder & Stoughton

Contents

Published by Hodder and Stoughton
A division of Hodder Headline PLC

Printed and bound in Great Britain by
Cox & Wyman Ltd, Reading, Berkshire

Hodder and Stoughton
A division of Hodder Headline PLC
338 Euston Road
London NW1 3BH

SANDRA BENÍTEZ

Extract from her new novel

A Place Where the Sea Remembers

A *Place Where the Sea Remembers* is available now at your local Dillons store priced £5.99.

Bring this voucher with you to obtain £1.00 off the publisher's prices at all Dillons stores.

A PLACE WHERE THE SEA REMEMBERS
by Sandra Benítez

This voucher entitles you to *£1* OFF *A Place Where the Sea Remembers by Sandra Benítez*

CONDITIONS

- *This voucher is only redeemable at Dillons Bookstores.*
- *Only one voucher may be redeemed per transaction.*
- *This voucher may not be used in conjunction with any other offer and is not exchangeable for cash.*

Promoter: Dillons Bookstore, Berwick House, 35 Livery Street, Birmingham, B3 2PB
Offer closes 31st October 1995

Candelario Marroquín

El Ensaladero (ensaladero, n.m. salad-maker)

On the day after his promotion to salad-maker, Candelario
Marroquín painted the door of his house a robin's egg blue.
The color blue was an obsession for him. Since his youth he
had found comfort in the special blueness of new mornings.
The azure stars that edged Our Lady's mantle inspired him
almost always to pray. And the glinting cobalt of the sea
produced in him such excitement that he was forced at
times to turn his back on it. 'When it comes to blue,' his
wife Chayo said, 'who can understand him?' She was away
when he began to paint the door. She had taken a basketful
of paper flowers to the beach in hopes of selling them to
tourists.

Candelario worked at his door in an act of quiet cel-
ebration. Each stroke of the brush soothed him and left
him more at peace. Now that he had advanced from a mere
waiter to the salad-maker, he would wear the cummerbund
and the stiff bow tie. His small, thick body would look
distinguished and important in the room where so many

dined. Salary and tips would increase too. In the years since they had married, Candelario and Chayo had worked hard and earned little. It was the way of life here in Santiago. When he lived behind the mountain range that stretched all the way to Mexico City, Candelario had tended the bulls that later would be sent to fight. His work had been brutal, but there was always enough to eat and, most times, enough pesos left over for a glass or two of pulque in the cantina.

Since marrying he had become a much more serious man. At Chayo's insistence he had given up the bulls for a more tranquil life. He did not drink anymore, for the pesos he made at the restaurant would not allow such indulgence. Chayo, too, felt the weight of life's difficulties. The tourists were sometimes so clever at bargaining that she could never count on much from the sale of her bouquets. But all that was in the past. Now that he was the salad-maker, their lot was sure to improve.

It was a good day for painting. The sun was high and there was hardly a breeze. Candelario Marroquín stepped back to admire his handiwork. The enamel had taken smoothly to the metal door. At the top, where the paint was nearly dry, the door reflected the brightness of the morning. I can thank the *patrón* for this, he thought. Don Gustavo del Norte owned the restaurant in which Candelario worked. Don Gustavo was a large man, soft-muscled but surprisingly quick in manner. He had opened his establishment not long after moving to Santiago. Five months before, he had left Guadalajara, where he had lived for many years. There he had owned a glass factory in the nearby village of Tlaquepaque. Candelario Marroquín had never been so far away and could not himself imagine a village spilling over with tiny shops, all dependent on the whims of tourists. He had asked Hortencio, the wine steward, about this. Hortencio had worked for don Gustavo in the glass factory, and he knew about merchants and about the ways of a city like Guadalajara.

'Why did Don Gustavo leave one business for another?' Candelario asked. 'Doesn't Don Gustavo know more about glassmaking than about food?'

Hortencio had not answered either question. Instead, he had shrugged his shoulders and continued to polish the silver cup that dangled from the chain he wore around his neck.

Candelario squatted to paint the bottom third of the door. It was not for him to question the *patrón's* motives. Don Gustavo was a man of clever ideas. It was his most recent belief that the tourists of Santiago deserved other things to eat than tacos and enchiladas. Just last week he had told Candelario that he would offer something different, feature some specialty for which the restaurant might become known. He had settled on the Caesar salad. Don Gustavo himself had instructed Candelario on how to make it. 'For a perfect Caesar,' the *patrón* said, 'the correct bowl is essential.' He had brought just the one from Guadalajara. It was wide at the base and lacquered black with squat, bowed sides. 'You must prepare this salad with a flair,' don Gustavo said. Candelario Marroquín had taken to this requirement. Secretly, he was proud of his ways in the bullring. Now he would transfer his bravura to the salad cart.

'We have anchovies,' Candelario said as he finished up the painting. He mimicked don Gustavo's instructions, wrinkling his nose at the acrid smell of the paint. 'Then comes the mustard, then the lemons.' The sun now struck the door with an intensity that made him squint. 'We have the eggs and then the romaine.' Candelario Marroquín pictured his cart: the narrow side-racks holding bottles and small shakers, the bottom shelf stacked high with plates, on the rims of which were stenciled delicate birds the color of his door.

Candelario propped his brush in the paint can and sat on the ground, his back against the wall of the house. He wiped his forehead with the back of a hand and glanced down the dry riverbed that fronted the house and led all the way to the sea. In the dry season the arroyo was used as a road, and now Chayo strode up it on her way back from the beach. Chayo's sister, Marta, came along too. Marta was fifteen, four years younger than Chayo; each had the same dark mole, high on the cheekbone under the left eye. Candelario Marroquín noted that Marta's pregnancy was not yet visible and he was glad of it. When her condition became apparent, there would be more than enough time for the town to talk.

That Chayo and he were childless he was certain the town already discussed. It perturbed him to think that his and Chayo's names could lie on the lips of so many. He often asked himself if it were pity that people felt for them. 'Poor Chayo,' he imagined people saying. 'In these two years there could have been two babies.' Candelario Marroquín bristled at the thought. He had no use for people's pity. He himself felt divided about his wife's condition. He knew that while having sons would show him to be the man he truly was, more mouths for him to feed would be a considerable burden.

Now Chayo and Marta approached Candelario. When she saw the blue door, Chayo rolled her eyes. 'It's not surprising,' she said.

Candelario said nothing, but he was pleased nonetheless at his wife's observation. The three went to sit under the lime tree growing at the edge of the yard, for they could not enter the house until the paint dried on the door handle.

'I sold all my flowers today,' Chayo said, tucking her skirt neatly under her legs. 'One tourist wanted my basket, so I sold that too.'

'She made sixteen thousand pesos,' Marta said.

'It is a fortunate day,' Candelario replied, a wave of contentment washing over him. Of late it seemed that his life had turned around. Things were going right again. 'We will buy more paint with the money. Now I can paint the inside of the house.' Candelario and Chayo's house had only one room and one window. Their marriage bed sat under the window, one side against the wall. The furniture had belonged to Chayo's mother. 'When I'm gone, I wish you to have it,' she had said.

'In a few days the doctor will be in town,' Marta said. She smoothed her dress over her belly. 'If I'm to put an end to my situation, it must be done soon. Time is running out.'

What's this? Candelario asked himself. He usually paid no attention to the women when they talked. It was his observation that, in one way or another, women always spoke of life or death. Candelario Marroquín preferred more practical subjects. Today, however, he paid close attention to what the two said.

'I don't know if it's the right thing,' Chayo said.

'It's right,' Marta replied. Although young, she had a determination and intensity of manner rare among the girls of Santiago. 'It's right because Roberto did this when I did not want it.' She struck her belly with a clenched fist. 'If I have this child, I will hate it for all my life. I will hate this child like I hate Roberto.'

Chayo said, 'Have the child. Tía Fina will help you raise it.' Marta lived with tía Fina, the women's aunt, in a rooming house in Santiago.

'Tía Fina can't do it. With her heart like it is, she can't look after children. Besides, I don't want to have a baby. I want to see the doctor when he comes. *El doctor* is the only one to help me.'

Chayo said, 'I have heard of infection, of death, resulting from what you want.'

'*El doctor* comes from Guadalajara. He has learned many things in the city. He will not harm me.'

'If you do this, you will harm your soul,' Chayo said.

Marta wrenched a handful of grass from the ground. 'Perhaps souls can be mended,' she said, allowing the grass blades to slip like rain through her fingers.

Chayo shook her head. 'Padre Mario will condemn this.'

'*El cura* cannot see into my heart. It is not for him to judge.'

For a moment the two fell silent and Candelario thought that the subject was closed and that it was Marta's straight-forwardness that had ended the conversation, but then Chayo asked, 'What about Remedios? Surely *la curandera* could tell you what to do.'

Marta turned her gaze up the arroyo. 'I don't need the healer. I know best what's good for me.'

'And the doctor?' Chayo asked. 'How much does he charge?'

'One hundred thousand pesos,' Marta said. 'I have money saved, but I still need more. If I made enough, I'd pay for this myself.' Marta cleaned rooms in the best hotel in town.

Candelario creased a lime leaf in half and let its essence escape. He rubbed the leaf's edge against his fingers dotted blue with paint. One hundred thousand pesos. If tips were good, it would take him weeks to earn that amount.

'Are you sure of the cost?' Chayo asked.

'As sure as I can be,' Marta said. 'Luz told me.' Luz worked in the hotel with Marta. She lived in the same rooming house where Marta and her aunt lived.

'*Yo soy el ensaladero*,' Candelario Marroquín said. 'Have the child. Chayo and I will take it.' He had not known that he would say this. Where had the idea come from? Could he take it back?

'Cande,' Marta said, her face going soft. She looked over at her sister whose eyes had widened and who was staring at Candelario. Marta turned to look at him too. 'Cande, are you sure?'

Candelario Marroquín squared his shoulders to show a little earnestness. 'Now that I'm the salad-maker, we will have money to raise your child.' What else could he say? He had made the offer, and it is a man's duty to honor what he says. He did not question his own decisions, no matter how hastily they were made. With the bulls, a moment of uncertainty could get you a sharp horn in the side. He looked at his wife but detected in her face only a slight pallor that caused the mole under her eye to appear darker.

Marta lightly touched her sister's shoulder. 'Chayo, will you really do this for me?'

'Cande says so, therefore it will be done.'

Marta said, 'I will hate the child less if you raise it.'

Some months later, very late at night, Candelario Marroquín arrived home from work. He placed his cummerbund and bow tie on the dresser and, because he was not sleepy, he opened the front door and stood there, looking out. Across the arroyo the little houses that stood in a row appeared like chalky bundles in the moonlight. The odor of wood smoke left behind from the day's labors drifted in, and Candelario savored this sign of his neighbors' industriousness.

'I had a dream,' Chayo said from their bed. She had been asleep when Candelario came in, but now she was propped up against the wall, her legs drawn up against her chest. Her long hair hung loose and fell like a dark mantilla over the tucks and gathers in her nightgown. She told him of the dream from which he'd awakened her.

She stood at the edge of the sea. Rhythmically the waves reached her, wetting first her toes, and then her ankles and finally her calves. She looked out to sea and tossed a sapphire-tinted flower onto each new cresting wave. She dreamed of watching her paper blossoms ride out to meet the sharp line of the horizon.

'Do you think it was a bad dream, Cande?' she asked.

'How can it be,' he replied, 'when there was so much blue in it?'

After a time, as the two lay nestled in bed, Candelario whispered, 'Don Gustavo will have important guests tomorrow. The doctor will come, the one with the clinic, the one from Guadalajara.' A cool breeze entered through the window and Chayo pulled their blanket more securely around them. 'The doctor and his wife are friends of don Gustavo. He is eager to impress them.'

Chayo was silent for a bit, but then she said, 'He is the one Marta would have gone to. He is the one who helps the women.'

Candelario had had some time to think how their life would change once Marta's baby arrived. Over the months a new thought had come to him. Could the presence of the child induce Chayo's womb to yield him up a son? He would love Marta's child for that. He knew without question that he would. In a moment of clarity, he allowed himself to look ahead. He pictured himself, in some hazy future time, the head of a family of many sons. He imagined his children eyeing with admiration his cummerbund and bow tie. Candelario sighed contentedly. 'I am a fortunate man,' he said. 'We do not need the doctor's help.' Chayo's body stiffened and she turned away and he blamed the gesture on the coolness in the room. 'I'll make the Caesar for them,' he added. 'It'll bring a good tip.'

'And if they don't like the salad?' Chayo asked. 'What will happen then?'

'You must not worry,' he said. 'If they are hard to please, I will enlighten them as I always do with the fussy ones.' In the months that he'd been salad-maker, Candelario had received some complaints about the salad, but always he had managed to ease misunderstandings. No need to involve the *patrón* in this, he'd thought. Candelario explained to the guests that this was don Gustavo's Caesar and as such it was special and very different. Candelario himself knew how different the salad was: all those greens coated with mustard and beaten egg. On one occasion he had tasted the dish and vowed never to again. How can people eat this? he had asked himself. But then, who was he to question the foods the rich enjoyed? Didn't they eat mashed potatoes and that concoction named yogurt? Candelario gave a little shudder at the thought.

Chayo said, 'The doctor and his wife. They are rich. They will drink imported wine. Hortencio's tip will be greater than yours.'

'It is not important,' Candelario said. 'I only wish for my share.' He turned and pressed himself against his wife's back, taking in the musky fragrance that was always caught in her hair.

On the following evening Candelario Marroquín watched as the visitors were seated by don Gustavo himself at a table with the best view of the sea. Candelario stood off to the side and waited for the snap of the *patrón*'s fingers. When he was called to service, he rolled his cart toward the guests. 'Good evening,' he said to the couple. He laid linen napkins across each of their laps. Don Gustavo hovered behind the doctor, a middle-aged man whose large belly kept him at a slight angle from the table. The doctor's wife was thin and very tanned; there were thick gold bracelets around her wrists. Long ago, Candelario had observed that women who were rich seemed to struggle to be thin. It was a curious thing. To have food in abundance and yet to choose to eat little.

'We'll have the Caesar,' the woman said to Candelario. 'It's a favorite, and for me, it'll be a meal.'

The doctor said, 'In addition, I'll have the beef steak and a potato.' Turning to don Gustavo, he said, 'But first, won't you join us for a glass of champagne, Gustavo? María Elena and I would like to toast your new business venture.' With an upturned hand, he made a sweeping gesture to point out the room.

'Jumping from glassmaking into the restaurant business seems to me an interesting move,' the wife said. The discs that dangled from her bracelets struck each other and made a happy sound.

'An interesting move full of hard work,' don Gustavo replied. Turning to the doctor, he added, 'It will be my pleasure to join you for a glass, but only if you're my guests.' He sat, ordered the wine from Hortencio, who stood by the table, and then clapped at Candelario to begin the salad.

'I'll watch him make the Caesar,' the woman said.

Smiling down at the cart, Candelario laid two anchovies in the bottom of the bowl. With the back of a fork he mashed them into a paste. Because the woman was watching, he put some style into the mashing.

'I passed the clinic today,' don Gustavo said. 'There was a line stretching out into the street. You're a very busy man.'

'When we come here, I don't see him until nightfall,' the doctor's wife said. 'I spend my day at the beach.'

Candelario looked up to see her take a sip from her water glass. She used a napkin to dab the corners of her bright red mouth. Candelario dipped a tablespoon into the mustard jar and dolloped three spoonfuls into the bowl. He mixed the mustard with the anchovy paste, pleased that the *patrón* could see how faithfully he executed the recipe.

Candelario glanced up again for a quick check of the table and was disappointed to note he'd lost his audience.

Hortencio had appeared with the long-legged ice bucket. He made a show of uncorking the champagne, and poured the wine into three tulip-shaped glasses.

'You do so much for the women of Santiago,' don Gustavo said after the doctor had made a toast and Hortencio had gone on to another table. 'So many babies would not survive but for your clinic.'

'It's the least I can do,' the doctor replied, settling himself more comfortably in the chair. 'You know how successful my practice is in Guadalajara. I've been very lucky. I come here periodically to provide for those who can't provide for themselves. When life is good, it's only right to give.'

'The people need to be educated,' don Gustavo said. 'Some are filthy. Their children are filthy. It's no wonder so many sicken and die.'

Candelario Marroquín thrust his fork deep into the flesh of half a lemon. He squeezed its juice into the bowl. *Educate them.* How often had he heard these words? It shamed him that at twenty-eight he could not read, that the only writing he could do was to scratch out his name. If he were to be educated, who would teach him? How easily the rich spoke of solutions. How untroubled and simple their lives seemed to be.

'It's not always the people's fault for the filth that surrounds them,' the doctor said. 'Filth is a symptom of the corruption in our society. It's a disease that flourishes in poverty. I try to do my part. I wish I could do more.'

His wife said, 'You do much for the people, Federico.' Turning to don Gustavo she said, 'He delivers babies practically for free. If therapeutic abortions are indicated, he does those equally as cheap.'

Candelario broke two eggs into the bowl just as he'd been taught to do. He followed with keen interest the bent of the conversation.

Don Gustavo made a clucking sound. 'Abortions,' he said,

lowering his voice and glancing quickly around the room before turning back to the doctor. 'You know abortions are illegal.'

'My dear Gustavo,' the doctor said, 'of course they are. María Elena is very precise about medical terms. Perhaps you'd feel more comfortable if she referred to therapeutic abortions as terminations of pregnancy. These are legal, you know, if there is good cause.'

Candelario whipped the eggs into a froth. His fork clicked against the sides of the bowl.

'And what would you consider good cause?' don Gustavo asked.

'Jeopardy of the mother's life due to the fetus,' the doctor replied. 'Certain deformities of the fetus.'

'*Violación*,' the woman said.

'Rape?' don Gustavo said.

'In my estimation,' the doctor said, 'rape is a legitimate reason for this procedure.'

'Both the law and the Church would quarrel with you on that,' don Gustavo said.

'My dear man,' the doctor replied, 'I am used to quarreling with the Church.'

Candelario set his jaw. He could feel the cords in his neck straining against his bow tie.

'But how can you know it's rape?' don Gustavo asked. 'Surely you don't believe all the women who cry rape.'

Candelario placed his fork upon the cart. His face was hot. He wiped the palms of his hands against his apron.

'And who would you have him believe?' the doctor's wife asked. 'Do you think Federico has the luxury of interviewing the men in question?'

'María Elena,' don Gustavo said with a little laugh, 'you sound so North American.'

The woman replied, 'No, no. It's not that. These are the 1980s, you understand.'

After a pause, don Gustavo asked, 'You do this free of charge?'

'I charge only a modest fee,' the doctor said.

'He charges twenty thousand pesos,' the woman said. 'That is an affordable amount for any woman to pay.'

Candelario took two plates from the bottom rack of the cart and placed them next to the salad bowl. He gave the salad a final toss. The romaine leaves glistened with eggy coating. Twenty thousand pesos. He should have known. Why had Marta listened to her friend, Luz? Luz was excitable, and she was a dreamer, and who could trust a person like that? Candelario served each guest, dusted the salads with cheese and then rolled the cart to the side of the room. He wished fate had not placed him at the table. He wished that, months ago, he had not been a party to the change in Marta's life.

Soy el ensaladero, he reminded himself. I do not need to fear the future. He went into the kitchen to select the greens for his next salad.

Candelario was at the refrigerator when don Gustavo rushed up.

'There's a problem at the doctor's table. It's the salad. They can't eat it. What have you done?'

'How can it be?' Candelario said. 'It was made as it should be. I must speak with them.' He reached to center his bow tie and then he hurried into the dining room, the *patrón* at his heels.

'May I be of service,' Candelario said to the doctor and his wife. Each had their salad before them, the woman's looked untouched, the doctor's had barely been eaten.

'It's nothing,' the woman said. 'We told Gustavo that it was nothing.'

'None of that, none of that,' the *patrón* said with a shake of his hand. 'A mistake has obviously been made. If you can't eat the salad, there has been some mistake.'

'Well,' the doctor said, 'there is no garlic here and no oil.' He lightly touched the edge of his plate.

'There is a reason for this,' Candelario said, stealing a quick look at the *patrón*.

'I'm sorry,' the wife said, 'but it's just too eggy for me.' She pushed her plate into the middle of the table.

Don Gustavo addressed Candelario, 'Explain what you have done.'

Candelario nodded and he informed the guests about don Gustavo's Caesar. He thrust out his thick chest and he told of the anchovies and the mustard and then the lemon and finally the eggs. 'Oh, I ask your pardon,' he said. 'I meant to say, finally the cheese.'

There was a silence after the litany. The doctor and his wife looked at each other. Don Gustavo looked around him. Other guests had stopped eating and were now intent on what occurred at this table.

Taking all this in, Candelario felt a rush of foreboding. 'I make the salad as I was taught,' he said. 'Perhaps there are many ways to prepare it, but I prepare it the only way I know. I follow the recipe just as it was explained to me.' Candelario knew that his words were hurried. He should slow down, be more thorough, but panic drove his thoughts and propelled him to explain, to try to shake them all from this misjudgment.

'I'd like to know who it was that taught this *indio*,' don Gustavo said. 'Who has heard of a Caesar without garlic, without oil.' He puckered his lips in distaste. 'It's nothing but ridiculous.'

'There should be croutons, too,' the woman blurted and then clapped a hand over her mouth.

'Of course, croutons,' the *patrón* said.

The doctor rose from his chair. 'Gustavo, for the love of God,' he said. 'You make much of nothing. This is not important.'

'It's important to me,' don Gustavo said, striking his chest. Turning to Candelario, he added, 'I will see you in the kitchen.'

Candelario was on his way down the hall when don Gustavo caught up with him.

'Do you understand what you have done?' the *patrón* said. He reached into his coat pocket and extracted a handkerchief and mopped his face. 'The doctor and his wife are friends of mine. They are two very important people. You have embarrassed me in front of them.'

'But Don Gustavo, I did nothing wrong.'

The *patrón*'s face was very red. 'You made the salad and they could not eat it. Everyone in the restaurant saw they could not eat it.'

'But it was your salad, Don Gustavo. It was you . . .'

'¡*Basta!* I will not have a salad-maker who cannot make salads. Tomorrow, *indio de la chingada*, you can look elsewhere for work.'

Candelario Marroquín extinguished the candles that graced the tables of don Gustavo's restaurant. Some candles he blew out, others he smothered with the tips of two fingers. He welcomed the quick pain. It was a distraction from the humiliation he'd suffered earlier, from the humiliation he still felt at having to finish out the evening before collecting his pay. When he reached the last candle, his fingertips were numb. Still he touched them to his tongue as if the gesture would make a difference.

Candelario placed each chair upside down upon its table. He swept the floor and mopped the tile until it darkened to the color of wet stones. He switched off the lights and looked out to the sea. The sea did not cheer him. Don Gustavo's words echoed in his head like pounding waves.

He went into the kitchen. Hortencio was near the sink.

His face looked pale in the eerie glow of fluorescent lighting.

'Where is Don Gustavo?' Candelario Marroquín asked.

'He has left. If you are finished, I have your pay.'

'I am finished.'

Candelario Marroquín untied the cummerbund from around his waist, the bow tie from around his neck. He placed both on the table. Silently, he picked up his money and stepped out into a starless night.

PETER BENSON

Extract from his new novel

Riptide

Riptide is available now at your local Dillons store priced £5.99.

Bring this voucher with you to obtain £1.00 off the publisher's prices at all Dillons stores.

RIPTIDE
by Peter Benson

This voucher entitles you to **£1** OFF *Riptide* by *Peter Benson*

CONDITIONS
- *This voucher is only redeemable at Dillons Bookstores.*
- *Only one voucher may be redeemed per transaction.*
- *This voucher may not be used in conjunction with any other offer and is not exchangeable for cash.*

Promoter: Dillons Bookstore, Berwick House, 35 Livery Street, Birmingham, B3 2PB
Offer closes 31st October 1995

ONE

I got surfer's feet from my mother, and a fear of meat by-products. I got blue eyes and thin hair from her. I took a photograph of her and Dad on a Cornish beach from Marcus and Susan's photo album. Marcus and Susan, my uncle and aunt. I get a postcard from my mother every birthday, always from somewhere different, never more than two dozen words, never addressed. My room's at the back of the house, over the kitchen. There's surfing stuff on the walls: a wide shot of the Portuguese wave called Supertubes, stills from *Endless Summer*, Wingnut Weaver smiling on a Hawaiian beach, Tom Curren ripping Waimea Bay.

For my nineteenth birthday I was given a hundred quid, blank tapes, strawberry Sex Wax, a leash, my mother's postcard and I got the mistake she had to make. She had left the postcard for her hotel to post, and they had franked it RIVER COVE HOTEL, ST IVES, CORNWALL. I was shocked when I read this. Over breakfast I said, 'I think I'll go to Porthleven for a few days.'

'OK,' said Susan.

'Maybe a week.'

'Have you got enough money?'

Marcus already had his hand in his wallet. 'Here,' he said, and he passed me another fifty. 'Don't run out of petrol.'

'Thanks.'

'Don't thank me,' he said.

'Who should I thank?'

Marcus looked at Susan, Susan lowered her eyes and her face turned the colour of rain. She stood up and carried her cereal bowl to the sink. 'I'm not saying,' she said to the window, and her garden.

My Dad died when I was ten, in an accident at a pie factory. Someone somewhere ate part of my Dad, and that would have pleased him, because he was a generous man.

My mother couldn't cope with the nightmares that followed, shopping, other people's kitchens or me; she left me with her sister Susan and her husband Marcus, and their two children, and disappeared off the face of the earth. She has never been spoken about, it is as if she died and the postcard comes from beyond the grave. Smelling of damp, wormed earth, propelled through sulphurous air, over mountains and valleys I only know the names of, dropped on the doormat, lying face down. Maybe my mother is a ghost, maybe she always was. My nineteeth-birthday card was of a surfer slashing up on Fistral beach, and read, 'I always think of you when I'm in Cornwall. Happy Birthday, with all your mother's love.'

Once we were a happy family in Margate. We went on holiday twice a year, we lived in a big terraced house with a long garden, a view of the sea and more bedrooms than we needed, and we ate grapefruit and hot rolls for Sunday breakfast. We used to take evening walks along the promenade and sit outside a pub for a drink. Mother would howl with laughter at something Dad said, and he'd buy me two bags of crisps. He'd see people he knew and they'd wave as they passed, she'd admire his profile, and forgive his habit of looking at the waxy bits he found in his ears. He had big ears, and they were very hairy. Mother had ears like the little whorls you see on iced cakes, and thin lips that used to make me think of gardening. They were crinkled like the edge of rose petals, damp after a heavy dew. She had trouble with her hair; she never knew what to do with it. One week it was up and brown, the next it was down and coloured a lighter shade. Then she had it cut off and wore it like a man; tired of that she didn't go near a hairdresser for six months, letting it grow long again. Then, at the first opportunity, she had it permed. I think different hair kept Dad excited, not knowing what sort of head he was going to wake up to next. Maybe remembering one and then finding another; who knows now?

Apart from the hair and its changes, my memories of my mother are broken in pieces, so when I recall them, I see only edges of the complete picture. Here are her whorly ears, and here's the edge of her voice, telling me to eat cabbage. And here is the edge of her dress, curling over me. The edge of her touch, my head folding into her, or her hands on my back. The scent of Peau d'Espagne on her neck blowing towards me on a steady onshore wind. A knowing look on her long, thin face. Some surfers search for the perfect ride on an empty wave that runs for ever, barrelling over a smooth and kind reef, but I search for my mother. Here is her hand, raised and waving from a beach, and here her back at a kitchen sink, and me ready for school. There's a curl of black hair, or is it russet, or blonde? I'm pulling it out of a plate of macaroni cheese and dropping it quietly on the floor.

My memories of my Dad are fixed, frozen in places; on a beach in Cornwall, in a guest house that smelt of lard, steadying a ladder he was climbing, passing him an oil can when he was trying to fix a squeaky kitchen stool, walking the cliffs, at home watching telly, him coming home from work with flowers and a book for Mother. Him pushing me out on my first board – a log – one he made from a door.

There's not much surf at Margate, but down the road, at Joss Bay, the waves are the best in Kent. I saw my first big wave there. It was short but it tubed perfectly, and as I watched it someone I hadn't noticed suddenly appeared. A surfer.

He was awesome, dressed in a plain black wet-suit, riding an orange and white thruster. He lived inside each wave he caught, low and perfectly balanced for each radical man-oeuvre. He spoke to the water and it talked back to him. The sun was hot and the sea was blue. Seagulls drifted above him, inclining their heads, riding the thermals, adjusting their positions with small movements of their tails. The surfer pumped down on his board and turned around on his waves. As he approached the shore he died as the surf died, disappearing beneath it and coming up smiling. His smile was small and peeped out from his mouth like carefully considered words. 'I want to do that,' I said. That was the only excuse Dad needed.

Dad let the car stand out all winter while he made the board in the garage. First, he beat the door to death with a claw-hammer, then unscrewed the hinges, the lock and the handles, and sawed the panel to a rough shape. He took a plane and began to shave the edges; he was a perfectionist, and spent weeks getting the shape just right. And when it was exactly right, he bought a can of varnish the size of a grown man's head and gave the board four coats. He sanded between each coat; my Dad's board was heavy, and its balance was screwed from the moment it stopped being a door, but I used it for three seasons and it never maxed me out.

The holidays were always spent by the sea. Weymouth, Dawlish, Newquay, Porthleven, St Ives, Salcombe, Sennen Cove, Bude, Exmouth; we stayed in all these places, usually in bed-and-breakfast houses run by middle-aged women and their pets.

I was seven when the board was made, and we tried it first

at Bude. I paddled out over sluggish breaks until I was caught by a mellow that turned me round and the nose of the board up. The board said 'Go', and I said 'Now'. I was instinctive, I wore thick blue trunks, I stood up, grew my first erection and, for five or six seconds, I rode my first wave. I was hooked. I looked towards the beach. My Dad was jumping up and down. My mother waved. She was holding a fat novel in her free hand. I put up my hand. The sun was hot. The board sank.

I still feel those five or six seconds. As the sea rushed beneath me, I was singing through my feet, and the board amplified my song through the water. The song was from *Porgy and Bess*, the words were in the sea and the melody was whistled by my Dad, given trills Gershwin had never intended. I don't know: 'Summertime', 'A woman is a sometime thing', 'One of dese mornings you goin' to rise up singin''? One of these or another? I saw the whole sky shine, and other surfers, riding behind and above me, appeared like members of the chorus. A single gull soared over me, and each cloud hung as if attached by cotton. The sea crested over the nose of the board, and when I shifted my weight forward, I accelerated. I leaned back and slowed, I heard the wake I left; when I focused on the beach, the people there looked as though they were illuminated by spotlights. I felt lit within, I felt immortal; at that time, my mother never had a passion as I had surf. This was her tragedy, and the reason she could not cope. Surf was my salvation. I lost my Dad but found him again in the ocean, and his song was mine, and that song sang from my feet.

In bed. You haven't seen your mother for eight years. She left you without explanation. You might meet her the following day. What are you going to ask her? What are you going to tell her? What is she going to say to you? Is she waiting for you? I have been waiting for this moment, and have no answers.

When I was left with Marcus and Susan, I pushed the shock and misery deep with one thing that could not be taken from me. They live at Norman's Bay, Sussex, where there is always a good swell, but not always good waves. It's always enough though, and I became king of the deliberate wipeout, and this took my grief away.

You wipeout when you fall off your board; I could take a wave and hold it in my hand, I would be able to teach it Greek, introduce it to my Geography teacher, call it names or take it on holiday; I would be able to ride it to shore but instead I'd lean forward, grab the nose and flip the board over my head, falling backwards over the lip and down the back of the wave, out of sight, with nothing but a strip of sky above me and folds of sea on either side. These elements were my clothes, I do not feel the cold. Physical cold is grief's brother, and my brother is my board. I am not sentimental about my board, my eyes, my balance, my low centre of gravity, my big, wide feet, waves or the combined power of these things.

What is this power? It is the power of forgetting, wipeout of the mind. Great surfers have died in wipeout, beaten by the waves, sunk by it and crushed by tons of falling water. The air is stolen from their lungs, they have lost consciousness and slammed into the sea bed and filled with sand. Sometimes their bodies are not found. Fit men with brown bodies and women ashore. The sea is a killer, and feathers and lead. You are in a doctor's waiting room and a woman comes in. She has a bone to pick with the doctor and shouts at the receptionist for five minutes before sitting down next to you. She's about twenty-one. She has long, straight blonde hair, and is wearing tiny pearl ear-rings. Her nails are painted pink and beautifully manicured. Her eyes are blue and do not blink. She is carrying a small dog beneath a smart black coat. The dog is beautifully groomed. The waiting room is hot, you feel faint, you have to blow your nose but you haven't got a tissue. You look at the woman's knees, then her hands, her arms, her neck, then her face. She is waiting for you to look in her eyes, and when you do she smiles. The smile is an old woman's smile, her teeth are brown, and she has a diseased tongue. This is the sea.

Can't sleep. 'I always think of you when I'm in Cornwall.' I wonder if she knew the hotel would frank the card. She could not bring herself to tell me where she was, as she could not bring herself to bring me up alone. The River Cove Hotel had to tell me, people I have never met. She makes me angry, and I can't get the anger out of my head. It picks at my mind and strips it of reason; I turned on the light, sat up and studied her handwriting. Was there something in the slope of her letters that gave me another clue, or the way she dots her i's? The dots appear over the letter in front, like spume flying off the crest of a wave, though the waves pull against the current. Is she sad or is she threatened?

I couldn't sleep, so I dressed and crept out of the house. Marcus was snoring lightly in his bedroom, Susan was still up. As I passed her room, she came to the door and said, 'Can't sleep?' It was as if she had been waiting for me.

'No.'

'Going to the beach?'

'Yeah,' I said.

'Want some company?' She reached out and touched my hand. She was cold.

'Dunno.'

'Come on,' she said.

'OK.'

Susan and I walked together in the moonlight. It was a still night, warm, and it smelt of sugar. Sugar in molten columns that rose from the earth and pierced the sky. Susan took my arm, and we walked slowly from the house to the beach.

Susan has never told a lie. She and Marcus are honest, they never fooled themselves into loving me as their own. Their children – my cousins – are older and different to me. Ronald is a doctor in Australia, Isabel is in Manchester and works in retail sales. Marcus is in insurance, and his hobby is insurance. Susan's passion is her garden, more sand and pebbles than flowers, but she grows huge potatoes and onions the size of footballs.

'Duncan?' she said.

'Yeah?'

'I saw the card.'

'Did you?'

'When you go down, are you going to try and see her?'

'Yeah.' I coughed and wiped my mouth with the back of my hand. 'If she's there.'

'If you do,' she said, and she turned towards me so the moon haloed behind her head, 'give her my love.'

'Of course. Anything else?'

She looked into my eyes, and there was no doubting them. 'I never told you before, maybe it's time to,' she said. She swallowed. Her eyes looked cast in steel, and glittered at their corners. The sea dragged the beach to itself, and threw what it didn't want back. It sounded as if it was unwrapping parcels of china and bells in front of a crackling fire.

'Told me what?' I said.

'I was sworn,' she stuttered, 'to secrecy.'

'Told me what?'

She held my eyes and did not flinch. 'I've never broken an oath,' she said.

'Are you going to now?'

'I think . . .' she faltered.

'You think?'

'It's a big thing for me . . .

'What?'

'. . . but I think it's more important that I break this one than keep it.'

'What is it, Susan?'

'Diana.'

Diana is my mother. 'What about her?'

'For the last eight years, she's sent me money for you. That fifty this morning; that was from her. And the money for your car. Most of that came from her.'

'You've known where she was?'

'Not all the time. She's moved a lot.' She coughed to clear her throat. 'She's never told me exactly what she's been doing, but I can read between the lines.'

'And?' I'm not angry, but I'm amazed. I understand that Susan took an oath, and how she must feel now. I feel that I'm about to catch a wave the size of a street.

'And she's found a man.'

'A man?' The wave lifted me up and I rose with it, climbing the water as if it was rock and I was wearing suckers on my feet.

'A man.'

'Who?'

'I don't know his name,' she said. 'I don't know anything about him.'

'No?' The wave was solid but moved as if it was water, flecked with spit and blood.

'No.'

'Oh,' I whispered.

'I'm sorry.'

'Why?' The wave began to curl above me and barrel behind; the faster I moved the faster it moved, and I heard it whispering about dealing with me. I kicked up and back, flew into the air and dropped down behind it. 'You don't have to be,' I said.

'No,' she said.

How do I feel? I expected this day, so I did not force it. I am patient. Surf teaches patience, anticipation and faith. It displays calm in fury. Below us, as we walked, the sea swept on to the beach in long, shallow sets. Fairy's surf. When the moonlight hit the lip of each wave it flashed along its length, unravelling into the night. Gobs of spume flew up and disappeared into the dark. I tasted salt in my mouth and my ears began to ring. Night surfing, I break the rules. The ringing stopped. 'Come on,' she said, and she took my arm again, and we walked across the pebbles to the tide-line.

A fisherman was sitting on a stool, six feet from the water's edge, his unshaven face lit by a hissing gas lamp. As we passed, he didn't take his eyes from the top of his rod. His line was taut, and dissolved into the dark, then the sea, weighted and baited at the end. The fisherman held a dead cigarette between his teeth. A miasma of guts and luncheon meat hung around him. He had erected a canvas wind-break, and wore a heavy waterproof cape. His rod was supported by a cradle, but he kept his hands on it. His fingers clasped and unclasped, otherwise he was motionless. He had a box of food on the beach beside him and a flask. The wind-break cracked in the breeze, and his line whistled softly.

'She told you about him in a letter?' I said.

'Yes.'

'Where from?'

'Essex,' she said. 'I think he was working there.'

'You said you didn't know anything about him . . .'

'I don't, Duncan. I was just reading between the lines.'

'Do you remember how the lines went?'

'No. Not precisely.'

'Imprecisely?'

'No, Duncan. I've already told you too much . . .'

'That means you haven't told me everything.'

Susan stopped walking. 'She told me,' she took a deep

breath, 'that she loved him. That's it.'

Essex. There're waves there, but they're broken things, fragile, dead-blown, that lapse towards the shore, insecure and paranoid. Those shores are lost to me. They are starved, thin as cats, grey and cold; if you offered them love they would spit it back in your face. I would not take my board to Essex, but I would follow my mother there. If she is being hassled I will be there.

She was staying in Southend. Remember? We went there.'

I remember. How could I forget Southend v. York at Roots Hall, where the birds fly upside down because there's nowt worth shitting on. The sight of a Southend striker bearing down on goal, three boys and an old man standing by the hot-dog stall at the back of the empty terrace, the cheers of thirty dedicated supporters rattling the loose rivets that held up the roof. Marcus took me to the match. We were walking past the ground when the gates opened, and the gateman pleaded with us to buy tickets. Marcus takes pity easily; he said, 'OK,' and offered the bloke a twenty-quid note for two on the home terrace. 'No,' said the gateman, looking at the note, 'I only wanted you to buy a couple of tickets, not the whole club.'

Half-way through the match it began to rain, and it rained in solid sheets and pooled on the pitch. The ball skidded and stopped as it was passed, so men who had not expected to find it at their feet found it at their feet and were forced to do something about it. Ball games give the player too much time to think, the best decisions are made without the luxury of time. Team games give the player too many chances to make excuses. Those Southend footballers did not like the conditions, they ran from them and lost 5–0.

'What was she doing there?' I said.

'She didn't say.'

'What's she been doing since she left me?'

'I don't know. She had some compensation, and she sold

the house, so she had some money. She travelled a lot. I had cards from lots of different places. Spain, Ireland, Canada, New Zealand. I think she was trying to lose herself, or find herself. I never knew which.'

I never knew which. Susan's straight, she doesn't worry herself. Other people mostly baffle her. She doesn't smoke and she rarely drinks, she eats plain food and never wears patterned clothes. Her bafflement has bred the ability to cut to the heart of some things; I was in a pub with her, and two blokes were steaming. They had insulted the barmaid, they had broken glasses, and were fooling around on the tables. No one was going to sort them out, so Susan stood up and forced herself between them and demanded to know why they were ruining everyone else's evening. For a moment, they were transfixed, amazed that anyone should ask them the question. And a middle-aged woman in plain brown clothes with a handbag in her hand. She wore no jewellery, she wore flat shoes, and no make-up. One of the blokes turned to his mate and said, 'What's the boiler on about?' Susan did not flinch. She said, 'I beg your pardon?' God, the two blokes laughed, then they dropped their laughs like stones and looked serious. Mean. Time in the pub was caught like a breath, or like the moment before a fast wave breaks and you have no time to stretch from prone to standing; the sea is roaring but you hear nothing. 'I beg your pardon?' one bloke mouthed. 'I beg your pardon?' said the other. They banged their heads together and then turned to stare at Susan. She stared back, put her hand to her shoulder and flicked away a ball of fluff. 'You're annoying people,' she said, and now she leant towards them and said, 'Nobody wants you here, so I think you'd better leave.' All the people in the pub stiffened, the stiffening could be felt in the air, the barman stepped from behind the bar with a baseball bat. Susan looked at him, then at her feet, then tapped her handbag with the palm of her hand and came back to where I was sitting. Susan drinks tonic water with a slice of lemon and sucks the slice dry when she's finished. The blokes left, promising to be back, but they never were.

I have never thought of her as my mother, just the woman I stayed with until I found my mother. 'I'm sorry,' she said. 'I broke my promise to Diana, and I'm afraid for you.'

'Why?'

'I can't say. It's between you and her; I've got nothing to do with it.'

'Only that you looked after me ten years.'

'Your mother suffered ten years, more than I know. She always did, even when she was a baby . . .'

'Everyone suffers.'

'Everyone can hear,' said Susan, 'but some can't enjoy music. They actually don't understand it. Can you believe that?'

'What's that got to do with Mother?'

'I've never heard you call her Mum.'

'I can't,' I said.

'That's it?'

'Yes.'

'Yes . . .'

'Did you ever think about telling me all this before?'

'Yes.'

'Why didn't you?'

'I promised her . . .'

'You've broken it now.'

'I had to one day; the time had to be right for you. I think she knows it too, and knew the hotel would stamp the card. She couldn't tell you herself, and at this moment she's sitting in her room, knowing we're having this conversation, knowing she's going to have to face you.'

'You think so?'

'It's possible. Anything's possible with Diana. She's never done the expected.'

'Maybe the expected never happened to her. Dad going like that . . .'

'The expected rarely happens to anyone,' said Susan.

'And I want her.'

TIM GEARY

Extract from his new novel

Spin

Spin is available now at your local Dillons store priced £5.99.

Bring this voucher with you to obtain £1.00 off the publisher's prices at all Dillons stores.

12

It was the day of Dawn Hope's birth into the fraught and wonderful world of soapland, and Annie was nervous as hell. She had been awake for most the night, her mind on the six a.m. alarm she'd booked with the telephone company. Though she had moved the phone unit close to the bed, and turned the volume up high, and put an alarm clock on a table just out of reach of her flailing, sleep-warmed arm, she had been troubled by the notion that something might happen and that she wouldn't wake in time. This had kept her in a state of jittery semiconsciousness. Also, she'd made the mistake of going to bed too early, so desperate had she been for a good night's rest. As the night had worn on she'd lain listening for a tick from her digital clock or for the ring of the phone. In a half-dream, she had pictured God's heavy fingers curled around the end of a black blanket, slowly lifting until dawn's light sneaked in around the edges to envelop her with a new day. Dawn's dawn! Something else to think about and keep her awake . . .

It was five forty now, but there was no way she was going to get up a minute before six. She had to look her best! Instead she tried to remember her first lines and the concentration sent her into a sudden deep sleep that could have lasted for hours had the phone not exploded with sound, jolting her heart and sending her shuffling towards the shower.

She made it to the studio on time. It felt a lot like going to a new school, the only difference being that she recognised the faces of all her classmates. It was odd being introduced to people she felt she knew. When she shook Stefano's hand, she wondered whether he would try to seduce her as he had all the girls on the show. Could Bobby *really* see, though he played a blind man? And were Johnson Bell and Olivia Rourke as affectionate off camera as the couple had been on screen, playing William and Mary, husband and wife, for almost twelve years straight?

Now, sitting on a cold metal folding chair like the ones they'd had at Cornell Williams, she glanced down at her script, checking her lines once again. Suddenly a shadow fell on the page. Lifting her eyes, Annie saw two red high-heeled shoes. She knew at once to whom they belonged.

'Hello, Faith,' she said, standing up. 'How are you?'

Faith, who hadn't given up her leaning, brushed her cheeks against Annie's in a lipless kiss.

'Welcome to our show,' she said.

'Thank you.'

Whatever physical features Annie had found laughable in the actress before – the lacquered, showy eyelashes like the thighs of an insect cancan troupe, heavy breasts like sweating balls of mozzarella in fishnets – seemed not lessened but exaggerated now. Faith was not Barbie, but Ken in drag, more woman than most women would ever want to be.

'Have you met the family?' she asked, her eyelashes kicking high.

'You mean the others? Yeah. Most, anyway.'

'If they're not friendly it's because we see so many of you. So many actresses coming, and then going. It's impossible to get personally involved with everyone.'

'I suppose so.'

'No, we can't, Annie!' Faith said as if contradicting her. 'They come and go.'

'Maybe I'll be here a while.'

'Get used to the early mornings then,' she said, 'or Make-up's going to hate you.'

Annie was going to reply but Zoë Dunlop had come into the room to start the rehearsal. If Annie worried that she herself looked awful, she knew Zoë looked worse. With a styrofoam cup of coffee in one hand, a cigarette in the other, her ginger hair sticking up in all directions and her thick, black glasses sloping across her face, Zoë looked as if she'd spent the night on the streets. Despite this, she seemed ready to start work. Putting down her breakfast, she began to pull the chairs into the centre of the space. Once they were in position, marking out the boundaries to be imposed on set, the actors could start blocking the first scene, beginning a day that would last twelve hours at least.

By lunch, Annie was wondering whether she'd made a mistake. This wasn't work, it was slave labour. She hadn't taped a single second yet, though she had done dry runs with the technical crews as well as being made-up and fussed over before running through the scenes again. In between rehearsing she hung around with the other actors on the sets. It felt as odd to sit on the Sheridans' marital bed as it had done meeting the couple. Having become so familiar with the room on TV, it almost felt as if it belonged to a friend. She recognised the fabric and furnishings, the bedside clock, even the glass of water that Mary kept by the neat pile of books on the bedside table.

It was almost three by the time the stage manager, Monty Prindle, came up to her, grinning. 'All ready for the big take-a-rooni, are we?'

'As ready as I'll ever be, Monty,' she replied.

Annie liked Monty, a large, gentle man in his late fifties with an avuncular grey beard. He reminded her of Lee Marvin, with a stomach that bulged out over his black jeans and strained the buttons of his brown check cowboy shirt. Monty seemed to be everyone's best friend, and it was from him that the cast and crew received their instructions on the set. While the taping was taking place, the director and line producers congregated in the production booth on the ninth floor. Monty, receiving instructions through his headphones, had to mastermind the operation on the eighth.

Annie's first scene was in the hospital ward where four of the crash victims were being tended. This was the storyline that Alex had imagined: the Brendan Air plane, carrying twelve of the soap's star characters, had come down soon after takeoff from Chicago. In need of urgent medical attention, they'd been brought to a hospital in the city, home to one of the Senators, the high-flying and beautiful Dawn Hope. Dawn, a compassionate woman running for the State Governor's seat, was visiting the hospital to see the injured characters, completely unaware that she was to reveal a past that would change their lives.

From within the production booth, Zoë Dunlop, headphones on and cigarettes by her side, told Monty that they were ready to tape. To Zoë's right sat her assistant director, who was following the taping with a stopwatch to ensure that it was running to time. To her left was the technical director responsible for switching between the three cameras on set when Zoë wanted a new angle. For soap operas, this was every few seconds. All of them, together with the line producer and the lighting engineer, followed the action on a wall of monitors in front and listened through speakers to the side. Each camera fed its picture onto a separate monitor and the one in use at any given time relayed its images to the larger preview monitor in the centre of the wall. Simultaneously, in the audio booth, sound effects and music were added.

On the studio floor Monty, sounding like a bingo compère, threw his booming voice over the hubbub.

'Here we go-go, gang. Opening places please.'

Annie stood on her spot, her heart thudding with nerves.

'We need some hush here,' said Monty.

Two of the male leads stopped their game of knuckles.

'Stand by. OK, and it's *Unto the Skies*, episode 11857, aaaaanda, take one.'

Joel, on camera two, moved in on the face of a nurse studying a clipboard at the end of William Sheridan's bed. She looked to her side.

In the booth, Zoë snapped her fingers. 'Three.'

The main monitor switched to camera three, a full-length shot of Dawn Hope and the doctor approaching the nurse.

Another snap of the fingers. 'One,' said Zoë.

Gormand's wrinkled, worried face appeared.

DR GORMAND
Nurse Mullholiland, this is Senator Hope. She's come to see the victims.

DAWN
How are they, Nurse?

NURSE
It was a horrible accident. It's a miracle there were so few casualties.

DAWN
A miracle and a credit to the emergency services. Nurse Mull – Mullholy – Mullyho – Oh shit!

Annie slapped her hands against her thighs with exasperation, and rolled her eyes. 'I'm sorry,' she said.

'Cut,' Zoë called out to the crew, then over the public address, 'Don't worry about it, Annie.'

'Do I have to say her name?' Annie asked, talking to Zoë through the camera.

'Jesus fuck,' the line producer said in thick Brooklynese, 'we've got an actress who talks back. What is this, *Tootsie Two*?'

'Hang on,' Zoë said over the PA. She turned to the producer. 'Mullholiland is a stupid name, Neil. Does she need it?'

'It's in there, so there's a reason for it.'

'What reason?'

'Don't ask me. Maybe her family built the hospital. But in soaps, sweetheart, there's a reason for everything.'

Zoë made a snap decision, assuming that she had more power than she did. She spoke again to the studio. 'Cut the name and let's take it from the top.'

The scene was repeated, and ran smoothly. Annie was soon standing by William Sheridan's bed. He was covered in bandages and bruises and had a crude scar on his face. Lou on camera three had silently rolled the podium for a close-up of the star's battered visage.

DAWN
Mr Sheridan, I'm Senator Hope, and you're a lucky man.

WILLIAM
Lucky, Senator Hope? My wife, she . . .

DR GORMAND
Don't give up. We're doing everything we can. Everything possible. And more. We know what a good woman Mary Sheridan is. She is a caring human being and we're going to care for her in return.

WILLIAM
Thank you, Doctor.

DAWN
(TAKING GORMAND ASIDE)
How is Mrs Sheridan?

'Go in very close on this one, Lou,' Zoë said.

DR GORMAND
Senator Hope, I'm going to be straight with you. She's not good. She's suffering from bilateral acute renal failure. If we can't get a donor soon, I'm afraid she might die.

'Keep tight on William's face, Joel. And,' she clicked her fingers, 'one, and three.'
The monitor showed the image from camera one, the doctor's face, then to three, of Dawn.

DAWN
Is there nothing we can do?

DR GORMAND
(CROSSING HIS FINGERS)
We keep doing this until we find a compatible organ.

Pauly, one of eleven members of the Lucci family who worked as a grip on the show, whispered to his neighbour, 'My organ's compatible with that new actress's, no question.'
'Your organ,' replied his cousin, 'is compatible with your right hand, and that's the end of it.'
'You can talk!' said Pauly.
Monty turned around and held a finger to his mouth.

On set, Dr Gormand and the Senator were still in deep conversation.

DAWN
How long has she got?

DR GORMAND
How long? It's hard to say. She's a problem case. We need to find the perfect match for her tissue type, and that's not going to be easy.

While camera one had been trained on Dawn and the doctor, camera two had repositioned itself by Mary Sheridan's bed. Unconscious, she was surrounded by what looked like enough equipment to send the space shuttle to Mars. She had tubes in her nose and drips in her arms and an oxygen pump by her head. Her son, Jamie, played by the actor Philip Shaw, sat by her, a bandage round his own head.

JAMIE
(STROKING HIS MOTHER'S HAIR)
(TEARY)
Remember that time I fell off the horse, Mom-Mom, and the doctors said I wouldn't pull through and you came and sat by me, day after day you sat by me, and you stroked my hair just like this? You were the only one who believed I'd live, and it was because of your strength, your courage and your prayers that I survived. I want to repay that debt to you. You gave life to me twice over, Mom-Mom. The least I can do is help you hold on to yours.

NURSE
(TAKING JAMIE BY THE SHOULDERS)
Mr Sheridan, you have to come away now.

'Remember I want full-length of the curtain being drawn around her,' said Zoë. 'Then two on Jamie and Dawn.'

DAWN
Jamie? Jamie Sheridan?

JAMIE
(BAFFLED)
Yes?

DAWN
Hello. I'm Dawn Hope. I'm running for Governor in November.

JAMIE
Excuse me, Lady, but this isn't the time or the place for your campaigning.

DAWN
Wait! Please don't go!

JAMIE
Didn't you hear? This isn't the time. Or the place. There's been an accident, a terrible accident. My mother is suffering from acute renal failure, my wife could be dying in front of my eyes and here you are trying to get votes, I . . .

DAWN
I'm not campaigning, Mr Sheridan. I'm here because I think I can help.

JAMIE
Wait a minute. Do I know you?

'Keep in on Jamie's face, in, in, and three on Dawn and two . . . one . . . and we're up,' Zoë said. Then, over the PA, she said, 'Good work, everyone. Nice start, Annie.'

There was a moment when all the actors stayed in position before Monty said, 'Tapes are good.'

'Then let's go to Four A,' said Zoë.

The scenes were shot not in chronological sequence, but by set, to save money and time. One of the problems it gave the actors was that they had no time to brush up their lines on new scenes and, as endless repetition was an important part of every soap, it was often difficult to remember dialogue written for the start of a scene that varied only slightly from that spoken at the end of a scene taped five minutes before.

On the set, Monty had come to give Annie a kiss.

'Never easy on your first day, kid,' he said, patting his stomach. 'You were magnifico.'

'I didn't have much to do, Monty.'

'Try saying that to some of the Method boffins,' Monty said. 'Oh boy, oh boyo! The headcases we've had. Wait a mo,' he said, 'I've got the voice of God coming through my headphones.'

He listened to the instructions arriving from the production booth, gave the thumbs up to one of the cameras, and then said, 'Four A, from el toppo, gang. Joel, repo here.'

Joel repositioned his camera to its new starting place.

Monty spoke again. 'Ready, all?'

The house lights were dimmed once more. Jamie Sheridan and Dawn Hope were standing in the hospital set, as they had been at the end of the scene before, though when the show aired two other scenes and a commercial break would be separating this scene from the last.

'Very still now,' Monty said, holding out a clipboard. 'Give me some hush-a-rooni. And five . . . four . . .

three . . .' The last two digits were unspoken before the red light shone on camera two, indicating that taping had begun.

JAMIE

You said you think you can help?

DAWN

It's possible, Mr Sheridan.

JAMIE

I think I know you. I'm sure I've seen you somewhere before.

DAWN

I am quite well known. I'm the youngest female Senator in the Senate.

JAMIE

I'm very impressed, but there's something else . . .

In the audio booth the technicians were adding the bleeping and whirring of hospital machines in commotion. Two nurses ran past Jamie and Dawn, followed by a surgeon and Dr Gormand. Jamie extended an arm to stop him.

JAMIE

Doctor, what is it?

DR GORMAND

I wish I knew.

'Cut,' said Zoë, speaking over the PA system. 'The doctor's line is, "I wouldn't like to say, Jamie, but it sounds very serious." Not "I wish I knew."'

The actor playing the role replied, 'I meant I wish I knew what the line was!'

'Have you got it now?' Monty asked.

The actor had the line repeated, and they did a second take from the top. This time, it ran smoothly.

The next scene belonged to Annie, played beside the silent, comatose Mary Sheridan. Her husband William was seen to be listening from the neighbouring bed. Once the other actors had left for the day and Olivia Rourke had had the chance to breathe for a while without tubes rammed into her mouth, the crew settled down to tape. This was to be the last scene of the show when it was aired two weeks from now, and the most important in persuading viewers to tune in again. Alex had decided that Annie was good enough to carry it alone. Zoë, though she had decided to begin the scene with an establishing shot of Mary flat out in the hospital bed, was concentrating for the most part on Annie's face. The lighting engineer had given the scene a mood of mysteriousness by dimly lighting Annie's face from below.

'Yup,' Monty said in response to a question through his headphones, 'ready when you are, boss.'

He counted the scene in, and the cameras stealthily moved in towards Annie. She was sitting on the bed, holding Mary Sheridan's hand, talking softly so as not to be heard. The curtain was drawn about them.

DAWN

Please don't die, Mary. I've met your family and your friends today and never in my life have I known such warmth and love shown to someone. You must be a very, very special lady. I knew you would be. I've followed you in the papers whenever you and William were in the news. I saw the Society pictures when Jamie and Vanessa were married and it made me happy to see you happy. He sensed something today, Jamie. He sensed something about me.

'Camera three on reaction shot of William. Aaand,' Zoë snapped her fingers once more, 'back to two.'

DAWN

It's funny how things work out, isn't it? All these long years I've been thinking of how to do this, and whether you'd be proud of me.

As tears came to Annie's eyes, the line producer leant forward in his chair and said to Zoë, 'Why's the stupid bitch crying? She's meant to be strong.'

'I like it,' said Zoë. 'She's getting inside the character.'

'In my script,' he added, 'it says, "Dawn laughs self-mockingly."'

'What's the difference, Neil?'

'The difference is that this isn't a movie. In soap you play by the rules!'

Dawn's speech was coming to an end. The technicians on the floor had no such doubts about Annie's performance.

DAWN

I don't know what I'd do if you never woke up, Mary. I want you to be proud of me. I want you to look at me and say, 'You did OK, Dawn! You did OK.' I don't want you never to know who I am. Please God, let this woman live so I can tell her who I am.

As the camera pulled back, the audience was left with the final image of William Sheridan straining as he sat up in his hospital bed and listening in amazement to what this Senator was saying to his wife.

'Tapes are good,' said Monty. 'And it's a one hundred per cent wrap-a-roo.'

Almost as soon as Annie stepped away from the bed, the grips moved in to dismantle the set.

Zoë, looking exhausted after two straight days on the set, emerged from the booth to join Annie. 'I'm bloody knackered,' she said. 'Can you come for a quick drink?'

'Never in my life,' said Annie, rubbing her make-up off with a towel, 'have I needed one more. I'll be with you in five.'

JOANNA HINES

Previously unpublished short story

Jordan

The Fifth Secret, Joanna Hines latest novel, is available now at your local Dillons store priced £5.99.

Bring this voucher with you to obtain £1.00 off the publisher's prices at all Dillons stores.

Jordan

Although she was only fifty-five and her last illness had been considered a tragic curtailment of a full and happy life, Lindsey Potter was reasonably ready to meet her maker. Throughout most of her life she had endeavoured to do the Right Thing – but not too strenuously, of course. There was no virtue in being a fanatic.

Heaven forbid.

And now there was movement, like a membrane detaching. She floated free of the squalor of disease, pausing for a moment to look back on the scene in which she had just been – and was still apparently thought to be – the main performer. In an ideal world, she reflected, death would be accompanied by a fanfare of violins and trumpets. The reality was that she was being serenaded from this life by the lachrymose honks of her nearest and dearest as they blew their noses into paper handkerchiefs. A sound somewhat reminiscent of geese passing over salt marshes.

Still, Lindsey thought, as she spiralled pleasantly towards the light, it was a touching scene she left behind her.

The nurse appeared, efficiently sympathetic, to let her family know their presence at the bedside had become superfluous.

Janet, her daughter, said, 'Time to go home, now, Dad.'

Their son Alan added, 'I suppose we'd better start ringing people.'

Ronald looked from one child to the other in a baffled sort of way, but after a few minutes he allowed himself to be shepherded from the hospital room and out into the car park.

Lindsey, ascending gracefully through a cone of light, wished she could tell him not to grieve, to tell him that she felt wonderful. Loving him as she did, she longed to lift the burden from his hunched shoulders and ease his pain. but also, because she was only human (though was that still true?), she had to admit just the teeniest twinge of gratification. It was, after all, most satisfying to know that they regarded her death as such a catastrophe. She accepted her sorrow as a tribute to her qualities as a wife and mother.

But for the first time in over thirty years, her husband was beyond her reach. Besides, she knew that it was right for him to grieve. An appropriate period of mourning would enable him, in time, to rebuild his life without her. Perhaps even to marry again. After all, Alan wasn't sixty yet.

Irritation wriggled through her at the thought of his recovery, but she smothered the emotion at once. Not very long ago she had read in a wonderful book (just at this moment she could not remember its name) that true love is never possessive, but desires only what is best for the beloved. The memory of this wise counsel made it much easier to let him go, and to be grateful for their long and mostly happy marriage. As she had worked hard to achieve both its length and its happiness, she did not intend to blot her copybook now by being selfish and possessive. It was a pity there was no way of letting Alan know about his emotional release – but from his point of view it would probably be premature.

By now Lindsey was definitely enjoying herself. She had an awareness of movement, though as she couldn't actually see anything moving around her it was difficult to say precisely where the sense of motion came from. All the same, the feeling was both exhilarating and comforting – like whizzing around a fairground ride while cocooned in cotton wool.

So she was almost sorry when it ended.

She was on some kind of towpath. The air was chill against her face and it had that pungent smell of dirt and salt which is often to be found where rivers spread and dawdle in the last stage of their journey to the sea. She was standing on a grass-covered bank which led down to what she supposed must be an estuary of some kind. On the far side she could just make out a greenish blur of what looked like woods and hills. A sudden longing took hold of her: she must find a way to reach that far shore. The desire to get across was overwhelming, a tug of homesickness she had not felt since childhood. She assumed there must be some kind of bridge further upstream.

She walked beside the river for a little while (it was marvellous to walk again, after all those weeks in the hospital), wondering when she was going to find someone who would tell her what she had to do next.

Further ahead she noticed a little pier. An odd collection of boats was clustered nearby and one or two more were on the water – apparently some kind of ferry service was being organised. About time too, thought Lindsey with relief. Her feet were beginning to ache with so much walking.

It took much longer than she had expected to reach the pier and by then she was worn out. Lack of exercise has made me unfit, she thought. And then realised what a stupid remark that was.

The urge to cross the river had become so strong it was a physical craving, but she couldn't find anyone who was in charge of the boats. Surely no one was expecting her to get across the river on her own?

'Hello!' she called out gaily.

No one.

She examined the boats more carefully and a very bizarre assembly they proved to be: long, thin ones like canoes, round ones (coracles?), odd-looking rafts and punts, and many others that she could not put a name to. Apart from the odd trip in a motor launch on their holidays, Lindsey had no knowledge of boats at all, and she was not about to try her luck in one of those little bath-tub toys. Not unless someone in authority made it absolutely clear that she was supposed to attempt the crossing alone.

She decided it was best to wait. Sooner or later someone was bound to come along who could explain the proper procedures to her. Obviously death was a new kind of country (hadn't she heard that somewhere before?) and it would be irresponsible to go putting her foot in things on her very first day.

She didn't have long to wait. A man appeared from somewhere behind her and began doing one of those complicated and wholly absorbing things that people do around boats. After watching him for a little while she decided it was time to introduce herself.

'Hello there!' she called. 'I'm sorry to interrupt you but I wonder if you could help me?'

The man paused in his work and turned to face her. She was disappointed to see that he was much younger than she had at first thought; she would have like to talk to one of the people in charge. But perhaps this man could tell her where they were to be found.

He left his boat and came down the pier towards

her. He had thin features and grey eyes and he looked almost bored.

'Yes?'

Lindsey wasn't sure how to begin. 'I'm Lindsey Potter,' she said. 'I arrived about an hour ago.'

'Oh.'

He was definitely playing this in a non-committal way. Lindsey sensed it was important to win him to her side and anyway, she had always found it easy to get along with young people. She smiled at him. Or rather, she used her smile to project the warmth that she was feeling: it was a smile of sympathy and liking that had come in useful in the past when there were barriers to be overcome.

There was no visible sign that his attitude had mellowed.

'I'm trying to find my way across the river.'

'Of course.'

Lindsey was silent, suddenly afraid that he might reject her next question, which was to ask if he would take her across. Instead she asked, 'Does this river have a name?'

'Jordan,' he replied, still unsmiling.

She heard his answer with a shiver of recognition. 'How fascinating! The River Jordan. I always assumed it was a metaphor. And yet here it is, as real as any river I've ever seen.'

He stared down at her. Was that scorn in his cold, grey eyes? But, 'If you like,' was all he said.

'Yes. Obviously.' Lindsey had decided that a direct approach was going to be best with this young man. 'My problem now is how to get across?'

'Boats are usual.'

'And could you perhaps – I mean, it would be awfully kind of you if you could – I'd be so grateful—'

'I can row you over.'

'Oh, *thank you*. That would be wonderful.'

He turned away. 'But there's someone you might want to meet first.'

'Oh.'

Lindsey's heart sank. She had to pass some kind of test. It was only to be expected, of course. Straight is the gate. You don't get something for nothing. Bread and butter before cake. Make your bed and lie on it. Only yourself to blame.

She went back to a bench she had spotted earlier. It was on the bank near the start of the pier. There she sat down to prepare herself. Heaven knows, she reflected, she ought to be ready for this meeting with – whoever it was she was going to meet. In a sense you could say her whole life had been a preparation for this moment. Of course, she was bound to feel apprehensive. Who wouldn't at a moment like this?

She laughed nervously, smoothing her skirt over her knees as she often did at moments of stress. Just be natural, she told herself. People like you for what you are. It's no good pretending. And besides, she had always had very pleasant manners. She had made sure the children did, too.

Again the nervous gesture, smoothing her skirt. But I've always done my best, she thought, I've always tried to do what was best. How many times had she said, to comfort poor Janet as she struggled over her homework, 'You can only do your best'? One of those rather barbed phrases of consolation, she had always thought, the way 'only' and 'best' were linked together like that. Though, of course, it was perfectly true.

She waited patiently. Someone she ought to meet . . . well, there was nothing to worry about there. She had always enjoyed meeting people and had been reasonably popular. Take an interest in the other person and they'll always like you, that's what she had told Janet, when she was going through her shy teenager phase. Be a good sympathetic listener and you'll never be short of friends. Now she'd had a chance to think it over, she found that she was almost looking forward to the coming interview.

But who – or rather, *whom* (grammar was another of those things it was best to get right since people do still notice) – was she about to meet? If that wide, grey stretch of water was the River Jordan then there was every chance that she was about to meet St Peter himself. A nervous giggle escaped her. Even for someone as gregarious as Lindsey Potter, a *tête á tête* with one of the apostles was bound to be a somewhat daunting prospect. Whatever would they find to talk about? She imagined him as a rather hearty-looking fellow – and bearded, of course. A bit like one of the hikers they had met in the Lake District on that walking holiday a couple of years ago.

She didn't altogether relish the prospect of trying to justify her life to someone like him. How could she explain to him why she had gone back to art school when the children were still so small? He was certain to have strong opinions about what mothers should and should not do, and she'd never be able to make him understand how incredibly bored she had been with only two small children and a gerbil for company all day. Nor – and here a sensation of distinct unease fluttered through her – was he likely to condone the two (no, best to be honest, *three* lovers she had had before she married Ronald. As she reflected on her various shortcomings, her enthusiasm for the coming interview began waning fast. In fact, she hadn't felt so uncomfortable since she was thirteen years old and waiting outside the headmaster's study to be lectured for skipping games three weeks in a row.

Lindsey shivered. The air was clammy and cold with mist that had begun to trail like a grey scarf along the estuary. The longing to cross the river was now a desperate ache in the pit of her stomach.

River Jordan is chilly and wide, Allelu- ia,
Milk and honey on the other side, Alle- lu- u- ia!

She peered into the greyness. Was there milk and honey on the other side? Maybe. There certainly wasn't much of anything on this bank of the river. And was milk and honey really a top priority at this moment? Well, it would be a start.

A sudden chirruping of human voices startled her and she half-rose from her seat. A crowd of children were running down the grassy slope. They were jostling each other good-humouredly in their eagerness to reach the boats. With a shout of delight, the boldest of them leapt straight into a canoe and pushed off at once, paddling hard. Some of the others were more cautious but they, too, made their choice, untied their boats and struck out into the midst of the river. They should be wearing life jackets, thought Lindsey, and then giggled, as the irrelevance of this particular precaution dawned on her.

Her laughter faded when she realised that one child, a pale, dark-eyed boy who appeared to have some unfortunate deformity of his legs, was failing in his efforts to keep up with the others. Lindsey leapt to her feet to go and help him. She knew how strong was the urge to cross the river and she couldn't bear to think of him being left behind. (And, after all – though of course she would have helped him anyway – it was hardly going to count against her in the coming interview if she should first be observed in an act of spontaneous kindness. It might even do something to counterbalance the record of her inexcusable selfishness towards Ronald's mother.)

'Here, let me help you,' said Lindsey.

He didn't even bother to look up. His face was ashen with determination. 'I can manage,' he spoke through gritted teeth. Then he was in the tiny boat and dipping his oars into the water. He pulled away from the bank with inexpert and clumsy strokes.

He'll never make it, poor lad, thought Lindsey. At the same time she wished she could have gone with him. His self-sufficiency had disappointed her. Even though she was glad, naturally, for his sake.

She stood on the pier and watched the ragged flotilla of little boats scatter like sweet papers across the huge field of grey water. The shouts and laughs of the children grew fainter. A little while more and she could no longer distinguish even the crippled child.

The water lapped, bored and aimless, against the wooden posts of the pier. There were no birds to sing. No wind.

'Do you want to talk now?'

Lindsey turned quickly.

A woman was standing beside her on the bank.

'Hello. I never heard you come up. Haven't we met somewhere before?'

The words sounded ridiculous, uttered here and now, but she couldn't help it. There really was something horribly familiar about the woman who stood facing her now. She had greying hair and a strong, sympathetic face – it could almost have been Lindsey's own mother (some years before she died, of course), or even her sister Delia in Australia. Goodness, thought Lindsey, I hope Delia hasn't died too.

The woman smiled at her oddly but said nothing. She

walked a little way along the bank, and Lindsey stood up and followed expectantly.

'Shall we sit here?' The stranger gestured to a stretch of smooth turf.

Lindsey nodded. 'That's fine by me.' In fact she would have much preferred to conduct this interview seated on her bench, which was at least dry, but she wasn't about to start quibbling over details at an important moment like this. All that really mattered was to find a way to convince this oddly familiar-looking woman that she should be allowed to cross the river. The yearning to reach the far side had become almost unendurable.

Silence. Just who *was* this woman?

She decided to break the ice. 'I'm Lindsey Potter,' she said. 'We haven't been properly introduced, so I suppose I ought to start the ball rolling.'

'There's really no need,' said the woman.

Silence again. The not-quite-stranger looked across the river wistfully, as though she also longed to reach the far bank.

After what seemed like an age, the woman turned to her and said, 'You can't know who I am, you see, because I never existed.'

'You're a ghost?'

'No—'

'Then I'm afraid I don't understand.'

'Not yet. No.'

Riddles, thought Lindsey irritably, that's all I need at a time like this. Still, this woman must carry some weight around here. She would have to give an account of herself, she supposed, before she could get permission to cross the river. But why on earth did this strange woman just sit there, gazing into the mist? Why didn't she ask her any questions?

The real truth was that Lindsey was beginning to find

her companion a trifle intimidating. There was something very brisk and business-like about her, despite her lack of speech. She reminded Lindsey of the maths mistress in her High School, a woman who had been strict and very unpopular, but for whom Lindsey had always had a sneaking respect. She had called a spade a spade all right . . . this woman looked as if she would, too. That is, if she could ever be persuaded to speak at all.

The burden of silence was crushing.

'Well,' said Lindsey brightly (more brightly than she felt), 'I suppose you want me to give an account of myself. Of my life, I mean.'

The woman frowned, but still said nothing. So far Lindsey did not believe she was doing very well: if only she could work out what was expected of her.

'I've made mistakes, of course – who hasn't? No, I don't mean to sound as if I'm trying to justify myself because obviously you're not interested in that. Let's be honest, I *have* made mistakes. Sometimes I've deliberately done the wrong thing.'

'Who says so?' The woman was still looking puzzled.

'Well, for instance, there was that business with Mark. You know, the widower who moved in next door when the children were small. I thought it was all pretty harmless really, since I had no thoughts of being unfaithful to Ronald. But I suppose I could have been accused of leading him on. Well, his attention was flattering, and Ronald was away a lot. But as soon as I realised what the problem was, well, then I made the situation clear to him at once. And I set the catering business up to keep myself busy. Only in a small way at first, because of the children. But I am sorry if Mark got hurt.'

Lindsey looked at her companion to see how she was taking this. The woman stared at the horizon through half-closed eyes. It looked to Lindsey as if her face was changing somehow: not the features themselves, exactly, but the expression. No, it was more than that, it was the character behind the expression that was changing.

Lindsey soldiered on. 'I must admit that I wasn't always one hundred per cent above board with the business. Sometimes when people paid me in cash it didn't go through the books. But I always gave some of that money to the women who helped out – a small tax-free bonus for all of us, as you might say. So it wasn't entirely selfish. Less wrong than if I'd kept it all to myself.'

'Who says so?'

'Well—'

'The Inland Revenue?'

'Of course not.'

'Then, who?'

Lindsey wished she had never brought the stupid subject up. The woman had pounced on her petty misdemeanour and seemed to be blowing it out of all proportion. Oh no, she thought, it would be just my luck to be cross-examined by some kind of celestial tax inspector.

'It just didn't seem so bad that way,' she ended lamely. The woman grunted but did not speak. Rather than risk another of those endless silences, Lindsey said, 'Can I ask you something?'

'Anything you want.'

'It's just that I've been wondering whether . . . do you by any chance represent someone else?'

'In a sense. But, as I told you, that person has never existed.'

(So it wasn't St Peter, anyway.)

'But you keep asking all these questions, so I naturally assumed—'

'On the contrary, I have not asked you a single

question. You have been giving me all sorts of answers to the questions you imagined I wanted to ask.'

'Then you weren't interested in— ?'

'Not much. No, not at all.'

'Oh.'

Lindsey felt distinctly crushed.

'So, what are we supposed to be talking about?'

'Supposed? Who by?'

By whom, Lindsey corrected silently. Proof of her superior grammar bolstered her confidence. Was the other woman being obtuse on purpose?

She spoke very clearly, as if to someone with learning difficulties, 'I am extremely anxious to find a means to cross the river. But when I asked the man who appeared to be in charge of the boats, he told me there was someone I had to talk to first. So I naturally assumed that our conversation was to be some kind of reckoning, a sort of totting up, if you like. And then, if all went well, I could cross.'

'A judgment?'

'I suppose so . . . yes . . .'

'All the good deeds on one side of the scales and all the bad ones on the other and see which side was the heaviest?'

'That's putting it rather crudely, but—'

'But it is what you mean. So, you believe in the doctrine of Heaven and Hell?'

'Not in the literal sense, no. I don't believe in eternal fires or sitting on clouds but—'

'But still, a kind of test that your life either passes or fails?'

'Well, I don't suppose it's as clear cut as that . . .' Lindsey broke off, confused. She'd never had a clear picture of what precisely she believed in. Not like her Catholic friends, or that nice Pakistani family that had moved in next door. (Not wishing to be racist, Lindsey had always referred to them as 'that nice Pakistani family' even after one of them had accused Alan of running over their cat deliberately and had threatened to make a very unpleasant scene.) Having been raised in a vaguely Church of England atmosphere, Lindsey had thought it rather bad taste to be too dogmatic about big subjects like Heaven and Hell. Unless you were ethnic, of course, like the Pakistani family, in which case it was all part of your cultural heritage and perfectly natural. Still, she had always accepted that there were right decisions and there were wrong ones. It therefore followed that one was supposed to choose the right ones. She couldn't understand why the woman sitting beside her was making such heavy weather of it all.

Again that longing, fierce as frustrated addiction, to reach the far side of the river. So she found it all the more exasperating that this preliminary talk seemed to be getting nowhere fast.

Lindsey could restrain herself no longer. 'For heavens sake,' she burst out, 'who *are* you?'

'Surely you recognise me by now.'

'No.'

'I am yourself.'

'But how— ?'

'Yourself as you might have been.'

'If— ?'

'If you had chosen differently.'

'Then where did I go wrong?'

'Tst. There you go again. Right and wrong. I am merely one of an infinite number of possible Lindseys.'

'Really? Heavens, I'd love to meet them.' Even as the words left her mouth, Lindsey wondered if that wasn't the most whopping lie.

'You can't,' said the woman. 'You are the only possible Lindsey now. And always will be.'

'But if you were to help me—'

'How can I do that? I'm only you, after all.'

'Goodness, how complicated. Can't you even try to explain?'

'I already have.'

'Are you saying I ought to have been more selfish?'

'Or less.'

'But—'

'Or you might have done exactly the same in every case.'

'Oh dear, it's all such a muddle. You must think I'm terribly obtuse but I simply don't—' And then, with sudden anxiety because the woman had stood up, 'Please don't go so soon. What is supposed to happen now? Who will help me get across the river? Ought I to try rowing myself, like the children did, or—'

'No point asking me. It's up to you. It always has been.'

'So, do you think— ?' Like a frightened child at bedtime, Lindsey clutched at the woman's safety, but it was too late.

'Not even me,' said the woman. And it was true. She was no longer there.

And then there was nothing. No one. Empty water and empty sky.

The light was growing still more purple; a damson-coloured stain spread across the water she so desperately wanted to cross.

For a long time Lindsey remained sitting patiently on the bench. She gazed out over the wide river, and waited to be told.

THOMAS KENEALLY

Extract from his new novel

A River Town

Thomas Keneally's latest novel in paperback, *Jacko: The Great Intruder*, is available now at your local Dillons store priced £5.99.

Bring this voucher with you to obtain £1.00 off the publisher's prices at all Dillons stores.

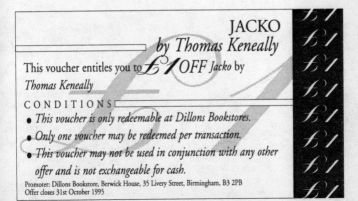

On the Sunday morning of the picnic, at the early Mass, Father Bruggy happened to speak of the Holy Name and the common abuse of it on low tongues.

'Ireland is a Catholic nation,' he said, 'and possesses a strong sense of the Ten Commandments. But there are two vices the Irish immigrant brings to New South Wales. The one, drunkenness – which shall be the subject of another sermon. The other – the undue invocation of the name of Our Lord and of his Blessed Mother. My English brother, Father McCambridge, comments on the fact that the Holy Name is most under threat from those who most honour it, the Irish emigrant to these shores. Here, his looseness with the Divine Name combines exactly with a colonial looseness of expression in general. I must warn Irish newcomers of their tendency to contribute to the general laxness of colonial, Australian expression. I would urge men to join the Holy Name Sodality, whose purpose is to stamp out the misuse of the Divine Name . . .'

Kitty was muttering at Tim. 'Takes an Englishman to remind us of all this. Put the Holy Name up on a shelf and rent it out for day-to-day use!'

Father Bruggy said that the Holy Name Sodality would meet at the end of Mass.

'Devil you'll join them!' Kitty told him. When she chose to obey priests she did it thoroughly. But she was discerning on the matter. Fortunately he lacked the inclination to stay behind.

After Mass, Mother Imelda and the other nuns observed a short thanksgiving period – as did their boarders perforce – and then rose and genuflected and processed out of the church. Their boarders in trim clothes and shining faces, behind them. Little Lucy Rochester amongst the boarders with her clenched features and her glowing eyes. The reformed climber. The repentant imperiller.

As already arranged, Mother Imelda brought Lucy to the Sheas. She nodded to Kitty and dragged Tim imperiously by the elbow a little way distant from the group. He could hear Annie say, 'That's Lucy, Mama. Lucy. She lives with the nuns.'

'The child,' Imelda murmured to Tim, 'has listened intently to everything, and Sister Philomena is astounded by her grasp of Christian Doctrine.'

Tim groaned – perhaps aloud. He knew what would now be said. 'She wishes to take instruction as a Catholic.'

Tim flinched. He had a duty by Albert. 'You're sure, Mother, she isn't just trying to please you?'

'Mr Shea, I have watched this occur with other children of Protestant parents. Give me some credit! I can sniff out what is genuine and what is merely opportune.'

'Her father's so recently dead, and he would not like this.'

'If our faith means anything, Mr Shea, it means he is now in possession of the *real* facts and is at peace.'

'Well, as much as I trust your discernment, Mother . . . Perhaps she should wait a little while. That's what I think.' Imelda staring him down. He shrugged, touched his hat. 'I'll talk to her on our picnic.'

Mamie had filled a hamper, and it sat in the dray along with a basketful of ale and a number of blankets. Joe and Mamie, shadowed by Johnny, who for some reason liked Joe and was quiet in his presence, climbed into Joe's uncle's plain yellow farm cart. It too carried an ample basket of ale.

Tim went and lifted Kitty up to the seat behind Pee Dee. Lucy and Annie were already in the dray, talking. Yet so hard as ever to hear what Lucy said!

All around, the carts of other communicants of St Joseph's Kempsey were pulling away from the church. Young men on ponies raced each other like young men of any communion at any time. Men with pipes in their hands who waited outside Kelty's – Kelty's opened up to certain Romans after Mass on Sundays, despite the licensing laws – took off their hats and waved to Tim. Did they also think he'd written the *Australis* letters and provoked bitter Billy Thurmond to his Patriotic Fund motion?

In Elbow Street in West, they encountered an astounding and ominous sight. The postmaster was out in the spare block beside the Post Office. With an axe, he was chopping through the timber uprights of the closed shooting gallery. The postmaster a mad-eyed Scot named MacAllen, and he paused and wiped his brow and nodded to Tim. 'The Shire won't take action. I've complained and complained about lads shooting away to all hours of the evening. Armenian bugger who runs the place is only squatting on this land anyhow.'

'Fair enough,' called Tim. Though secretly he was a little surprised by this kind of lawlessness in an official. MacAllen said, 'My wife sits up worrying about the children and the Sydney plague, and all we can hear is bang, bang, bang!'

'Very trying,' called Kitty, turning her short body with diffi culty towards the postmaster, but then covering a laugh with her lace-gloved hand.

'Better to agree with a man with an axe,' she muttered to Tim.

As the postmaster applied himself again, the sheet of corrugated iron which had roofed the gallery fell like thunder. The postmaster stepped back and was pleased.

They rolled on, convinced that this might be a good day to be away from the town.

At the Central punt in Smith Street, Bandy was waiting for them, smiling. On the same grey he'd been riding the day of Albert Rochester's tragedy, and the night of the illicit ride.

'Good morning, Sheas and Miss Kenna and Mr O'Neill. Prayers completed, the day now belongs to a totally decent picnic!'

Tim looked to the cart behind, because he was curious to see how Mamie reacted to this fulsome sentiment of Bandy's. She was rolling her eyes at O'Neill and laughing. Yet it did not seem to be in total mockery.

Annie touched Tim's arm from the back of the cart where she sat on a pile of rugs with the white-frocked Lucy. 'Bandy Habash is funny,' she sagely told him.

The exhilaration of being on the deck of a punt, all in a party, observing the thickness of fertile soil in the banks, the splendid mountains too bluely distant to show their burnt trunks.

They landed in East, Bandy leading his biddable grey and at the same time hauling Pee Dee by the bit, while Tim hallo-ed and urged. The road followed for a little way the path he and Bandy had taken to the plague camp. But went past the turnoff for a mile before itself veering back to the coast, becoming a sandy, claggy track. Ahead, between them and the sea, lay a huge mountain, Dulcangui. Covered with grey-green trees and displaying gnarls of sandstone, it rose up out of the low ground like a threat. When they reached the rise, the road now became a cutting through the mountain's rock. Kitty took over the reins of the Shea wagon. Tim and Lucy got down to walk. Bandy himself dismounted from the grey after making a number of experimental canters up and down the stony slope. Then he put Annie in the saddle, a place that seemed to please her very much, and began to lead the way up Dulcangui.

'Watch out for snakes!' cried Tim. For he did not want the grey shying with Annie in its saddle.

To make the ascent, Tim walked level with Pee Dee's neck, grabbing him by the harness to hold him to the mountain. After Pee Dee had shaken his head the required number of times to satisfy the Horse Union's idea of bloody-mindedness in a beast, he allowed Kitty at the reins to gee him up the first section of road. Rocks and saplings designed for impaling lay all the way down the murderous slope which fell away from the side of the track.

Mamie strode past Tim and Lucy, her neat knees ploughing away beneath the fabric of her white dress. A bit of an athlete, this one. She went ahead and walked and talked with Annie and Habash, while Joe O'Neill, alone except for Johnny and at the rear, learned to urge his uncle's cart up this severe track.

In country like this, the Patriotic Fund seemed barely a dent on human contentment. Yet Tim could hear Pee Dee snorting, the bugger. Just to make things interesting. Kitty tugged at him with her now-bare, red little hands and uttered both soothing and threatening non-words to get him over the hill.

Lucy beside him. The little would-be Papist. How horrified the Primitive Methodists would be.

'Well, you want to be a convert, do you?' he asked the child.

'Yes.' She walked with the gait of a grown woman.

'You wouldn't do that just to please the nuns, eh? You can't please them. I know it because I'm their grocer.'

He could tell by her up-tilted gaze that she knew it too. They were hungry goddesses.

'You'll have to remember,' said Tim, 'that your little brother at Mrs Sutter's won't be with you in this.'

Typical of her, she said nothing.

'Well, do you think he'd mind?'

'He's too young,' she told him. 'This is a business for me.'

'Why do you want to do it though?'

'I want to have God. But I want the angels too.'

'Wouldn't the other people let you have angels?'

'I want the Blessed Mother too.'

'You *are* an ambitious little woman, aren't you?'

'I want a Blessed Mother.'

A reasonable and pitiable desire in an orphan, he thought. He took one of the lollies he was keeping for the children out of his pocket and slipped it into her hand.

'I'll tell you this. Don't do it too easily. And don't do it to please anyone. Because you're stuck with it for life then and people think the worse of you. Suspect you of all sorts of things they don't suspect you of if you stayed Primitive Methodist.'

'I know. But.'

'*But*. But you have the angels and the saints?'

'Yes,' said Lucy. 'There's lots of them.'

'Some people consider that a problem.'

Kitty on the reins and Tim at the halter dragged Pee Dee and the cart around a last wall of rock, and now this was the top. A vast glitter of sea could be seen from up here. Its line broken only by Crescent Head's two famous headlands – the Little Nobby and the Big.

Down again towards the paperback swamps which lay between Dulcangui and the ocean. Bandy let Lucy lead the grey and came back to help control Pee Dee. Pee Dee fussy on the stony downslope. Mamie climbed up beside Kitty and took a hand at the reins. You could hear the bottles jiggling in their baskets. Before they got to the bottom, two in the hamper on Joe O'Neill's cart exploded.

Meanwhile, Lucy and Johnny, who had abandoned poor Joe for the greater excitement of the vanguard, between them led the grey down onto the corduroy road across the swamp to the sea. In the grey's saddle, Annie still sat. Entering into a fair imitation of her kingdom.

The picnic place finally chosen was on a sward above the surf at the bottom of the Little Nobby. They could look out over the sea and then across a small saltwater creek to the twelve miles of Front Beach. Mamie was enthused by this vigorous bright sight and was soon knee-deep in the creek with the children. Johnny, shirt off, began splashing round as he did in the river, but his strokes were interrupted by the shallowness of the creek and the playful current. Tim waded in too, his trousers rolled up. Standing still you could see mullet swim by. Annie, Johnny, Lucy kept trying to catch them in their hands.

Ashore Kitty lay on her back on a rug and under a parasol, pointing the unborn Shea child straight at the arc of blue sky. Near her, Joe O'Neill began smoking reflectively and plunking his banjo. The tune 'Bold Phelim Brady' was raggedly released into the air. His boots were still on. Perhaps he had an inlander's fear of the water. When Tim waded ashore, Joe and he began opening beer with flourishes. After the rough trip, the stuff fizzed out of the necks of the bottles.

'Porter, Mrs Shea?' asked Joe, putting a long glass of frothy stout in Kitty's outreaching hand.

'Oh, dear,' sighed Kitty. 'As lovely as you'll get.'

Meanwhile Bandy took the saddle off his grey's back. Steam rose gently from the crushed, damp hair. Tim was surprised to see Bandy take his shirt and pants off too, so that now he wore only a singlet and his long, white linen breeches. The singlet was low-cut and revealed in part a smooth, brown, hairless chest. Arms not like the arms of men from Europe. Both smaller and yet more sinewy. He jumped on the grey's back and urged it gently into the creek. It went placidly, standing to its belly in the water, seeming content amongst the little waves. Bandy turning to throw a salute to the shallows where Mamie and the children were prancing and yelling and trying to grab mullet.

Lucy now with her skirts tucked in her knickers looked more a child and less of a witness than he'd ever seen. Though sometimes she would cup up a palm full of saltwater and study it.

Having crossed the creek, Bandy put the grey into a gallop on the firm sand below the tidemark along Front Beach. All this looked splendid to Tim, half-naked Bandy leaned down to the grey mane, the lovely mare shattering its own reflection in the wet sand, and thundering away.

Whereas Pee Dee was up along the slope, turned out of the traces and eating grass as if he'd never go back to work again.

'You bugger, you're for the knackers,' Tim casually called to Pee Dee, who disdained to stop devouring the hillside.

At last, for love's sake, Joe O'Neill took his big boots off and rolled his trousers and went and stood in the rim of the creek. Kitty must have been able to see this from her lying position. 'Look out for them sharks, Joe,' she murmured.

They ate a drowsy lunch – sardines and cornbeef, beer and ginger beer. Chewing heartily, Mamie looked across to the larger headland, smooth and green and momentous. It took up a whole quarter of the sky.

'We'll be climbing that big feller there?'

He could see the children's eyes flick towards the Big Nobby. Not a question that it invited you!

'You and Joe can go up there after lunch,' said Tim. It was the right sort of physical feature for courting. It demanded that hands be reached to each other. But he didn't want mad Johnny up there.

'What can you see from the top?'

'The whole coastline of New South Wales,' said Kitty dreamily. 'At a total sweep. And the air. A lens, you see. The air like a bloody telescope.'

'Can we go, Papa?' asked Johnny bolt upright like a jack rabbit, on his knees. More than ready for high places again, the little ruffian.

'I'll take you over the creek to the beach,' said Tim. 'Mr Habash might take his grey again and you can ride. But not gallop, son, not gallop. I know you.'

'But can't the children come?' asked Mamie. It was as if she did not want to be left alone with Joe. 'We can all keep an eye. You'll be good won't you, Lucy?'

Lucy looked up at her levelly. 'I learned my lesson,' said Lucy in a way which implied canings and made everyone laugh.

Something entirely convincing about Lucy swayed Tim, as did the size of the day. He remembered too the gradual, accommodating lines of the Big Nobby.

'Then I'll go too,' said Tim. 'I'll keep an eagle eye out. And

you, Bandy. You come too if you would, and watch these little
blackguards.'

He felt sorry for Joe, the corner of whose mouth conveyed
disappointment. Mamie was a bugger of a tease.

'But first the tea,' said Bandy. He had made a fire a little way
down on the creek. He now went and fetched the excellent tea
he had brewed. Mamie stood up and asked to see into the billy
he was carrying.

'There's tree leaves in that tea,' she complained.

'That's gum leaves,' said Tim. 'Australians make their tea with
gum leaves thrown in. When there's a tree handy.'

So, it struck him now: Bandy was by habit an Australian.

They drank plenty of this tea to ready themselves for their
thirsty climb. When they were finished, Tim wanting to get
up there and down and have it over, they left Kitty lying on
a blanket in scant shadow, with her parasol leaned across her
face to give double shade. A strong sea breeze cooled her and
played with the tassels of the parasol.

On the flanks on the great whale-like Big Nobby, whorls of
tussocky grass made the climb easy. You stepped from one knot
of grass to another. Step by step, like climbing a pyramid. Johnny
kept racing ahead and looking down like a gazelle from some
nest of grass. But Lucy mounted the headland beside Tim,
whose hand was held by Annie. So they rose up the green
slope quite easily, Joe O'Neill chattering away, to the domed
top of the thing.

Bandy seemed to take care to be up there first, not it appeared
for rivalry's sake but as if he too wanted to prevent any madness
in Johnny. As Tim and Annie rose higher on the great headland,
they began to pick up the welcome southerly on their brows. Tim
finished the climb with Annie on his back, since the child did
not believe in wearing herself out. All the others were waiting
on top for them, looking south, Mamie exclaiming at what
could be seen. Joe had a wrestle-hold on Johnny, and Johnny
struggled in it, laughing. Lucy stood soberly there like one of the
adult party.

Arriving and dropping Annie so that she could take up her
normal august posture, Tim saw Back Beach and its wild surf
stretching away to Point Plummer, Racecourse Beach, etc, etc.

You could have seen Port Macquarie except that the day's haze blurred the scene about twenty miles south.

'Now you don't see a sight like that,' said Mamie, 'anywhere on the Cork or Kerry coast.'

'Because it's always wrapped in mist there,' murmured Joe.

From here it could be seen that the headland on which they stood had two tops, this one and another further to the south. In between, a green saddle with grass and little thickets of native shrubs. Beneath the saddle a partially seen great rock wall fell into the sea, which grew plum-coloured in the shadow of the black stone. You could hear and partly see the ocean raging down there, making caves. Of course there was no way, having got here, the party would choose not to walk on into the saddle towards the other, lower dome. Finding a way past the spiky banksias, and so to the Big Nobby's second summit. From there they would, of course, be able to look from safety directly down into the turmoil of rock and sea below.

'No shy-acking then, Johnny,' Tim called out. He didn't utter any warnings to Lucy. For she seemed a changed child. She knew about witnessing angels.

As they walked down into the saddle, dragging their feet through clumps of button grass, the Big Nobby maintained its gradual character. Not like cliffs elsewhere – not a case of grass running sharply to the definite and dramatic precipice, and then the sudden fall. You knew that somewhere to their left the black cliff began. But here, because of the headland's gentle angle and its thick grass tufts, each one a rung of its massive ladder, there was no sense that you could topple and roll.

'Prickly, prickly,' said Annie as they reached the thickets, flapping her long-fingered hands at him, pleading to be picked up. She had those delicate fingers utterly unlike Kitty's. They came from his sister Helen, who'd married the newspaper editor in Brooklyn.

He lifted her and followed the path the others had taken. These strange, olive green banksia bushes with their black cones. Splits in the cones like eyes and mouths. 'Look,' said Tim, holding one of the cones. 'The Banksia Man. He's an evil little fellow.'

Annie threw herself about in his arms with fake shudders.

They came back up out of the banksias to Big Nobby's grassy

southern crest. Ah yes, you could see down to where the grasses grew steeper and the rock layers began and the hungry surf worked away. A number of birds wheeled around the semi-circle of this rock wall. It seemed to Tim to be the mad energy of the waves that kept them up, since none of them flapped their wings. A little way up from the wall above the sea, a sea-eagle considered a dive. A sharp, pearly, commanding shape with black wingtips.

'That one there's a sea-eagle,' he told the others. 'When they dive, they bloody dive.'

'This is the place,' said Mamie. 'You could have a tea-house up here.'

'A pub perhaps,' amended Joe O'Neill, who was sure to crack more ale once they got down. Lucy stood beside Joe and on the other side of him, still quiet from respect for this soon-to-be uncle, Johnny. Good. They were still. They watched the sea-eagle. Its circles had them hypnotised. It had authority over the air. It put the frenzied children in their place.

'Will you carry me down like you carried me up, papa?' asked Annie ceremoniously, at his side.

'To walk will be good for your little legs.'

'I don't think that's true. My little legs don't agree.'

He heard Mamie laughing. The sea-eagle banked and Tim took a new sense of it, that it was no mere natural wonder of some kind. A sudden gust came up to them as if the bird had manufactured it for them with its banked wings. Tim felt the stirred air all around him. The damned wheeling thing had command of the day. Its very ease, he felt at once, was a frightful temptation and the young should not be exposed . . .

He heard Mamie shriek, and Habash cry, 'Stop this!'

Somehow the bird had by its malign circling and its sending a breeze engendered something unspoken but at once mutual between Lucy and Johnny. In all their campaigns, had they ever exchanged a word? If they had, no one had heard it. They planned it as if by fishing in each other's mind.

This was their venture now. They were running down the incline of the headland, their hands clasped. Johnny could be heard laughing in between Joe's shouting, but Lucy was silent. It was such an inviting slope, and from some angles you found it hard to imagine or give credence to the drop, the indented face below, the Nobby's true, black sting. So piteously confident were they of their impunity, that seeing them you were possessed by an absolute panic of pity. Pity could be heard in the way everybody howled.

Now they all followed – Bandy, Joe, Mamie. Then himself, dropping Annie's hand, since she could be trusted. All the party running with their heels thrust forward to avail themselves of the holding power of the grass. All yelling direly. Pleas not to be remembered afterwards word by word. Simply a general, frantic, fatherly pleading of the two little buggers running hand in hand. Ahead the feverish sapphire sea, and a sky of acid blue. Tim feeling his ankle yell at this strange usage as he ran madly towards the gulf. The younger men and the one young woman still ahead of him, all helplessly shrieking. *Noooooooooooo!* So steep now where the children were, and Johnny leaning back, Tim saw with hope, but Lucy thrusting skinny shoulders forward. Welcoming the fall. And still hands locked. Soon they would go flying over together. This beat the stern of *Terara*. This beat the Angelus tower. This so clearly a venue worthy of their shared will that he cursed himself for allowing anyone but Mamie and Joe to approach this climb.

But when the result seemed obvious, Johnny simply sat on a tussock. The grasp was as easily broken as that. Lucy sailed out alone. Shrilling but not with terror. And vocal now she had taken to the air. So close to the fall of the cliff was everyone that they saw only the first liberated segment of her fall. Tim continued down the awful grade and yanked Johnny upright by his collar. Johnny's face was ghastly. *He* had been playing. Had expected her to sit too after the joke had been played out. *Look, we are reformed! You only thought we were playing the old games!*

Nonetheless, Tim couldn't stop himself striking the boy on the head in a kind of horror and gratefulness. Bandy was working energetically around the rim, the only one not screaming and exclaiming. He wanted a better view. To see if Lucy was frolicking or fluttering in and out on the waves in that chaos down there. Everyone, whimpering and pleading, worked their way around the edge as Bandy had, so that they could see into the cauldron.

'There is nothing,' Bandy yelled against the wind. 'Nothing to be seen.' The hugh masses of white there contained none of Lucy's whiteness or white fabric. She had been swallowed.

Above them, Annie – who had had the best view – was wailing for him to come back.

STEPHEN KING

Short story taken from
Nightmares & Dreamscapes

The End of the Whole Mess

Nightmares & Dreamscapes is available now at your local Dillons store priced £5.99.

Bring this voucher with you to obtain £1.00 off the publisher's prices at all Dillons stores.

The End of the Whole Mess

I want to tell you about the end of war, the degeneration of mankind, and the death of the Messiah – an epic story, deserving thousands of pages and a whole shelf of volumes, but you (if there are any 'you' later on to read this) will have to settle for the freeze-dried version. The direct injection works very fast. I figure I've got somewhere between forty-five minutes and two hours, depending on my blood-type. I think it's A, which should give me a little more time, but I'll be goddamned if I can remember for sure. If it turns out to be O, you could be in for a lot of blank pages, my hypothetical friend.

In any event, I think maybe I'd better assume the worst and go as fast as I can.

I'm using the electric typewriter – Bobby's word-processor is faster, but the genny's cycle is too irregular to be trusted, even with the line suppressor. I've only got one shot at this; I can't risk getting most of the way home and then seeing the whole thing go to data heaven because of an oHm drop, or a surge too great for the suppressor to cope with.

My name is Howard Fornoy. I was a freelance writer. My brother, Robert Fornoy, was the Messiah. I killed him by shooting him up with his own discovery four hours ago. *He* called it The Calmative. A Very Serious Mistake might have been a better name, but what's done is done and can't be undone, as the Irish have been saying for centuries . . . which *proves* what assholes they are.

Shit, I can't afford these digressions.

After Bobby died I covered him with a quilt and sat at the cabin's single living-room window for some three hours, looking out at the woods. Used to be you could see the orange glow of the hi-intensity arc-sodiums from North Conway, but no more. Now there's just the White Mountains, looking like dark triangles of crepe paper cut out by a child, and the pointless stars.

I turned on the radio, dialed through four bands, found one crazy guy, and shut it off. I sat there thinking of ways to tell this story. My mind kept sliding away toward all those miles of dark pinewoods, all that nothing. Finally I realized I needed to get myself off the dime and shoot myself up. Shit. I never *could* work without a deadline.

And I've sure-to-God got one now.

Our parents had no reason to expect anything other than what they got: bright children. Dad was a history major who had become a full professor at Hofstra when he was thirty. Ten years later he was one of six vice-administrators of the National Archives in Washington, DC, and in line for the top spot. He was a helluva good guy, too – had every record Chuck Berry ever cut and played a pretty mean blues guitar himself. My dad filed by day and rocked by night.

Mom graduated *magna cum laude* from Drew. Got a Phi Beta Kappa key she sometimes wore on this funky fedora she had. She became a successful CPA in DC, met my dad, married him, and took in her shingle when she became pregnant with yours truly. I came along in 1980. By '84 she was doing taxes for some of my dad's associates – she called this her 'little hobby.' By the time Bobby was born in 1987, she was handling taxes, investment portfolios, and estate-planning for a dozen powerful men. I could name them, but who gives a wad? They're either dead or driveling idiots by now.

I think she probably made more out of 'her little hobby' each year than my dad made at his job, but that never mattered – they were happy with what they were to themselves and to each other. I saw them squabble lots of times, but I never saw them fight. When I was growing up, the only difference I saw between my mom and my playmates' moms was that their moms used to read or iron or sew or talk on the phone while the soaps played on the tube, and my mom used to run a pocket calculator and write down numbers on big green sheets of paper while the soaps played on the tube.

I was no disappointment to a couple of people with Mensa Gold Cards in their wallets. I maintained A's and B's through my school career (the idea that either I or my brother might go to a private school was never even discussed so far as I know). I also wrote well early, with no effort at all. I sold my first magazine piece when I was twenty – it was on how the Continental Army wintered at Valley Forge. I sold it to an airline magazine for four hundred fifty dollars. My dad, whom I loved deeply, asked me if he could buy that check from me. He gave me his own personal check and had the check from the airline magazine framed and hung it over his desk. A romantic genius, if you will. A romantic *blues-playing* genius, if you will. Take it from me, a kid could do a lot worse. Of course he and my mother both died raving and pissing in their pants late last year, like almost everyone else on this big round world of ours, but I never stopped loving either of them.

I was the sort of child they had every reason to expect – a good boy with a bright mind, a talented boy whose talent grew to early maturity in an atmosphere of love and confidence, a faithful boy who loved and respected his mom and dad.

Bobby was different. *Nobody*, not even Mensa types like our folks, *ever* expects a kid like Bobby. Not *ever*.

I potty-trained two full years earlier than Bob, and that was the only thing in which I ever beat him. But I never felt jealous of him; that would have been like a fairly good American Legion League pitcher feeling jealous of Nolan Ryan or Roger Clemens. After a certain point the comparisons that cause feelings of jealousy simply cease to exist. I've been there, and I can tell you: after a certain point you just stand back and shield your eyes from the flashburns.

Bobby read at two and began writing short essays ('Our Dog', 'A Trip to Boston with Mother') at three. His printing was the straggling, struggling galvanic constructions of a six-year-old, and that was startling enough in itself, but there was more: if transcribed so that his still-developing motor control no longer became an evaluative factor, you would have thought you were reading the work of a bright, if extremely naive, fifth-grader. He progressed from simple sentences to compound sentences to complex ones with dizzying rapidity, grasping clauses, sub-clauses, and modifying clauses with an intuitiveness that was eerie. Sometimes his syntax was garbled and his modifiers misplaced, but he had such flaws – which plague most writers all their lives – pretty well under control by the age of five.

He developed headaches. My parents were afraid he had some sort of physical problem – a brain-tumor, perhaps – and took him to a doctor who examined him carefully, listened to him even more carefully, and then told my parents there was nothing wrong with Bobby except stress: he was in a state of extreme frustration because his writing-hand would not work as well as his brain.

'You got a kid trying to pass a mental kidney stone,' the doctor said. 'I could prescribe something for his headaches, but I think the drug he really needs is a typewriter.' So Mom and Dad gave Bobby an IBM. A year later they gave him a Commodore 64 with WordStar for Christmas and Bobby's headaches stopped. Before going on to other matters, I only want to add that he believed for the next three years or so that it was Santa Claus who had left that word-cruncher under our tree. Now that I think of it, that was another place where I beat Bobby: I Santa-trained earlier, too.

There's so much I could tell you about those early days, and I suppose I'll have to tell you a little, but I'll have to go fast and make it brief. The deadline. Ah, the deadline.

I once read a very funny piece called 'The Essential *Gone with the Wind*' that went something like this:

'"*A war?*" *laughed Scarlett.* "*Oh, fiddle-de-dee!*"

'*Boom! Ashley went to war! Atlanta burned! Rhett walked in and then walked out!*

'"*Fiddle-de-dee*," *said Scarlett through her tears,* "*I will think about it tomorrow, for tomorrow is another day.*"'

I laughed heartily over that when I read it; now that I'm faced with doing something similar, it doesn't seem quite so funny. But here goes:

'*A child with an IQ immeasurable by any existing test?*' *smiled India Fornoy to her devoted husband, Richard.* '*Fiddle-de-dee! We'll provide an atmosphere where his intellect – not to mention that of his not-exactly-stupid older brother – can grow. And we'll raise them as the normal all-American boys they by gosh are!*'

Boom! The Fornoy boys grew up! Howard went to the University of Virginia, graduated cum laude, *and settled down to a freelance writing career! Made a comfortable living! Stepped out with a lot of women and went to bed with quite a few of them! Managed to avoid social diseases both sexual and pharmacological! Bought a Mitsubishi stereo system! Wrote home at least once a week! Published two novels that did pretty well!* '*Fiddle-de-dee*,' *said Howard,* '*this is the life for me!*'

And so it was, at least until the day Bobby showed up unexpectedly (in the best mad-scientist tradition) with his two glass boxes, a bees' nest in one and a wasps' nest in the other, Bobby wearing a Mumford Phys Ed tee-shirt inside-out, on the verge of destroying human intellect and just as happy as a clam at high tide.

Guys like my brother Bobby come along only once every two or three generations, I think – guys like Leonardo da Vinci, Newton, Einstein, maybe Edison. They all seem to have one thing in common: they are like huge compasses which swing aimlessly for a long time, searching for some true north and then homing on it with fearful force. Before that happens such guys are apt to get up to some weird shit, and Bobby was no exception.

When he was eight and I was fifteen, he came to me and said he had invented an airplane. By then I knew Bobby too well to just say 'Bullshit' and kick him out of my room. I went out to the garage where there was this weird plywood contraption sitting on his American Flyer red wagon. It looked a little like a fighter plane, but the wings were raked forward instead of back. He had mounted the saddle from his rocking horse on the middle of it with bolts. There was a lever on the side. There was no motor. He said it was a glider. He wanted me to push him down Carrigan's Hill, which was the steepest grade in DC's Grant Park – there was a cement path down the middle of it for old folks. That, Bobby said, would be his runway.

'Bobby,' I said, 'you got this puppy's wings on backward.'

'No,' he said. 'This is the way they're supposed to be. I saw something on *Wild Kingdom* about hawks. They dive down on their prey and then reverse their wings coming up. They're double-jointed, see? You get better lift this way.'

'Then why isn't the Air Force building them this way?' I asked, blissfully unaware that both the American and the Russian air forces had plans for such forward-wing fighter planes on their drawing boards.

Bobby just shrugged. He didn't know and didn't care.

We went over to Carrigan's Hill and he climbed into the rocking-horse saddle and gripped the lever. 'Push me *hard*,' he said. His eyes were dancing with that crazed light I knew so well – Christ, his eyes used to light up that way in his cradle sometimes. But I swear to God I never would have pushed him down the cement path as hard as I did if I thought the thing would actually work.

But I *didn't* know, and I gave him one hell of a shove. He went freewheeling down the hill, whooping like a cowboy just off a traildrive and headed into town for a few cold beers. An old lady had to jump out of his way, and he just missed an old geezer leaning over a walker. Halfway down he pulled the handle and I watched, wide-eyed and bullshit with fear and amazement, as his splintery plywood plane separated from the wagon. At first it only hovered inches above it, and for a second it looked like it was going to settle back. Then there was a gust of wind and Bobby's plane took off like someone had it on an invisible cable. The American Flyer wagon ran off the concrete path and into some bushes. All of a sudden Bobby was ten feet in the air, then twenty, then fifty. He went gliding over Grant Park on a steepening upward plane, whooping cheerily.

I went running after him, screaming for him to come down, visions of his body tumbling off that stupid rocking-horse saddle and impaling itself on a tree, or one of the park's many statues, standing out with hideous clarity in my head. I did not just imagine my brother's funeral; I tell you I *attended* it.

'*BOBBY!*' I shrieked. '*COME DOWN!*'

'*WHEEEEEEEE!*' Bobby screamed back, his voice faint but clearly ecstatic. Startled chess-players, Frisbee-throwers, book-readers, lovers, and joggers stopped whatever they were doing to watch.

'*BOBBY THERE'S NO SEATBELT ON THAT FUCKING THING!*' I screamed. It was the first time I ever used that particular word, so far as I can remember.

'*Iyyyy'll beeee all riyyyyht . . .*' He was screaming at the top of his lungs, but I was appalled to realize I could barely hear him. I went running down Carrigan's Hill, shrieking all the way. I don't have the slightest memory of just what I was yelling, but the next day I could not speak above a whisper. I *do* remember passing a young fellow in a neat three-piece suit standing by the statue of Eleanor Roosevelt at the foot of the hill. He looked at me and said conversationally, 'Tell you what, my friend, I'm having one *hell* of an acid flashback.'

I remember that odd misshapen shadow gliding across the green floor of the park, rising and rippling as it crossed park benches, litter baskets, and the upturned faces of the watching people. I remember chasing it. I remember how my mother's face crumpled and how she started to cry when I told her that Bobby's plane, which had no business flying in the first place, turned upside down in a sudden eddy of wind and Bobby finished his short but brilliant career splattered all over D Street.

The way things turned out, it might have been better for everyone if things had actually turned out that way, but they didn't.

Instead, Bobby banked back toward Carrigan's Hill, holding nonchalantly onto the tail of his own plane to keep from falling off the damned thing, and brought it down toward the little pond at the center of Grant Park. He went air-sliding five feet over it, then four . . . and then he was skiing his sneakers along the surface of the water, sending back twin white wakes, scaring the usually complacent (and overfed) ducks up in honking indignant flurries before him, laughing his cheerful laugh. He came down on the far side, exactly between two park benches that snapped off the wings of his plane. He flew out of the saddle, thumped his head, and started to bawl.

That was life with Bobby.

Not everything was that spectacular – in fact, I don't think *anything* was . . . at least until The Calmative. But I told you the story because I think, this time at least, the extreme case best illustrates the norm: life with Bobby was a constant mind-fuck. By the age of nine he was attending quantum physics and advanced algebra classes at Georgetown University. There was the day he blanked out every radio and TV on our street – and the surrounding four blocks – with his own voice; he had found an old portable TV in the attic and turned it into a wide-band radio broadcasting station. One old black-and-white Zenith, twelve feet of hi-fi flex, a coathanger mounted on the roofpeak of our house, and presto! For about two hours four blocks of Georgetown could receive only WBOB . . . which happened to be my brother, reading some of my short stories, telling moron jokes, and explaining that the high sulfur content in baked beans was the reason our dad farted so much in church every Sunday morning. 'But he gets most of em off pretty quiet,' Bobby told his listening audience of roughly three thousand, 'or sometimes he holds the real bangers until it's time for the hymns.'

My dad, who was less than happy about all this, ended up paying a seventy-five-dollar FCC fine and taking it out of Bobby's allowance for the next year.

Life with Bobby, oh yeah . . . and look here, I'm crying. Is it honest sentiment, I wonder, or the onset? The former, I think – Christ knows how much I loved him – but I think I better try to hurry up a little just the same.

Bobby had graduated high school, for all practical purposes, by the age of ten, but he never got a BA or BS, let alone any advanced degree. It was that big powerful compass in his head, swinging around and around, looking for some true north to point at.

He went through a physics period, and a shorter period when he was nutty for chemistry . . . but in the end, Bobby was too impatient with mathematics for either of those fields to hold him. He could do it, but it – and ultimately all so-called hard science – bored him.

By the time he was fifteen, it was archaeology – he combed the White Mountain foothills around our summer place in North Conway, building a history of the Indians who had lived there from arrowheads, flints, even the charcoal patterns of long-dead campfires in the mesolithic caves in the mid-New Hampshire regions.

But that passed, too, and he began to read history and anthropology. When he was sixteen my father and my mother gave their reluctant approval when Bobby requested that he be allowed to accompany a party of New England anthropologists on an expedition to South America.

He came back five months later with the first real tan of his life; he was also an inch taller, fifteen pounds lighter, and much quieter. He was still cheerful enough, or could be, but his little-boy exuberance, sometimes infectious, sometimes wearisome, but always there, was gone. He had grown up. And for the first time I remember him talking about the news . . . how bad it was, I mean. That was 2003, the year a PLO splinter group called the Sons of the Jihad (a name that always sounded to me hideously like a Catholic community service group somewhere in western Pennsylvania) set off a Squirt Bomb in London, polluting sixty per cent of it and making the rest of it extremely unhealthy for people who ever planned to have children (or to live past the age of fifty, for that matter). The year we tried to block-ade the Philippines after the Cedeño administration accepted a 'small group' of Red Chinese advisors (fifteen thousand or so, according to our spy satellites), and only backed down when it became clear that (a) the Chinese weren't kidding about emptying the holes if we didn't pull back, and (b) the American people weren't all that crazy about committing mass suicide over the Philippine Islands. That was also the year some other group of crazy mother-fuckers – Albanians, I think – tried to air-spray the AIDS virus over Berlin.

This sort of stuff depressed everybody, but it depressed the *shit* out of Bobby.

'Why are people so goddam mean?' he asked me one day. We were at the summer place in New Hampshire, it was late August, and most of our stuff was already in boxes and suitcases. The cabin had that sad, deserted look it always got just before we all went our separate ways. For me it meant back to New York, and for Bobby it meant Waco, Texas, of all places . . . he had spent the summer reading sociology and geology texts – how's that for a crazy salad? – and said he wanted to run a couple of experiments down there. He said it in a casual, offhand way, but I had seen my mother looking at him with a peculiar thoughtful scrutiny in the last couple of weeks we were all together. Neither Dad nor I suspected, but I think my mom knew that Bobby's compass needle had finally stopped swinging and had started pointing.

'Why are they so mean?' I asked. 'I'm supposed to answer that?'

'*Someone* better,' he said. 'Pretty soon, too, the way things are going.'

'They're going the way they always went,' I said, 'and I guess they're doing it because people were built to be mean. If you want to lay blame, blame God.'

'That's bullshit. I don't believe it. Even that double-X-chromosome stuff turned out to be bullshit in the end. And don't tell me it's just economic pressures, the conflict between the haves and have-nots, because that doesn't explain all of it, either.'

'Original sin,' I said. 'It works for me – it's got a good beat and you can dance to it.'

'Well,' Bobby said, 'maybe it *is* original sin. But what's the instrument, big brother? Have you ever asked yourself that?'

'Instrument? What instrument? I'm not following you.'

'I think it's the water,' Bobby said moodily.

'Say *what*?'

'The water. Something in the water.'

He looked at me.

'Or something that *isn't*.'

The next day Bobby went off to Waco. I didn't see him again until he showed up at my apartment wearing the inside-out Mumford shirt and carrying the two glass boxes. That was three years later.

'Howdy, Howie,' he said, stepping in and giving me a non-chalant swat on the back as if it had been only three days.

'Bobby!' I yelled, and threw both arms around him in a

bear-hug. Hard angles bit into my chest, and I heard an angry hive-hum.

'I'm glad to see you too,' Bobby said, 'but you better go easy. You're upsetting the natives.'

I stepped back in a hurry. Bobby set down the big paper bag he was carrying and unslung his shoulder-bag. Then he carefully brought the glass boxes out of the bag. There was a beehive in one, a wasps' nest in the other. The bees were already settling down and going back to whatever business bees have, but the wasps were clearly unhappy about the whole thing.

'Okay, Bobby,' I said. I looked at him and grinned. I couldn't seem to stop grinning. 'What are you up to this time?'

He unzipped the tote-bag and brought out a mayonnaise jar which was half-filled with a clear liquid.

'See this?' he said.

'Yeah. Looks like either water or white lightning.'

'It's actually both, if you can believe that. It came from an artesian well in La Plata, a little town forty miles east of Waco, and before I turned it into this concentrated form, there were five gallons of it. I've got a regular little distillery running down there, Howie, but I don't think the government will ever bust me for it.' He was grinning, and now the grin broadened. 'Water's all it is, but it's still the goddamndist popskull the human race has ever seen.'

'I don't have the slightest idea what you're talking about.'

'I know you don't. But you will. You know what, Howie?'

'What?'

'If the idiotic human race can manage to hold itself together for another six months, I'm betting it'll hold itself together for all time.'

He lifted the mayonnaise jar, and one magnified Bobby-eye stared at me through it with huge solemnity. 'This is the big one,' he said. 'The cure for the worst disease to which *Homo sapiens* falls prey.'

'Cancer?'

'Nope,' Bobby said. 'War. Barroom brawls. Drive-by shootings. The whole mess. Where's your bathroom, Howie? My back teeth are floating.'

When he came back he had not only turned the Mumford tee-shirt right-side out, he had combed his hair – nor had his method of doing this changed, I saw. Bobby just held his head under the faucet for awhile then raked everything back with his fingers.

He looked at the two glass boxes and pronounced the bees and wasps back to normal. 'Not that a wasps' nest ever approaches anything even closely resembling "normal", Howie. Wasps are social insects, like bees and ants, but unlike bees, which are almost always sane, and ants, which have occasional schizoid lapses, wasps are total full-bore lunatics.' He smiled. 'Just like us good old *Homo sap*s.' He took the top off the glass box containing the beehive.

'Tell you what, Bobby,' I said. I was smiling, but the smile felt much too wide. 'Put the top back on and just *tell* me about it, what do you say? Save the demonstration for later. I mean, my landlord's a real pussycat, but the super's this big bull dyke who smokes Odie Perode cigars and has thirty pounds on me. She —'

'You'll like this,' Bobby said, as if I hadn't spoken at all – a habit as familiar to me as his Ten Fingers Method of Hair Grooming. He was never impolite but often totally absorbed. And could I stop him? Aw shit, no. It was too good to have him back. I mean I think I knew even then that something was going to go totally wrong, but when I was with Bobby for more than five minutes, he just hypnotized me. He was Lucy holding the football and promising me this time *for sure*, and I was Charlie Brown, rushing down the field to kick it. 'In fact, you've probably seen it done before – they show pictures of it in magazines from time to time, or in TV wildlife documentaries. It's nothing very special, but it *looks* like a big deal because people have got these totally irrational prejudices about bees.'

And the weird thing was, he was right – I *had* seen it before.

He stuck his hand into the box between the hive and the glass. In less than fifteen seconds his hand had acquired a living black-and-yellow glove. It brought back an instant of total recall: sitting in front of the TV, wearing footie pajamas and clutching my Paddington Bear, maybe half an hour before bedtime (and surely years before Bobby was born), watching with mingled horror, disgust, and fascination as some beekeeper allowed bees to cover his entire face. They had formed a sort of executioner's hood at first, and then he had brushed them into a grotesque living beard.

Bobby winced suddenly, sharply, then grinned.

'One of em stung me,' he said. 'They're still a little upset from the trip. I hooked a ride with the local insurance lady from La Plata to Waco – she's got an old Piper Cub – and flew some little commuter airline, Air Asshole, I think it was, up to New Orleans from there. Made about forty connections, but I swear to God it was the cab ride from LaGarbage that got em crazy. Second Avenue's still got more potholes than the Bergenstrasse after the Germans surrendered.'

'You know, I think you really ought to get your hand out of there, Bobs,' I said. I kept waiting for some of them to fly out – I could imagine chasing them around with a rolled-up magazine for hours, bringing them down one by one, as if they were escapees in some old prison movie. But none of them had escaped . . . at least so far.

'Relax, Howie. You ever see a bee sting a flower? Or even hear of it, for that matter?'

'You don't look like a flower.'

He laughed. 'Shit, you think *bees* know what a flower looks like? Uh-uh! No way, man! They don't know what a flower looks like any more than you or I know what a cloud sounds like. They know I'm sweet because I excrete sucrose dioxin in my sweat . . . along with thirty-seven other dioxins, and those're just the ones we know about.'

He paused thoughtfully.

'Although I must confess I *was* careful to, uh, sweeten myself up a little tonight. Ate a box of chocolate-covered cherries on the plane —'

'Oh Bobby, Jesus!'

' —and had a couple of MallowCremes in the taxi coming here.'

He reached in with his other hand and carefully began to brush the bees away. I saw him wince once more just before he got the last of them off, and then he eased my mind considerably by replacing the lid on the glass box. I saw a red swelling on each of his hands: one in the cup of the left palm, another high up on the right, near what the palmists call the Bracelets of Fortune. He'd been stung, but I saw well enough what he'd set out to show me: what looked like at least four hundred bees had investigated him. Only two had stung.

He took a pair of tweezers out of his jeans watch-pocket, and went over to my desk. He moved the pile of manuscript beside the Wang Micro I was using in those days and trained my Tensor lamp on the place where the pages had been – fiddling with it until it formed a tiny hard spotlight on the cherrywood.

'Writin anything good, Bow-Wow?' he asked casually, and I felt the hair stiffen on the back of my neck. When was the last time he'd called me Bow-Wow? When he was four? Six? Shit, man, I don't know. He was working carefully on his left hand with the tweezers. I saw him extract a tiny something that looked like a nostril hair and place it in my ashtray.

'Piece on art forgery for *Vanity Fair*,' I said. 'Bobby, what in hell are you up to this time?'

'You want to pull the other one for me?' he asked, offering me the tweezers, his right hand, and an apologetic smile. 'I keep thinking if I'm so goddam smart I ought to be ambidextrous, but my left hand has still got an IQ of about six.'

Same old Bobby.

I sat down beside him, took the tweezers, and pulled the bee stinger out of the red swelling near what in his case should have been the Bracelets of Doom, and while I did it he told me about the differences between bees and wasps, the difference between the water in La Plata and the water in New York, and how, goddam! everything was going to be all right with his water and a little help from me.

And oh shit, I ended up running at the football while my laughing, wildly intelligent brother held it, one last time.

'Bees don't sting unless they have to, because it kills them,' Bobby said matter-of-factly. 'You remember that time in North Conway, when you said we kept killing each other because of original sin?'

'Yes. Hold still.'

'Well, if there *is* such a thing, if there's a God who could simultaneously love us enough to serve us His own Son on a cross and send us all on a rocket-sled to hell just because one stupid bitch bit a bad apple, then the curse was just this: He made us like wasps instead of bees. *Shit*, Howie, what are you doing?'

'Hold still,' I said, 'and I'll get it out. If you want to make a lot of big gestures, I'll wait.'

'Okay,' he said, and after that he held relatively still while I extracted the stinger. 'Bees are nature's kamikaze pilots, Bow-Wow. Look in that glass box, you'll see the two who stung me lying dead at the bottom. Their stingers are barbed, like fishhooks. They slide in easy. When they pull out, they disembowel themselves.'

'Gross,' I said, dropping the second stinger in the ashtray. I couldn't see the barbs, but I didn't have a microscope.

'It makes them particular, though,' he said.

'I bet.'

'Wasps, on the other hand, have smooth stingers. They can shoot you up as many times as they like. They use up the poison by the third or fourth shot, but they can go right on making holes if they like . . . and usually they do. Especially wall-wasps. The kind I've got over there. You gotta sedate em. Stuff called Noxon. It must give em a hell of a hangover, because they wake up madder than ever.'

He looked at me somberly, and for the first time I saw the dark brown wheels of weariness under his eyes and realized my kid brother was more tired than I had ever seen him.

'*That's* why people go on fighting, Bow-Wow. On and on and on. We got smooth stingers. Now watch this.'

He got up, went over to his tote-bag, rummaged in it, and came up with an eye-dropper. He opened the mayonnaise jar, put the dropper in, and drew up a tiny bubble of his distilled Texas water.

When he took it over to the glass box with the wasps' nest inside, I saw the top on this one was different – there was a tiny plastic slide-piece set into it. I didn't need him to draw me a picture: with the bees, he was perfectly willing to remove the whole top. With the wasps, he was taking no chances.

He squeezed the black bulb. Two drops of water fell onto the nest, making a momentary dark spot that disappeared almost at once. 'Give it about three minutes,' he said.

'What —'

'No questions,' he said. 'You'll see. Three minutes.'

In that period, he read my piece on art forgery . . . although it was already twenty pages long.

'Okay,' he said, putting the pages down. 'That's pretty good, man. You ought to read up a little on how Jay Gould furnished the parlor-car of his private train with fake Manets, though – that's a hoot.' He was removing the cover of the glass box containing the wasps' nest as he spoke.

'Jesus, Bobby, cut the comedy!' I yelled.

'Same old wimp,' Bobby laughed, and pulled the nest, which was dull gray and about the size of a bowling ball, out of the box. He held it in his hands. Wasps flew out and lit on his arms, his cheeks, his forehead. One flew across to me and landed on my forearm. I slapped it and it fell dead to the carpet. I was scared – I mean really scared. My body was wired with adrenaline and I could feel my eyes trying to push their way out of their sockets.

'Don't kill em,' Bobby said. 'You might as well be killing babies, for all the harm they can do you. That's the whole *point*.' He tossed the nest from hand to hand as if it were an overgrown softball. He lobbed it in the air. I watched, horrified, as wasps cruised the living room of my apartment like fighter planes on patrol.

Bobby lowered the nest carefully back into the box and sat down on my couch. He patted the place next to him and I went over, nearly hypnotized. They were everywhere: on the rug, the ceiling, the drapes. Half a dozen of them were crawling across the front of my big-screen TV.

Before I could sit down, he brushed away a couple that were on the sofa cushion where my ass was aimed. They flew away quickly. They were *all* flying easily, crawling easily, moving fast. There was nothing drugged about their behavior. As Bobby talked, they gradually found their way back to their spit-paper home, crawled over it, and eventually disappeared inside again through the hole in the top.

'I wasn't the first one to get interested in Waco,' he said. 'It just happens to be the biggest town in the funny little non-violent section of what is, per capita, the most violent state in the union. Texans *love* to shoot each other, Howie – I mean, it's like a state hobby. Half the male population goes around armed. Saturday night in the Fort Worth bars is like a shooting gallery where you get to plonk away at drunks instead of clay ducks. There are more NRA card-carriers than there are Methodists. Not that Texas is the only place where people shoot each other, or carve each other up with straight-razors, or stick their kids in the oven if they cry too long, you understand, but they sure do like their firearms.'

'Except in Waco,' I said.

'Oh, they like em there, too,' he said. 'It's just that they use em on each other a hell of a lot less often.'

Jesus. I just looked up at the clock and saw the time. It feels like I've been writing for fifteen minutes or so, but it's actually been over an hour. That happens to me sometimes when I'm running at white-hot speed, but I can't allow myself to be seduced into these specifics. I feel as well as ever – no noticeable drying of the membrance in the throat, no groping for words, and as I glance back over what I've done I see only the normal typos and strike-overs. But I can't kid myself. I've got to hurry up. 'Fiddle-de-dee,' said Scarlett, and all of that.

The non-violent atmosphere of the Waco area had been noticed and investigated before, mostly by sociologists. Bobby said that when you fed enough statistical data on Waco and similar areas into a computer – population density, mean age, mean economic level, mean educational level, and dozens of other factors – what you got back was a whopper of an anomaly. Scholarly papers are rarely jocular, but even so, several of the better than fifty Bobby had read on the subject suggested ironically that maybe it was 'something in the water'.

'I decided maybe it was time to take the joke seriously,' Bobby said. 'After all, there's something in the water of a lot of places that prevents tooth decay. It's called fluoride.'

He went to Waco accompanied by a trio of research assistants: two sociology grad-students and a full professor of geology who happened to be on sabbatical and ready for adventure. Within six months, Bobby and the sociology guys had constructed a computer program which illustrated what my brother called the world's only calmquake. He had a slightly rumpled printout in his tote. He gave it to me. I was looking at a series of forty concentric rings. Waco was in the eighth, ninth, and tenth as you moved in toward the center.

'Now look at this,' he said, and put a transparent overlay on the printout. More rings; but in each one there was a number. Fortieth ring: 471. Thirty-ninth: 420. Thirty-eighth: 418. And so on. In a couple of places the numbers went up instead of down, but only in a couple (and only by a little).

'What are they?'

'Each number represents the incidence of violent crime in that particular circle,' Bobby said. 'Murder, rape, assault and battery, even acts of vandalism. The computer assigns a number by a formula that takes population density into account.' He tapped the twenty-seventh circle, which held the number 204, with his finger. 'There's less than nine hundred people in this whole area, for instance. The number represents three or four cases of spouse abuse, a couple of barroom brawls, an act of animal cruelty – some senile farmer got pissed at a pig and shot a load of rock-salt into it, as I recall – and one involuntary manslaughter.'

I saw that the numbers in the central circles dropped off radically: 85, 81, 70, 63, 40, 21, 5. At the epicenter of Bobby's calmquake was the town of La Plata. To call it a sleepy little town seems more than fair.

The numeric value assigned to La Plata was zero.

'So here it is, Bow-Wow,' Bobby said, leaning forward and rubbing his long hands together nervously, 'my nominee for the Garden of Eden. Here's a community of fifteen thousand, twenty-four per cent of which are people of mixed blood, commonly called Indios. There's a moccasin factory, a couple of little motor courts, a couple of scrub farms. That's it for work. For play there's four bars, a couple of dance-halls where you can hear any kind of music you want as long as it sounds like George Jones, two drive-ins, and a bowling alley.' He paused and added, 'There's also a still. I didn't know anybody made whiskey that good outside of Tennessee.'

In short (and it is now too late to be anything else), La Plata should have been a fertile breeding-ground for the sort of casual violence you can read about in the Police Blotter section of the local newspaper every day. Should have been but wasn't. There had been only one murder in

La Plata during the five years previous to my brother's arrival, two cases of assault, no rapes, no reported incidents of child abuse. There had been four armed robberies, but all four turned out to have been committed by transients . . . as the murder and one of the assaults had been. The local Sheriff was a fat old Republican who did a pretty fair Rodney Dangerfield imitation. He had been known, in fact, to spend whole days in the local coffee shop, tugging the knot in his tie and telling people to take his wife, please. My brother said he thought it was a little more than lame humor; he was pretty sure the poor guy was suffering first-stage Alzheimer's Disease. His only deputy was his nephew. Bobby told me the nephew looked quite a lot like Junior Samples on the old *Hee-Haw* show.

'Put those two guys in a Pennsylvania town similar to La Plata in every way but the geographical,' Bobby said, 'and they would have been out on their asses fifteen years ago. But in La Plata, they're gonna go on until they die . . . which they'll probably do in their sleep.'

'What did you do?' I asked. 'How did you proceed?'

'Well, for the first week or so after we got our statistical shit together, we just sort of sat around and stared at each other,' Bobby said. 'I mean, we were prepared for *something*, but nothing quite like this. Even Waco doesn't prepare you for La Plata.' Bobby shifted restlessly and cracked his knuckles.

'Jesus, I hate it when you do that,' I said.

He smiled. 'Sorry, Bow-Wow. Anyway, we started geological tests, then microscopic analysis of the water. I didn't expect a hell of a lot; everyone in the area has got a well, usually a deep one, and they get their water tested regularly to make sure they're not drinking borax, or something. If there had been something obvious, it would have turned up a long time ago. So we went on to submicroscopy, and that was when we started to turn up some pretty weird stuff.'

'What kind of weird stuff?'

'Breaks in chains of atoms, subdynamic electrical fluctuations, and some sort of unidentified protein. Water ain't really H_2O, you know – not when you add in the sulfides, irons, God knows what else happens to be in the aquifer of a given region. And La Plata water – you'd have to give it a string of letters like the ones after a professor emeritus's name.' His eyes gleamed. 'But the protein was the most interesting thing, Bow-Wow. So far as we know, it's only found in one other place: the human brain.'

Uh-oh.

It just arrived, between one swallow and the next: the throat-dryness. Not much at yet, but enough for me to break away and get a glass of ice-water. I've got maybe forty minutes left. And oh Jesus, there's so much I want to tell! About the wasps' nests they found with wasps that wouldn't sting, about the fender-bender Bobby and one of his assistants saw where the two drivers, both male, both drunk, and both about twenty-four (sociological bull moose, in other words), got out, shook hands, and exchanged insurance information amicably before going into the nearest bar for another drink.

Bobby talked for hours – more hours than I have. But the upshot was simple: the stuff in the mayonnaise jar.

'We've got our own still in La Plata now,' he said. 'This is the stuff we're brewing, Howie; pacifist white lightning. The aquifer under that area of Texas is deep but amazingly large; it's like this incredible Lake Victoria driven into the porous sediment which overlays the Moho. The water is potent, but we've been able to make the stuff I squirted on the wasps even more potent. We've got damn near six thousand gallons now, in these big steel tanks. By the end of the year, we'll have fourteen thousand. By next June we'll have thirty thousand. But it's not enough. We need more, we need it faster . . . and then we need to transport it.'

'Transport it where?' I asked him.

'Borneo, to start with.'

I thought I'd either lost my mind or misheard him. I really did.

'Look, Bow-Wow . . . sorry. Howie.' He was scrumming through his tote-bag again. He brought out a number of aerial photographs and handed them over to me. 'You see?' he asked as I looked through them. 'You see how fucking perfect it is? It's as if God Himself suddenly busted through our business-as-usual transmissions with something like "And now we bring you a special bulletin! This is your last chance, assholes! And now we return you to *Days of Our Lives*."'

'I don't get you,' I said. 'And I have no idea what I'm looking at.' Of course I knew; it was an island – not Borneo itself but an island lying to the west of Borneo identified as Gulandio – with a mountain in the middle and a lot of muddy little villages lying on its lower slopes. It was hard to see the mountain because of the cloud cover. What I meant was that I didn't know what I was looking *for*.

'The mountain has the same name as the island,' he said. 'Gulandio. In the local patois it means *grace*, or *fate*, or *destiny*, or take your pick. But Duke Rogers says it's really the biggest time-bomb on earth . . . and it's wired to go off by October of next year. Probably earlier.'

The crazy thing's this: the story's only crazy if you try to tell it in a speed-rap, which is what I'm trying to do now. Bobby wanted me to help him raise somewhere between six hundred thousand and a million and a half dollars to do the following: first, to synthesize fifty to seventy thousand gallons of what he called 'the high-test'; second, to airlift all of this water to Borneo, which had landing facilities (you could land a hang-glider on Gulandio, but that was about all); third, to ship it over to this island named Fate, or Destiny, or Grace; fourth, to truck it up the slope of the volcano, which had been dormant (save for a few puffs in 1938) since 1804, and then to drop it down the muddy tube of the volcano's caldera. Duke Rogers was actually John Paul Rogers, the geology professor. He claimed that Gulandio was going to do more than just erupt; he claimed that it was going to explode, as Krakatoa had done in the nineteenth century, creating a bang that would make the Squirt Bomb that poisoned London like a kid's firecracker.

The debris from the Krakatoa blow-up, Bobby told me, had literally encircled the globe; the observed results had formed an important part of the Sagan Group's nuclear winter theory. For three months afterward sunsets and sunrises half a world away had been grotesquely colorful as a result of the ash whirling around in both the jet stream and the Van Allen Currents, which lie forty miles below the Van Allen Belt. There had been global changes in climate which lasted five years, and nipa palms, which previously had grown only in eastern Africa and Micronesia, suddenly showed up in both South and North America.

'The North American nipas all died before 1900,' Bobby said, 'but they're alive and well below the equator. Krakatoa seeded them there, Howie . . . the way I want to seed La Plata water all over the earth. I want people to go out in La Plata water when it rains – and it's going to rain a lot after Gulandio goes bang. I want them to drink the La Plata water that falls in their reservoirs, I want them to wash their hair in it, bathe in it, soak their contact lenses in it. I want whores to *douche* in it.'

'Bobby,' I said, knowing he was not, 'you're crazy.'

He gave me a crooked, tired grin. 'I ain't crazy,' he said. 'You want to see crazy? Turn on CNN, Bow . . . Howie. You'll see crazy in living color.'

But I didn't need to turn on Cable News (what a friend of mine had taken to calling The Organ-Grinder of Doom) to know what Bobby was talking about. The Indians and the Pakistanis were poised on the brink. The Chinese and the Afghans, ditto. Half of Africa was starving, the other half on fire with AIDS. There had been border skirmishes along the entire Tex-Mex border in the last five years, since Mexico went Communist, and people had started calling the Tijuana crossing point in California Little Berlin because of the wall. The saber-rattling had become a din. On the last day of the old year the Scientists for Nuclear Responsibility had set their black clock to fifteen seconds before midnight.

'Bobby, let's suppose it could be done and everything went according to schedule,' I said. 'It probably couldn't and wouldn't, but let's suppose. You don't have the slightest idea what the long-term effects might be.'

He started to say something and I waved it away.

'Don't even suggest that you do, because you don't! You've had time to find this calmquake of yours and isolate the cause, I'll give you that. But did you ever hear about thalidomide? About that nifty little acne-stopper and sleeping pill that caused cancer and heart attacks in thirty-year-olds? Don't you remember the AIDS vaccine in 1997?'

'Howie?'

'*That* one stopped the disease, except it turned the test subjects into incurable epileptics who all died within eighteen months.'

'Howie?'

'Then there was —'

'Howie?'

I stopped and looked at him.

'The world,' Bobby said, and then stopped. His throat worked. I saw he was struggling with tears. 'The world needs heroic measures, man. I don't know about long-term effects, and there's no time to study them, because there's no long-term prospect. Maybe we can cure the whole mess. Or maybe —'

He shrugged, tried to smile, and looked at me with shining eyes from which two single tears slowly tracked.

'Or maybe we're giving heroin to a patient with terminal cancer. Either way, it'll stop what's happening now. It'll end the world's pain.' He spread out his hands, palms up, so I could see the stings on them. 'Help me, Bow-Wow. Please help me.'

So I helped him.

And we fucked up. In fact I think you could say we fucked

up big-time. And do you want the truth? I don't give a shit. We killed all the plants, but at least we saved the greenhouse. Something will grow here again, someday. I hope.

Are you reading this?

My gears are starting to get a little sticky. For the first time in years I'm having to think about what I'm doing. The motor-movements of writing. Should have hurried more at the start.

Never mind. Too late to change things now.

We did it, of course: distilled the water, flew it in, transported it to Gulandio, built a primitive lifting system – half motor-winch and half cog railway – up the side of the volcano, and dropped over twelve thousand five-gallon containers of La Plata water – the brain-buster version – into the murky misty depths of the volcano's caldera. We did all of this in just eight months. It didn't cost six hundred thousand dollars, or a million and a half; it cost over four million, still less than a sixteenth of one per cent of what America spent on defense that year. You want to know how we razed it? I'd tell you if I had more thyme, but my head's falling apart so never mend. I raised most of it myself if it matters to you. Some by hoof and some by croof. Tell you the truth, I din't know I could do it muself until I did. But we did it and somehow the world held together and that volcano – whatever its name wuz, I can't exactly remember now and there izzunt time to go back over the manuscript – it blue just when it was spo

Wait

Okay. A little better. Digitalin. Bobby had it. Heart's beating like crazy but I can think again.

The volcano – Mount Grace, we called it – blue just when Dook Rogers said it would. Everything when skihi and for awhile everyone's attention turned away from whatever and toward the skys. And bimmel-dee-dee, said Strapless!

It happened pretty fast like sex and checks and special effex and everybody got healthy again. I mean.

wait

Jesus please let me finish this.

I mean that everybody stood down. Everybody started to get a little purstective on the situation. The wurld started to get like the wasps in Bobbys nest the one he showed me where they didn't otink too much. There was three yerz like an Indian summer. People getting together like in that old Youngbloods song that went cmon everybody get together rite now, like what all the hippeez wanted, you no, peets and luv and

wt

Big blast. Feel like my heart is coming out thru my ears. But if I concentrate every bit of my force, my *concentration* —

It was like an Indian summer, that's what I meant to say, like three years of Indian summer. Bobby went on with his resurch. La Plata. Sociological background etc. You remember the local Sheriff? Fat old Republican with a good Rodney Youngblood imitashun? How Bobby said he had the preliminary simptoms of Rodney's Disease?

concentrate asshole

Wasn't just him; turned out like there was a lot of that going around in that part of Texas. All's Hallows Disease is what I meen. For three yerz me and Bobby were down there. Created a new program. New graff of circkles. I saw what was happen and came back here. Bobby and his to asistants stayed on. One shot hisself Boby said when he showed up here.

Wait one more blas

*   *   *

All right. Last time. Heart beating so fast I can hardly breeve. The new graph, the *last* graph, really only whammed you when it was laid over the calmquake graft. The calmquake graff showed ax of vilence going down as you approached La Plata in the muddle; the Alzheimer's graff showed incidence of premature seenullity going *up* as you approached La Plata. People there were getting very silly very yung.

Me and Bobo were careful as we could be for next three years, drinke only Parrier Water and wor big long sleekers in the ran. so no war and when everybobby started to get seely we din and I came back here because he my brother I cant remember what his name

Bobby

Bobby when he came here tonight cryeen and I sed Bobby I luv you Bobby sed Ime sorry Bowwow Ime sorry I made the hole world ful of foals and dumbbels and I sed better fouls and bells than a big black sinder in spaz and he cryed and I cryed Bobby I luv you and he sed will you give me a shot of the spacial wadder and I sed yez and he said wil you ride it down and I sed yez an I think I did but I cant reely remember I see wurds but dont no what they mean

I have a Bobby his nayme is bruther and I theen I an dun riding and I have a bocks to put this into thats Bobby sd full of quiyet air to last a milyun yrz so gudboy gudboy everybrother, Im goin to stob gudboy bobby i love you it wuz not yor falt i love you

    forgivyu

  love yu

sinned (for the wurld),

WILLIAM McILVANNEY

Short story taken from Walking Wounded

Hullo Again

William McIlvanney's most recent novel, *Strange Loyalties*, is available now at your local Dillons store priced £5.99.

Bring this voucher with you to obtain £1.00 off the publisher's prices at all Dillons stores.

SEVENTEEN

HULLO AGAIN

Recognition came to him between dessert and coffee. He had noticed her earlier, sitting opposite another woman and talking with a slightly actressy animation, given to *ingénue* gestures that belied her age, as if life hadn't discovered her yet. He had seen a woman in her forties with hair that still looked naturally dark, eyes that were still interested and a body that was nicely substantial. When he realised that he knew her, that he owned, as it were, a small part of her past, his glances had become less cursory, more proprietary. She's weathered well, he thought. I wonder.

Recognising her was a moment of small adventure for him, a pulse of adolescence in a middle-aged day. The pretentious restaurant, chosen by his client, briefly seemed a place where something might happen and the deadness of occasion animate to an event. Even the proprietor's manner seemed less obtrusive. He was a small, numbingly bright man who had fixed an expression of jollity to his face like a Hallowe'en mask. He mistook interference for attentiveness and flippancy for wit. His blandishments had threatened the meal, for eating in his presence was like having everything drenched in syrup.

He appeared to know the client well and perhaps they deserved each other. The client was a self-made man who had long ago ceased to notice that most of the parts were missing. 'What I always say is' was what he always said. He had started out 'as a silly boy with nothing' and after years of unremitting effort and deals of legendary deviousness had successfully trans-formed himself into a silly man with nothing, except an awful lot of money. He had spent most of the lunch expressing his modestly oblique astonishment at why other people couldn't be more like him. 'What I always say is whiners create their own difficulties.' If everybody would get out and do as he had done, they could be in the same position as he was. The thought of a nation of near-millionaires seemed to present him with no logistical problems. He disarmed any suggestion of egotism with frequent references to how much he owed to God. He referred to God as if He might be a senior partner with a particularly astute sense of the market.

'I did it,' he was saying. 'And what's so special about me?'

His audience smiled and said, 'Excuse me. I've just seen someone I know. Do you mind? Won't be a minute.'

He rose and walked towards her table. He saw her glance towards him and back to her companion. He enjoyed the stages of her recognition. The first look had simply been acknowledging someone moving in the restaurant. When she looked back, it was because she had belatedly registered that he was looking at her. She stared, wondering why he should be coming towards her table. The need to understand focused her attention and he saw her eyes widen in surprise as he walked out of strangeness into familiarity. Being recognised for who he had been stimulated his own sense of the past and he remembered her name just in time. She half-stood up in confusion.

'Eddie Cameron,' she said.

'Marion. You haven't changed a bit. I recognised you right away.'

He kissed her on the cheek and, as soon as he had done it, knew the action was a moment of inspiration, for the kiss was a cipher of past intimacy. It made them a conspiracy of two in the crowded room.

'I was amazed,' he said. 'There's Marion, I thought. I was going to come over earlier but you both seemed so engrossed.'

'Oh, this is Jane Thomas. Jane, Eddie Cameron.'

As he shook hands, he noticed that the woman, whose back had been towards him, was as plain as a loaf and he wondered again if pretty women sometimes chose their friends like accessories to highlight themselves. Marion had sat back down.

'It's Jane's birthday,' she said. 'We work in the same office. We're out celebrating.'

'If celebrating's the word,' Jane said.

'Anyway, congratulations or condolences, Jane. Choose your pick. You look good on it, anyway.'

'The wine,' Jane confided.

'You should keep taking the medicine then.'

'Thank you, doctor.'

He was glad that their brief coquetry caused Marion to butt in like someone at an excuse-me dance.

'What are you doing here?' she said.

'Business. It's a long time since I was in this town. It's changed so much.'

'Not for the better,' Jane said.

'I'm lost in it now,' he said. 'What about you, Marion?' He glanced at her rings. 'Happily married with ten of a family?'

'I'm a widow.'

She didn't say it casually. Her voice went into mourning and he wondered how recently it had happened.

'God, I'm sorry, Marion,' he said and felt a quickening of interest. 'Obviously, I didn't know. That was clumsy.'

'You weren't to know. It's been seven years now.'

The information made the tone in which she had declared her widowhood seem a bit extravagant. He was reminded of a woman he knew who was inclined to intone every so often, 'Father would have been ninety-five by now.' Or ninety-six. Or, the following year unsurprisingly, ninety-seven. It had led to a joke with his wife. 'Father would have been a hundred and forty-two by now. Pity he died at nineteen.'

'Any children?' he asked casually.

'Two,' Marion said soulfully, as if the shadow of dark wings had fallen across the cheese-board. Inexplicably, he felt the prospect of the evening brighten.

'That's good,' he said. 'Best invention in the world, children.'

He sensed Jane's face opening towards him like a flower.

'I know what you mean,' she said. 'They can be a trial. But they're what it's all about as far as I'm concerned. Mine are taking me out tonight. I'd better sober up before then. They're choosing the restaurant. Wait till you see. John, he's the oldest. He's been taking charge of all arrangements. Won't let Michael – that's my husband – even know where we're going. And Darren, the youngest, he's been threatened within an inch of his life if he reveals the dreaded secret. He's been bursting to tell me all week.'

'Lucky you,' Eddie said, hoping to forestall the taking of snapshots from her handbag. 'I'll probably go and read the cemetery. Catch up on news of old friends.' The gaffe of being flippant about death so soon after Marion's mention of her dead husband made him move on quickly. 'And what about you, Marion? What wild plans have you got for tonight?'

Marion's close-lipped smile was wan as a fading rose in memory of her husband.

'She doesn't go out nearly enough,' Jane said. 'I've been telling her that.'

'So you should,' Eddie prompted.

'An attractive woman like her.'

'A *very* attractive woman like her.'

Their pincer movement was neatly trapping Marion in their sense of her. She seemed to be enjoying the mild embarrassment.

'It's such a waste,' Jane said.

'You get out of the way of going out,' Marion was on the defensive. 'Mixing with people.'

'I know what you mean,' Eddie said.

'It's no excuse,' Jane said.

'Here!' Eddie said, as if it was something that had only just come into his mind. 'What about dinner with me tonight, Marion? You'd be doing me a favour. It's either that or counting the perforations in the tea-bag in my hotel room.'

'Eddie!'

'Why not?'

'Why not, Marion?' Jane said.

'For old times' sake,' Eddie said. 'An innocent meal between old friends. A good way for you to break the ice again. No complications.'

'I don't think I could take another bite after this,' Marion said.

'Then we'll eat the ambience. What you say?'

'She says yes.'

'Jane!'

'Well, you do.'

'I don't know. What about Michael and Lucy?'

'Look. You two going back to your office now?'

Jane nodded.

'Okay. You think about it, Marion. If you give me the office number, I'll phone you there this afternoon. It's all right. If it's no, I promise not to take an overdose.' Jane had already taken a pen from her handbag and she wrote the number on the flap of an envelope, tore it off and handed it to Eddie.

'Sweet lady,' he said. 'A birthday beverage for you. What's it to be?'

'Oh, I've had enough. I'll be singing at the switchboard.'

'Please. Let me make the gesture. People should sing on their birthday. Maybe a sad song. But they should sing. A liqueur. What's your favourite liqueur?'

'She likes Tia Maria,' Marion said.

'What about you, Marion?'

Marion was hesitant, as if saying yes once might develop into a habit.

'I don't know that I should.'

'I'm not drinking on my own,' Jane said.

'Green Chartreuse then.'

Even egregious sycophancy has its uses. The proprietor's overeagerness meant that Eddie's gesture was interpreted as it happened. He was grateful, for he could remember other occasions when he had thought he would have to let off a flare to get a waiter. This time the moment came clean out of the films of his boyhood. The small ceremony complete, he asked the proprietor to add the drinks to his bill.

'Happy birthday, Jane,' he said. 'Nice to have met you. Marion. You'll hear me calling you.'

They were laughing as he left. The client wasn't. His conversation was a lecture. He didn't like it when the audience walked out. Eddie offered more coffee like paying a fine and put on his listening expression while his thoughts went off on their own.

The piece of paper in his pocket interested him: the first number in the combination to a safe. What would be inside? He looked back at Marion and she sketched a toasting gesture with her glass. She smiled and he smiled back, exchanging sealed communications – billets-doux or blank paper? It occurred to him that neither knew what the other meant. It occurred to him that they didn't know yet what they meant themselves.

The room pleased him now. It had lost its predetermined crassness, sanctified for him by his renewal of the sense of mystery. Its garish brightness had become luminous and, hearing the faint clash of cutlery and the voices baffled into an indecipherable human murmur by his mood, he felt the happy strangeness of being there.

He watched Marion and her friend rise and begin those female preparations for leaving that he loved, the retrieving of scarves and umbrellas, the finding of handbags, the gathering of coats – not so much a leaving as a flitting. It was as if they briefly set up house wherever they went. As they were walking out, they waved. He waved to Jane. Towards Marion he pointed his right hand like a gun, winked along his forefinger and clicked down his thumb.

'How do you know her?' the client asked.

As the wine wore off during the afternoon, Jane grew doubtful about her part in getting Eddie to phone the office. She had a determinedly married woman's superstition about the things that might threaten the comfortable stability of her marriage. It was a kind of psychological housewifery: leave crumbs and you get mice. What irritated her late in the afternoon was that she had left crumbs.

Her attitudes were usually well dusted and neatly in place. The overall structure that housed them was simple but substantial: marriage is too important to play around with. Inside that monumental certainty all her responses fitted comfortably. Whatever situation cropped up, she knew where it went. If a man tried to chat you up, you didn't allow it. You didn't involve yourself with married friends who were interested in other men. If you got out of work early, you did shopping or came home.

Coming back from the restaurant in the taxi they had to take because they were late, Marion had said, 'But he's married!'

'How do you know? He doesn't wear a ring.'

'He must be married. And he mentioned children.'

'Maybe he's divorced.'

'He would have said.'

'We didn't ask him. Or maybe he'll get divorced after tonight.'

The glibness of the remark turned acid in her conscience. How could she have said that? She felt she had betrayed some unknown woman. She felt she had betrayed Michael and the children. She believed that to be dismissive about other people's marriages was somehow to tempt providence in relation to your own. She shouldn't have taken so much wine, she thought. When she was relieved at the switchboard to get her coffee, she was still troubled.

'That Eddie Cameron,' she said to Marion. 'How do you know him?'

'We used to know each other years ago. When we were still in our teens.'

'First love,' Jane's love of categories suggested.

'First something.'

'And you haven't seen him since?'

'More than twenty years. I don't know how he recognised me.'

'You made up your mind yet?'

'I thought I might leave that to you. You seem to have decided everything else for me.'

'No complications, he said.'

Jane said it to herself as much as to Marion and she took the thought away with her like a plea for the defence. She had acted in all innocence, she told herself. But she couldn't avoid the thought that she wouldn't like Michael to behave like Eddie Cameron. She couldn't believe that he would, for very practical reasons. Their marriage was a highly efficient radar system by which each could plot the exact position of the other at any given time of day or night. There wouldn't have been room for another woman in Michael's life unless he was secretly making one out of hardboard in his work-room or growing her from a seed in the greenhouse.

Hearing Eddie Cameron's voice on the phone and putting him through to Marion, Jane felt herself an accomplice in a crime. At the end of the day, as they both collected their coats, Jane asked Marion a question with her eyes and Marion nodded.

'Michael and Lucy are going to my sister's,' she said.

Jane hurried home to hold on to her domesticity like a talisman.

During dinner they tried to find out who each other was. Her married name was Bland and when she mentioned 'Harry' (which she did often enough for the word to be a conjunction, about as essential to her expression of herself as 'and'), Eddie suspected that he had known her late husband. He didn't mention the fact. If he was right, his sense of Harry Bland hardly squared with Marion's hushed reverence. Entering the sanctum with hobnailed boots was no part of seduction.

'He was a salesman, too, you know,' Marion said.

'Hm,' Eddie said.

She mentioned Jane Thomas's worries about what Marion might be getting herself into and waited. He dutifully explained about his separation and divorce, and how often he saw his daughters. He told her about the time he had worked in the bookshop and noticed her soften slightly, confronted with a man of some sensitivity, who had concerns beyond the material.

As the evening progressed, he noted a certain morbid tendency in her to refer to death. He forestalled it with levity. It was as if Harry's death had given her a Ph.D. in the subject. Once she mentioned the beatific expression on Harry's face as he stared towards the ceiling before he died. 'He was probably thinking he'd never have to paint another cornice,' Eddie said to himself but not to her.

'Have you ever watched anyone dying, Eddie?' she said.

'I suppose I have.'

'Have you really?'

'You sound surprised.'

'I wouldn't have guessed somehow.'

'What it is,' he said, 'I'm not wearing my death-watcher's badge tonight.'

Shared moments from the past made up much of the talk. They sat like lepidopterists comparing specimens. It was encouraging how well their memories matched. It was only occasionally that he had a Red Admiral and she had a moth. By the second bottle of wine, those fragile butterflies seemed to be shaking themselves free of their pins and fluttering in the room around them, there to be caught all over again. The air seemed full of possibilities.

'Eddie,' she said. 'You know that I can't take you home with me. It's been too long. I just can't.'

'Of course not,' he said. 'I understand.'

At her place they drank coffee. While their mouths discussed how soon he would have to leave, the physical sensations they had generated in each other circled their conversation like patient muggers, waiting for their moment. He precipitated the moment by getting up to leave. He crossed to the door.

'Eddie,' she said. 'Put out the light.'

He didn't question her. He put out the light. He stood in the darkness, listening to the sounds of her undressing beside the couch where he had left her. As if hypnotised by those sweet, furtive whisperings of cloth, he began to do the same. He started to feel his way towards her.

'Please don't be rough, Eddie,' she said.

'Darlin', I may never find you,' he said.

But he did and, by the unromantic light of an electric fire, her with one of her suspenders flapping loose, him with his socks still on, they made that mysterious and awesome transition from having sex to making love. Their bodies led them out past attitudes to wander looking for each other in an authentic darkness lust had made. His clever mouth went infant. Seduction was a second language he had never effectively learned and he reverted to honest, desperate babbling and ate her as the uttermost expression of his meaning. In the heat Harry was incinerated. The past was cast like clothes and she became sheer, voracious present. They forged their bodies into weird shapes and cooled into strangers, not to each other, to themselves.

It was strange to sit holding each other and, watching the fire, wonder who you were.

Bed seemed a kind of solution. They talked gentle irrelevancies to each other and kissed and tried to sleep. But they couldn't sleep. How do you sleep when you're lying in a stranger's body? They got out of bed and tried to find roles to play.

Marion made more coffee. Eddie suggested fixing a screw to the handle of the door but Marion didn't know where there was a screwdriver. The jokes this led to between them were a relief. Finding themselves laughing, they both began to use jokes as a discreet conspiracy, dead leaves with which to smother the awkwardly living thing they had made between them.

Marion found an old photograph of them with Eddie striking a rather dramatic pose. They remembered the wincing pretentiousness of his teens. Marion went in search of a phrase he had been fond of using that would illustrate exactly how pretentious he had been. Eddie was trying to help her.

'I've got it, I've got it,' she said.

'Good,' Eddie said unconvincingly.

'You said,' she said. 'You said – wait for this. You were going to live life . . . It wasn't to the hilt. That's not what you said. Curmudgeon or something. Dudgeon. That was it. You were going to live life to the dudgeon. You said that. Whatever the hell it means.'

'It means the same as hilt,' Eddie said. 'I think I was trying to show I'd read *Macbeth* at school. "And on the blade and dudgeon gouts of blood." Jesus, that's embarrassing.'

'Live life to the dudgeon. How about that? That's what you should call your memoirs. "How High Was My Dudgeon"!'

Eddie thought she was going to wet herself. He laughed loudly and waited. As they talked on, trying to exorcise the hours of darkness until normalcy could resume, both sensed how frenetic the conversation was becoming and how much closer to cruelty it was moving. But perhaps because of the guilt of what they were deliberately, if discreetly, doing or perhaps because daylight was coming near and there were still disturbing signs of life under the dead leaves, they made no attempt to stop themselves. They orchestrated a quarrel. It was as if they had tacitly agreed, 'If the bloody thing won't lie still, let's use shovels.'

Harry provided the soil. Marion had found some photographs of him. She didn't just show them to Eddie. She kept setting them in gilt-frames of anecdote, touching them up into icons. She was re-installing Harry in his shrine and doing penance before it for her unworthiness, as exemplified, presumably, by what they had done tonight.

'Selective embalming,' Eddie said.

Marion's smile became a wound.

'Why do you say that? You don't know what a good person he was.'

'If that's what bothers you, you can forget it. Because I knew him.'

'You're lying. How could you be so sure?'

'Harry Bland. Worked for Maynard's, didn't he? I thought I knew the name. And the photos clinched it.'

'You're lying. You would've said before this.'

'I don't like desecrating shrines.'

'You seem to manage.'

'I didn't know then that the deity was malign.'

'Oh, you're lying.'

'Maynard's. Area Supervisor. Right? I met him more than once. Conferences. Once in London with people I knew. Not official biographer status, right enough. But enough to get a perspective. I always remember he had the top of a finger missing. How's that for a birthmark?'

'That's right.'

Marion gathered all the photographs and replaced them in the shoe-box. She put the lid on very carefully, nursing the box on her lap.

'If you knew him at all,' she said, 'then you'll understand how lousy I feel in comparison.'

'No.'

'Then you didn't know him.'

'I know that he chased tail. With what amounted to dedication. Not too successfully but keenly.'

'Get to hell out of my flat!'

'I'm not dressed for a dramatic exit.'

'Just leave! Get out!'

'Oh, piss off,' he said. 'You're like a sparrow thinks its being victimised by winter. Nobody's after you. It's just if you talk you're liable to bump into the truth now and again. You better stop letting your thoughts run around in sentences. They'll get knocked down. And if you insist on clinching with people, naturally you'll burst your oxygen tent. And you'll have to breathe real air.'

'What you're saying isn't the truth.'

'Of course, it is.'

'How do you know?'

'Because I heard people who knew him well say it. Without malice. And I saw him trying to operate a couple of times.'

'With women?'

'It was all boringly heterosexual.'

'You're a bastard!'

'Accolades, accolades.'

'I don't believe you.'

'Then don't.'

They went on and Marion painstakingly outlined to Eddie just what an utterly pathetic object he was. He was, it seemed, a superannuated philanderer, a case of severely arrested development and someone who had – triumphant moment of finding the killing phrase – 'acne of the eyes'. He infected whatever he looked at with his own disease.

Eddie constructed a rococo verbal edifice in his defence. The way he lived was, apparently, the nature of the game. You had to lose a lot of conventional attitudes trying to find that occasional chord which put the jangle of coincidence in tune. Private lives were getting slightly *passé*, anyway. They had the television for a mirror. Pretty soon they would all be able to copulate by post. It was old-fashioned of him to want to confront his privacy in a full-length, wasting mirror every so often. He made himself sound slightly heroic.

They went on, she in her dressing-gown and slippers, he in trousers and bare feet with his jacket over his naked body, his paunch protruding coyly. Coffee dregs congealed and were thawed out with fresh brewings. The cigarette-stubs sank in a sea of ash.

Among the sound of the first starlings, she said, 'I believe you.'

'Sorry?'

'I believe you.'

'How do you mean?'

'About Harry. Damn you!'

'As long as you don't damn him. He didn't ask to be canonised.'

'I feel like not bothering to go on.'

'No you don't. You've only lost something you never had. Nothing to be done about that.'

When it was fully light, he brought in the milk and made more coffee and toast. They breakfasted in silence. He dressed and came over to her. She stood up. They embraced and felt the earth move – not the world, just the rubbish they had heaped on that moment of disturbing love they had experienced together. The feeling was still alive. They looked at each other.

'Are you going to phone?' she asked.

He winked.

'Maybe from Mars.'

She smiled.

'I'll be out.'

He went back to the hotel and showered and shaved and put on fresh clothes. He saw two clients in the morning but his conversations with them were like transatlantic telephone calls. He was aware of a recurring gap between what they said and his assimilation of it. His eyes were sparking. He began to think that, functioning like this, he should be on commission from a rival firm.

He was back in the hotel by 12.30. He lunched in a dining-room where two women whispered among the empty tables and through the window two old men played the nine-hole putting-green in anoraks. The way their caps, unresisted by any hair, fitted themselves to their heads saddened him. They tottered about the grass like a vision of the future. He saw his life relentless as a corridor. From now on there wouldn't be many doors that opened off it.

Upstairs, he stripped to shirt, trousers and socks and lay on the bed. He didn't sleep. He regretted telling her about Harry. He didn't regret telling her about Harry. He regretted the way he had told her about Harry. He could be a cruel bastard.

He remembered Allison, his ex-wife – whom God preserve, but far from him – engaging in one of her scenes from the Theatre of the Absurd, during one of those dramatic quarrels that made Eugene O'Neill seem laconic. She had emerged from the bathroom to announce grandly that she had been trying to slit her wrists. He had made the mistake of rushing towards her to comfort her. A magnifying glass could have detected a red line across each wrist. His anger at himself for falling for yet another of her fakeries had made him bitter.

'You won't win any death-certificates with that,' he had said.

'You'd think it was funny if I *was* dying,' she had said.

'Considering the rate at which you're losing blood, you can't have more than twenty years. With a tourniquet you might stretch that to thirty. You should get an elastoplast. It's not very dramatic to die of septic wrists.'

He didn't like himself for having said that. He didn't like what he'd become. How long was it since he had thought of Margaret Sutton, who had loved him and who had killed herself? He was the one who as a teenager couldn't watch anybody cry without finding tears in his own eyes. He felt some of that softness re-activate as he thought of Marion. He wanted to protect her. Perhaps he wanted her to protect him, too. He wanted his head examined.

He thought of a joke card he had bought and put in the alcove in the sitting-room of his flat. It showed a tall, bare-breasted woman standing in the middle of a maze. A small, down-trodden man was standing outside the maze, looking at her and saying, 'The last time I went into one of those it took me five years to get out.' The small man had been lucky.

My life is orderly, he told himself. So is a headstone, he told himself. You want to play that game again? he asked himself. You know another one that matters? he asked himself. At the moment Marion and he were two separate, contained confusions. Together, they could grow into a disaster. Neither of them needed that. But, beyond rationality, small images were budding in his memory, irrelevant as flowers. The softness of her upper arms. The way her head had found his neck before they parted.

He got up and walked about the room. 'No way,' he said aloud. But it was years since he had felt so alive. He became idiot with anonymity in the hotel room. He whistled and danced to himself in the mirror. He made pum-pum noises and snapped his fingers as he crossed the floor. He lay flat on the bed, reading the 'For Your Information' leaflet. Then he laid it on his face and carefully tested how hard he had to blow to blow it off. He noticed how squat his feet were in his socks. He found one tendril of dark cobweb dangling from the ceiling and for minutes watched it wafting gently.

'Chambermaid,' he said loudly. 'If your proficiency doesn't improve, you will be beaten to death with a feather-duster.' He laughed like the villain in a bad film.

He got up and crossed to the phone and dialled. He hoped she would speak to him. Jane Thomas's voice answered and, when he introduced himself, she was effusive in her welcome. It was presumably relief because Marion had explained that he wasn't married with fourteen of a family. The omens were propitious.

'Hullo,' Marion said.

'Hullo again,' he said and was talking not just to her but to what was left of the young man he had been.

ALLAN MASSIE

Short story taken from Telling Stories 4

Bertram's Funeral

Bertram's Funeral

They knew him in the village as 'the writer', but none of them had read his books. That didn't make them remarkable. His success, once considerable, was a bit back. When he brought out a novel now, it was reviewed as one in a batch, often at the tail-end, and his telephone didn't ring. He read interviews with more fashionable novelists instead.

The cottage garden was overgrown and the wind bent the brown thistle-heads. It was too early for a gin. Most days that wouldn't have bothered or stopped him, but he was going to the funeral of an old friend. He didn't want to topple into the grave.

The old friend was a painter. When Graham started out as a writer, he had known people who went and did all sorts of different things. His own father had been an engineer and the people he put in his first two books were engaged in the sort of occupations that demand regular hours; he had characters who wouldn't themselves read novels. Now he knew only other writers, painters, failed actresses, and the layabouts drawing dole money who were numerous in the county where he had come to live. That was after his wife left him, or he left her – he couldn't be sure which had made the decisive move, if indeed there had been one – the marriage came to the point when there were no leaves left on the tree.

The cat came to the window. He let it in and it asked for food. He scratched it behind the ear, but it shook its head, and he went to the refrigerator and took a chunk of cod he had cooked yesterday and put some on a saucer. He gave himself that gin to keep the cat company.

It was a beautiful cat, a long-haired Red Self, half Persian. He had swithered about having him neutered, and then done nothing, and put up with the spraying. The cat was called Trajan, after the emperor, and slept on Graham's bed and sometimes nibbled his ear in the dark.

The church was five miles away. He drove through the lanes at twenty-five miles an hour, hooting at junctions. He sat upright in his big black car. The wings were spattered with mud. He had had the car twenty years, and the marque was long discontinued as a result of a series of mergers and what they called rationalisations. It would last some time yet. He didn't do 3,000 miles in a year and usually he remembered to garage it in the old barn which went with the cottage. He sang, off-key, as he drove:

> We plough the fields and scatter
> The good seed on the land,
> But it is fed and watered
> By God's almighty hand . . .

He didn't go to church now, except for funerals, but he sang hymns while driving, shaving, or taking a bath.

There were already a lot of people in the church, and, in the English fashion, they had filled it from the back, so that he had to advance well up the aisle to find a place. He dropped on his knees on a worn hassock, extruding stuffing, to say a long-remembered, long-disused prayer. 'Visit this habitation, we beseech thee, o Lord . . .' Why did the word, 'beseech', vanished from ordinary parlance, where, in any case, if used, it would be condemned as feeble, sound so right here?

He sat back and fingered his black tie. The last funeral he had attended, he had been the only man wearing a black tie, and he had hesitated before knotting it this morning. He had looked at himself in the glass, with the tie dangling loose, at the face he had not liked when young, though some found it attractive, but which he had grown fond of as it deteriorated, and then he had sighed, and knotted the tie, thinking, as he seldom did, of his mother who used to ask if he had put on clean underclothes in case he was knocked down by a car and taken to hospital.

There was a good turn-out for Bertram. Graham had been to services at crematoria where there had been so few that a hymn was out of the question. He made a point of going to the funerals of friends, and there were a lot of them now as gin, whisky, cigarettes, anxiety, loss of hope, took their toll. He hated crematoria though. The assumption there was that the dead were simply inconveniences to be shuffled off; his presence was a silent protest.

A woman, heavily veiled, was advancing up the aisle. That was perhaps a bit much. One of Bertram's old mistresses making a point, staking a claim, stealing the scene? Then she passed him and he saw it was a young black man with dreadlocks. The trailing skirt he had caught in the corner of his eye belonged to an overcoat. The young man's head was bowed which was why it had looked as if he was wearing a veil. Graham felt a giggle steal up on him: it was a joke Bertram would have liked.

Besides the mistresses, Bertram had had three wives, not concurrently, and six or seven children. There might have been other children born out of wedlock, Graham didn't know. He had scattered his image freely enough. Graham made a sign to Annie, the second wife, the one he had known best and liked least.

The vicar read the Twenty-third Psalm, from green pastures to the valley of the shadow of death. Tears came into Graham's eyes. Another lesson: in my Father's house are many mansions . . . as many, he wondered, as the bed-sitters of Pimlico, where he had been living in a drab room with yellow walls, when he had first met Bertram? He had shared it with a young man called Richard. Neither of them had any work, but they spoke of how they would dominate the world. One evening, Richard said: 'Do you and Bertram have to be drunk every night?'

They stood to sing. 'The ancient Prince of hell/Hath risen with purpose fell . . .' 'Ein festes burg ist unser Gott . . .' In his youth Graham worked at night, often finishing at two, three in the morning. Then he went out into the city and walked. It was a time when even the bad things that happened seemed fruitful.

'The blessing of God Almighty, Father, Son and Holy Ghost . . .' Eight young men, at least three of them Bertram's sons, carried the coffin out of the church.

The rain had stopped. Bertram had loved painting rain. He did it well, better than anything else. There was one painting he had kept for years, refusing to sell, of ploughed fields in rain. The fields rose from the bottom of the canvas towards a line of winter trees. It was grey and brown, half a dozen different greys and browns, except for a dot of pink placed by a church spire that rose between the trees. There was a figure in the foreground, but Graham couldn't remember if it had been male or female. It didn't matter. It was just there, and maybe it was meant to be insignificant. Then Bertram sold the painting and probably it was hung in an American gallery now.

He squashed his hat on to his head and buttoned his overcoat. It was an eastern county and all winds were sharp from October to March. There was a big sky and the chug of a tractor. Jackdaws flew about the little church with its square tower. He was standing near a woman whom he recognised as his daughter. He hadn't seen her for six or seven years, and the line of her jaw was stronger than it used to be. She hadn't seen him, her gaze was fixed on the grave. Old words floated towards him. He took off his hat and shoved it into his pocket. He bent his head. Bertram was her godfather. That was why she was here, and it was right. They would have to speak, later. He used to call her 'Nutkin'. He doubted if she would like to be called 'Nutkin' now. Her coat was good and expensive. She had her arm round a young blond boy. It must be his grandson.

One of the young men holding one of the cords let go too soon. The coffin lurched feet first into the hole. For a moment it looked as if Bertram would have to be buried vertical. Then adjustments were made. The descent was accomplished. Handfuls of earth were thrown. The crowd began to disperse. Graham waited, then scratched up some of the blue-grey clay soil, and let it fall on his friend. That was that. He wondered if they had put a paint brush and palette in the coffin. He hoped they had, not that he would ask for a typewriter in his. There wouldn't be this sort of turn-out when it came to his turn to turn in.

He touched his daughter on the shoulder.

'Susie,' he said, not daring 'Nutkin'.

His fingers left smears of clay on the good navy-blue cloth. He hoped she wouldn't notice till she got home and that she wouldn't then connect it with him.

'You should have let me know you were coming. I'd have given you lunch.'

The boy was looking at him. He had the kind of face illustrators used to draw in school stories, for the hero – frank, open, manly; obsolete, unusable epithets. Graham thought of other boys he knew, or saw around on his rare visits to London, and wondered how long this boy could keep that look in today's world.

Susie said nothing. She left the word 'lunch' hanging in the thin autumn air.

'You don't know me,' he said to the boy. 'I'm your grand-father.'

How old was he? Thirteen, fourteen? Something like that. He was a nice-looking boy, and he had nice manners, because he smiled now, not embarrassed, even as if pleased to meet him.

'This is the first funeral I've ever been to,' he said. 'I've only come because I'm on half-term.'

'Good,' Graham said. 'I'm glad you've come, Susie. Old Bertram was always fond of you.'

'He sent me a painting last Christmas,' she said. 'I could see it was good, but I only hang abstracts. But he said it was valuable and I suppose it is.'

'Take it to his dealer if you want it valued. But I should hang on to it. Bertram said his paintings will be worth more in ten, fifteen years than they are now. That was quite recently. He always had a good eye for market values.'

He hoped he didn't sound bitter. The words could seem bitter, but they weren't meant that way. Still, they helped get over the awkwardness and ease them on their way from the churchyard to the house. But the awkwardness couldn't be altogether avoided.

'Is your mother here? I didn't see her in the church.'

It was mad that he hadn't thought they might be here.

'No,' she said. 'She's not. In fact, she's ill. In fact she's in hospital.'

The wind twitched at the thin branches, ruffled his hair. He pushed his hat back on his head.

'I'm sorry,' he said. 'Is it serious?'

'Only tests. They're doing tests.'

'Nutkin', he thought again. I suppose she really does dislike me. He ought to know which school the boy was at.

'Tests?' he said.

'Yes,' she said. 'It begins with tests, doesn't it?'

SUSAN MOODY

Extract taken from

The Italian Garden

The Italian Garden is available now at your local Dillons store priced £5.99.

Bring this voucher with you to obtain £1.00 off the publisher's prices at all Dillons stores.

'Fuck it,' Susie said. '*Fuck* it.'

'Language, old girl.' Hannah was lying in the hammock slung between a corner of the house and a handy tree. The heat had increased; even the nights now were almost unbearably warm, sleep difficult.

Susie slammed the garden table with her clenched fist. 'Damn them to hell.'

'For heaven's sake.' Hannah tried to sit up. 'What on earth's the matter?'

'My bloody parents.' Susie scowled at the letter which had arrived that morning from her father. 'It looks as though I shall have to go to Rome after the weekend. *Fuck* it.'

'Why?' Although she kept her voice unconcerned, Hannah could already feel a flutter of tension in her stomach. Susie was building up into one of her spectacular rages.

'Why? Because my *bloody* parents have made an appointment for me to see someone, that's why.' Susie spoke through gritted teeth.

'What about?'

'Nothing much.' Furiously, Susie scraped her chair back and then, with slow deliberation, grabbed the edge of the table at which she had been sitting and tipped it over, sending the remains of their breakfast flying. Crockery smashed, fruit and bread were showered with shards of broken porcelain, a juice glass rolled to the edge of the grass.

'Calm down, Sooz,' Hannah said, without any hope that Susie would do so. When she was really angry, she was like some elemental force, completely out of control.

'On top of that, Pa wants me to talk to his lawyers about something. Which, knowing Italian lawyers, could take days. Even weeks. And Rome'll be bloody *sweltering* at this time of year.' Susie stamped the ground and then, her face clearing, looked suddenly hopeful. 'Why don't you come with me?'

Hannah groaned inwardly. The last thing she wanted was a hot drive down to the crowded city. 'Do I have to?'

'Pa can damn well pay for the hire of a car. We could drive down together, make a trip of it.'

'I'd much rather stay here.'

Susie frowned, face contorting with anger, then shrugged. 'OK. Suit yourself.'

'I've got masses of reading to do.' Hannah did not add that, so far, she had scarcely opened her books. 'With you away, it'll be a good opportunity for me to get on with it. Finals next term and all that.' She had no wish to spend time in the enervating heat of Rome, nor did she wish to get caught up in any more of Susie's rage than she had to, knowing from experience that it would take hours to simmer down. Then she reminded herself that Susie was her friend. Hastily, she added: 'I'll come if you really want me to, of course.'

'Not if you don't want to,' Susie said. 'Actually, now I think about it, it might be quite a good idea if I went alone.'

'Why?'

'Because, my dear, much as I love you, there are times when two's company and three's a crowd.'

Hannah tried to sit up, the hammock rocking dangerously beneath her. 'I see. And where will you be staying in Rome, might I ask?'

'Ma's got this cousin with a flat near the Colosseum.'

'And is this cousin young, male, gorgeous and loaded?'

'As a matter of fact, *she*'s ninety-two and looks like a cross between the Hunchback of Notre Dame and one of the Ugly Sisters.'

'Is there a young, gorgeous, loaded male living on the premises? Or close by? Or somewhere in Rome?'

'Since you ask,' said Susie, 'there just might be something of the sort.'

'All I can say, old girl, is jolly good luck to you.' Relieved, Hannah lay back again in the hammock and swung herself slowly back and forth. Used to solitude, she could almost taste the pleasure of being on her own in the Giulia, with its echoing rooms, its dusty sunlight and dim, grey mirrors. And lying beneath that pleasure, there was, too, the tingle of some not-quite-acknowledged anticipation which she did not care to examine too closely.

After Susie had left, she went to the kitchen to make a mug of coffee. A majolica bowl lay shattered on the floor; frowning, Hannah found a broom. Susie must have come in here before she left and flung it violently at the wall. Her rage of the other day had not abated over the intervening weekend, then, though she had managed successfully to conceal it after her initial outburst. She wandered slowly through the empty house, drifting across the polished floors while swirls of dust rose like moths in her wake. Standing on the balustraded terrace, she looked between the big urns towards the town. It was noon. The sun burned; the fields of ripe wheat glittered. Later, when the long shadows began to move up from the plains, the scene would change, the colours turn from fawns and terracottas to shades of cinnamon and chocolate.

A hot breeze stirred. She watched it shiver among the leaves at the edge of the grass and die down. Overhead the air was milky, a blue so fragile that if she were to reach up and touch it, the whole sky might shatter and fall about her in dagger-sharp fragments, like the majolica plate.

Sweat rolled down her back, under her thin blouse. It was cooler in the house, but the pool, deep among the trees, was more inviting. Crossing the grass, she pushed between the shrubs, leaves stroking her skin. Heat waited even in the green tunnels; where the sun penetrated, it burned like a flame. It was too hot to do anything more than endure, lie comatose like a lizard and simply wait for the dark.

The surface of the pool was warm, almost hot, but cool and shadowed underneath. Ripples moved across the black water and stirred the water-lily leaves; the fat buds rocked, bamboo rustled and whispered.

She caught a glimpse of white in the shrubs which crowded behind the two marble columns. Someone was watching her again. Lucas? Or some archaic spirit of the trees? In the melting heat, she felt herself to be at one with all that was around her. It did not matter who watched; they too were part of the green woods and black water.

Towards evening, when the sun had moved lower in the sky, she cycled along the flat roads towards the town, to buy bread and fruit. The shadows were longer now; behind the castle on the brow of the hill, a ghost-white circle of moon hung from the cloudless sky.

In the piazza she saw Lucas slouched at a table, a cold beer in front of him. He raised a hand and called her name; she pretended not to have heard him. Since the afternoon at the pool she had managed to avoid him, pleading a series of headaches, saying she had work to do, or was tired. Carrying a disc of crusty bread, she hurried away from him between high, pink walls. In the coolness of the dairy, she waited while they wrapped the creamy cheese which was a speciality of the region. She bought fat tomatoes, gleaming purple-black aubergines, yellow capsicums. She hoped he would not follow.

But, as she was choosing wine in the dark little grocer's shop, she felt a hand on her shoulder.

'You can't run away for ever,' he said, behind her.

Hannah did not reply. He was close enough to her that she could feel his voice against the back of her blouse. He touched one of the knobs of her backbone with a finger; she arched away as though singed by a flame.

'You're too thin,' he said, and his breath brushed the side of her neck.

'Am I?'

'Much, much too thin. Let me take you out to dinner tonight.'

'No thank you,' she said hastily, bending her head, reaching for a bottle, any bottle so that he would not realise how awkward she felt.

'Why not?'

'I just . . . couldn't.'

'Of course you could.' He took the bottle from her, taking her hand, turning her round so that she faced him. 'I wouldn't buy that – it's quite disgusting.'

'Oh.' He burned like a candle in front of her.

'Look. I know you're all alone at the Villa Giulia – Susie rang and told me she was going to Rome. She asked me to look after you, see that you were all right.'

'I'm perfectly capable of taking care of myself, thank you.'

'I know you are. So will you come for my sake? I too am alone at the moment.'

'I'd really rather not.'

'Please, Hannah.'

She turned her back to him, considering. She did not wish to have dinner with him; the memory of his rejection still flooded her with embarrassment whenever she thought of it. And she knew, without analysing exactly how, that if she went with him, she also would be, as he had said, endangered.

Yet he sounded as if he wanted her to come. And it might be fun. And he was a—

'*Hannah* . . .' The unspoken word rang inside her skull.

'All right,' she said. She turned to face him. 'What time?'

'I'll come for you at eight.'

How easily the wrong road was taken.

The moon was almost overhead when they came out of the restaurant, round and golden against a sky splattered with stars. Hannah had enjoyed herself. Lucas was an entertaining and informed companion; his knowledge of the classical myths was at least equal to her own. And he had never once given any indication that he remembered her unsolicited advances beside the pool, never glanced at her mockingly or suggestively, not even touched her.

She stared up at the dark as they walked towards Lucas's car. 'Look at those stars.'

'Glorious. Seeing them, I realise why I never feel quite at home in England.'

'It'd be chilly by now, if we were there now,' Hannah said. 'The air's still warm here, even though it's so late.'

'Careful,' Lucas said. 'You nearly bumped into that car.' He took her hand.

Hannah did not pull away. They walked in silence. In the car, instead of starting the engine, he sat with his hands on the steering wheel, staring ahead. Then he sighed: 'I must take you home, Hannah.'

'Yes.'

The road out of the town wound uphill for a while before dipping down to the plain. The huge, sombre-faced moon was sometimes behind them, sometimes ahead. At the top of the hill, Lucas pulled to the side of the road.

'Look,' he said softly.

Up here, the moon seemed flatter, paler, pasted against the sky rather than hanging from it. Beneath it lay a landscape smoothed out by darkness, sheened like silk. The moonlight was not silver but grey, as though a blanket of cobwebs had been spread over it. In the middle of the vast flatness, riding the dark fields like a boat, reared a small ridge crowned with a pink four-square house which looked out over the lonely countryside all round it. The windows were shuttered; there were four trees, one at each corner, black in the pearl-grey light. The scene had the simplicity of a child's painting.

'Oh,' Hannah said.

'Isn't it beautiful?'

'I wonder who lives there.'

'A friend of mine,' Lucas said. 'A good friend. She's – the house is empty at the moment.'

Hannah turned to him. In the strange light, his eyes were almost opaque, the colour of the moonlight itself. 'Listen,' she said.

'What to? I can't hear anything.'

'Exactly. There's no noise. Absolutely nothing.'

'Cicadas,' Lucas said.

'But no traffic, no sense of other people. Not even night sounds, like owls.' Beads of green fire hung in the air around them. 'Fireflies,' whispered Hannah.

'Magical, isn't it?' Lucas was still staring at the pink house under the moon; momentarily, the long lines of his face seemed to deepen. He was so still that he seemed not to be breathing.

He shook himself and turned towards her.

Hannah. She heard the word, though his lips did not move.

He reached across the car for her, lifting her face to meet his. She knew she ought to resist, but could not.

As his lips touched her mouth, images of regeneration and metamorphosis filled her mind; butterflies and chrysalises, ice and water, buds and flowers. He stared down at her; she could feel herself disintegrating under his sombre gaze, her old self tearing like paper, transmuting into something new and shiny. Under the pressure of his mouth, she groaned.

He took a deep breath. When he took her into his arms, the material of her dress touched her breasts and the sensation filled her with a peppery excitement. It was the heat, she told herself, nothing more than that, the will-sapping heat. But still, she yearned. She wanted to lose herself, take his hand and push it into the hot moist place between her legs, feel his hands opening her, his mouth learning her. Proprieties dissolved. The wine, the candles, the slow flicker of the fireflies, the stunning heat and in front of them, the ghost-coloured fields spreading away towards the black hills: there was an urgency in the night to which, although unconversant, she longed to respond.

Then, remembering his rejection of her by the pool, she forced herself away from him. 'You'd better take me back,' she said. Her voice was not quite under control.

'Yes. I suppose I had.'

She looked at him from under her lashes. His profile was black against the moon which seemed so close that it could have been lying on the windscreen, staring in at the two of them. He turned his head and their eyes met. Were hers as full of longing as his, she wondered? Did they contain the same expression of regret, of might-have-beens, of something precious which had slipped from their grasp?

'Some things are not meant to be,' he said quietly, and searching her mind for a response, she could not come up with one and so remained silent.

'And some things which are, should never have been,' he added, his voice harsh.

She did not ask what he meant. Her hands ached to reach out to him, her mouth longed to feel his again. She wished she was like those others, those girls who so lightly swapped their beds and their men. She wished she could enjoy sex as they did, without needing the complications of love.

He dropped her at the foot of the terrace steps, and then turned in a spin of sandy gravel and drove back down to the road which led to his own house. He had not kissed her again.

She was sitting in the piazza two days later, trying to make sense of the local paper, when someone stopped at her table.

'At least today you are not trespassing,' a voice said and, looking up, she saw the man who had almost run her over a couple of weeks before.

It was a slight remark, and one to which, in view of the heat, she could scarcely be bothered to reply. None the less, she smiled and, when he asked if he could join her, pointed to a chair.

'You are English,' he said, after ordering a *cappuccino* from the waiter, 'yet you look like an Italian. Much too—' He clicked his fingers in the air, searching for a word, 'too skinny, of course. But you have the colouring of the women of our country.'

'Just because I have dark hair—'

'It's more than that,' he said. He looked her over and she felt herself begin to blush. 'Even in that terrible dress, you have a kind of – of excitement about you. A . . . sexiness.'

'Thank you very much.'

'You are not pretty, but when you are old you will be beautiful.' He leaned back and put one hand in the pocket of his slacks.

'Hasn't anyone ever told you that it's very impolite to make personal remarks?' she said.

For a moment he looked at her with a puzzled expression on his face. Hannah could see that he did not know how to react. Then he laughed, throwing back his head.

'You are right.' He reached quickly across the table to touch her hand. 'I have been very ill-mannered—'

'And it's not the first time, either,' Hannah said prissily. 'You were pretty bloody-minded the afternoon you ran me over.'

'*Almost* ran you over.' He laughed once more. 'But you see, there I was, driving along on my own land—'

'I thought you said it was your wife's land.'

'It is the same thing,' he said carelessly, 'and what do I see in front of me but a girl on a bicycle. A very furious girl.'

She wondered how old he was. Ten, maybe fifteen years older than herself? He was dark, tanned, handsome, his body full of energy. 'How could you tell?' she asked.

'Every line of your body registered rage,' he said. 'And not only were you furious, but you were wavering about—'

'Do you mean weaving?'

'Weaving is with a—' He mimed the actions of someone at a loom. 'To make fabrics, no?'

'Yes. But it's also teetering from side to side, like a – like a drunk.'

'Exactly. Like a drunk. This girl, I say to myself, this stupid girl, is not only furious, but also drunk, and I must be careful.'

Hannah giggled.

'And possibly crazy as well,' he continued. 'This, I say to myself, is a girl to avoid.'

'Except that you *didn't* avoid me.'

He spread his hands. 'I had no choice.'

'You practically ran me over.'

'Believe me,' he said, 'no one could be more thankful than I that my brakes were in such good condition. And when I say that, I am not joking.' His face was serious; although she knew that what he said was no more than the gallantry which came with being Italian, inside Hannah something contracted for a moment, as though her heart had been squeezed like a sponge and then wrung out. He leaned towards her. 'It is good to see you laugh, rather than cry.'

She watched a cat stalk across the sunny square, its tail held high, and settle down in the shade of the plane trees. 'My parents will be pleased to hear that you maintain your car so well,' she said lightly.

'Ah. Your family. Tell me about them.'

She spoke of her parents and as she did so, the two of them, awkward and dull, assumed a gentler outline, time or distance softening their angularities, lending them some distinction. They were both eminent in their field; were she not their child, she might well have seen them as parents to be proud of. Susie was always saying that she would never inflict the misery of being an only child on another human being: would her own inner loneliness have been assuaged by a sibling? It was one of those questions to which there could never be an answer.

'And your house,' he said. 'Tell me how you live. I am anxious to know.'

'Why?'

'Because you seem to be a fascinating woman, a woman of contrasts. And I ask myself: what makes a woman like this, why is someone so lively at the same time so afraid? How can a woman be so full of fire and yet so frozen?'

Before she could answer, he smiled. 'But perhaps you will accuse me once more of making personal remarks. I am sorry.' He put out a hand. 'Perhaps I should introduce myself: my name is Faustino Castelli.'

'Hannah Carrington.'

'Anna Carrington. Good.'

'Hannah,' she corrected. 'You said you live in Rome.'

'We have a flat,' he said. 'A big apartment near the Via Veneto.'

'And how often do you come down here?'

'My wife is often here in the summer. I come once or twice. I have work to do, patients to see. Besides, I prefer the city to the country.' With a kind of bow at her, he added: 'But now I have met you, perhaps I shall change my opinion.'

'But of course,' Hannah said, her voice sardonic. 'You're a doctor, are you?'

'A psychiatric doctor, yes.'

She stood on the balcony of her bedroom. Overhead, fierce stars burned. As she watched, one detached itself from the sky and rushed across the darkness in a thin trail of fire. Ignorant of the night skies, Hannah could only identify the Plough. It seemed wrongly positioned here and – or did she merely imagine it? – brighter than in England. Behind her, in the bedroom, there was a sound and she turned. In the glimmering half-light she could see a figure standing just inside the room.

She should have been afraid but was not. 'Who's there?' she said calmly. And heard his voice calling her across the room, beating like a moth against her brain.

Hannah. Hannah.

'Lucas.' For a moment she stopped breathing, seeing again a

composite set of images: white breasts, green water, the long leaves of the bamboo.

'I had to come,' he said. 'I couldn't . . . not.'

He had been leaning against the wall. Now he came slowly towards her. She was powerless. Even when he pressed a hand against the small of her back, almost lifting her from the ground, she could not move, or speak. She wanted to lie down with him among flowers, under warm pine trees. She wanted him to linger over her naked body, to kiss the secret moistness of her. She wanted to make love with him. As if in a dream, she felt him lift the dress over her head; she raised her arms like a child when he asked her to. Slowly he began to undo his shirt and somewhere at the back of her mind, she asked herself: *do you really want this?* But body and mind seemed dissociated as he ran his hands down her back to her buttocks. The soft places in her melted. She felt as though she had been poured full of sunshine as he laid her down on the bed.

Why did she yield so easily? It was a question which, afterwards, she was never able to answer. At the time, it seemed to her that there was nothing else in the world except the two of them and the heat of the empty house, the sheets beneath.

'Hannah,' he said, and this time she felt the tender movement of his mouth against her shoulder.

It was as though she no longer had a will of her own. Lucas called to her, and his voice was compelling. Helplessly, she would stop what she was doing and walk through the hanging leaves, down the mossy paths towards the pool. Sometimes he was there waiting for her; he would take her without speaking, open her, stare deep into her eyes as he slowly entered her. At other times, ducking between the tumbledown railings which marked the boundary line of the villas, she would make her way along the paths between the bushes – here, at the Diana, kept raked and sanded – up to his house.

Sometimes he would be on the terrace, naked, his body white, already erect. Sometimes he would draw her after him, up the marble stairs to his bedroom, the twin of hers, and then make her wait. Sometimes she would see him standing between the half-closed shutters of his room, watching as she made her way towards him across the grass. Always, after that first time, she went to him.

He rarely spoke. He used her body like a piano, playing her like someone for whom the sounds he drew from his keyboard were memories of raptures once experienced, all the joy he would ever know. Eyes half-closed, their secret fires hidden, he would watch while her body sang for him.

'Lucas,' she would sigh, moan, scream. But he did not answer her, nor did he call her name. She was transfixed by him, melting, arching, clasping; whatever he wanted, she let him do. Sometimes he would take her almost as soon as they came together. At others, he would lie above her, tracing the line of her body, skilfully arousing her with his fingers, his mouth, his tongue. Through him, she learned the secrets of her own sensuality, discovering herself as he discovered her.

Once, she felt tears on his face.

And when it was over, when his sweat had dried on her body, she would stand and dress herself in silence, turned away from him, afraid that if he looked into her eyes, he would see that despite the totality of her yielding, she was none the less able to keep back one small piece of herself, a tiny corner of her mind where she did not allow him to enter. Then, leaving him on the bed, she would walk along the passage to the top of the sweeping stairs and go slowly down them, his juices still oozing from her, and out of the terrace door into the violent heat. He never offered to accompany her; she never asked that he should. She was aware, occasionally, of doors quietly closing as she passed, of eyes which watched from the end of passages, of corners just turned; sometimes, looking back, she would see a shape at one of the windows.

Reaching the pool, she would take off her clothes and plunge into it, up to the neck, to rid herself of Lucas. Sometimes there was a violence about him which hovered on the edge of being perilous. She did not question why she allowed him to use her as he did, to turn her into nothing more than an object, but away from him she could always see that what they did together was altogether degrading. Until the next time he called.

Need me, she begged him silently. *Want me. Ask me for something.* He made no emotional contact with her. She felt unclean, yet the pleasure he gave her was intoxicating, a drug whose habit she had acquired.

'Need me,' she said once, standing over him after he had rolled away from her and her body had regained its normal pulses.

'What?' He turned on the damp sheet and looked up at her from under tousled hair.

'You use me, Lucas.' She shrugged into her cotton shirt and began to do up the buttons.

'Don't you like it?' He reached out a hand and caressed her hip.

She stepped away from him; his arm dropped to the side of the bed and his fingers trailed on the floor. 'You know I do. But I hate the – the impersonality of it. Surely there ought to be something more than just—'

'Just fucking?' He laughed. 'Isn't that enough?'

She pressed her lips together for a moment. 'Not for me,' she said quietly.

He hoisted himself up on one elbow. 'Come on, Hannah. You're a grown woman.'

'Am I?' She did not feel it.

'You know what it's all about.'

'I suppose I do.' But she did not. Fucking without feeling: she had supposed that even so there would be murmurs, kisses, whispered sweetnesses. She had not thought it would be this brutal. Or this lovely.

'Please, Hannah. You aren't going to talk about—' he paused, '*love*, are you?'

'Of course not.' She reddened. 'I just wish you—'

'What?'

'*Needed* me more than you do.'

He sat up. 'Oh, I *need* you, Hannah. Don't make any mistake about that. I really do need you. In fact—' he glanced down at himself, 'if you come back to bed, I'll show you just how much.'

She did not wish to. But he reached out and pulled her towards him, holding her wrist so tightly that the small bones grated. He lifted her shirt, kissed the base of her stomach. She felt his tongue caress the slippery places of her and her body yearned towards him. 'No,' she said faintly. 'Not like that.'

But it was too late. He threw her down, kneeling between her legs, kneeing them apart, wider and wider, before coming into her in a series of violent movements which had her shaking with ecstasy.

'I need you,' he said. 'Do you believe that?'

'Yes,' she said, exploding around him. 'Yes, I do. Yes.'

Afterwards, it seemed pointless trying to explain that that was not what she had meant at all.

MARTINA NAVRATILOVA

Extract taken from

The Total Zone

The Total Zone is available now at your local Dillons store priced £5.99.

Bring this voucher with you to obtain £1.00 off the publisher's prices at all Dillons stores.

Chapter One

The last time I was in front of the TV cameras, millions of people saw me get annihilated by a sixteen-year-old girl with her hair in pigtails and braces on her teeth. I never went back to Wimbledon, or any other tennis tournament for that matter, although not entirely as a personal choice. Now I was in front of the cameras again, and it all came back in the blitz of flashes – the headiness of the attention, the cheers of the crowd, the adrenaline that raced through my body as I braced to run the gauntlet. Except this time I wasn't playing for the crowd; I was in it. I wasn't out to win; I was out of the game. And I wasn't getting an award; my former opponent – now my client – was. I walked purposefully ahead on the red carpet, joining the crush of celebrities, entourage members, and wannabes, simultaneously hoping that somebody would recognize me and dreading the prospect. Suddenly I felt a hand wrench my shoulder and reach past my neck with a sharp chop to my throat. Something shoved the small of my back. A metal object grazed my skull, and a heavy combat boot smashed down on my instep, tripping me to my knees. A blinding light flashed before my eyes.

Paparazzi.

An exclusive shot of a major star was worth thousands of dollars, and these guys would probably kill for it. The legitimate press was one thing. The tabloid guys, however, were a whole other breed. If they didn't get a shot, they'd create it by stripping one star's head onto another's body, or whatever it took. Nothing personal. I was irritated, and

a little shaken, but I knew I was not the intended prey –
a shot of me was worth about five cents, if my mother
had change in her purse. I was just blocking somebody's
viewfinder.

I was rescued by a Garden security officer, who grabbed
the photographer and yanked him unceremoniously off
me. 'Where's your pass, mister?' he grilled the man, as
another guard raced to offer me a hand and two or three
more men in uniform materialized.

'Media,' the photographer mumbled.

'You don't have a pass. Get over here,' commanded the
guard, as he and his uniformed friends formed a wedge,
lifted the photographer up by the elbows, and deposited
him back behind the velvet rope.

'Are you all right, miss?' asked the guard who'd helped
me up. He held his walkie-talkie at the ready.

'I'm fine. It was an accident. I think.' I'd escaped pretty
much unscathed, except that I'd ripped my stockings when
I fell and a huge run was making its jagged way down the
length of my left leg. And, of course, I'd skinned my knee.
But then, that was in character.

There are some people, like Fred Astaire, Ginger
Rogers, fashion models, and society-page habitués, who
can wear formal gowns and tuxedos as comfortably as a
T-shirt and jeans. I, Jordan Myles, am not one of them.
I blame this on the fact that, until a few years ago – five
years ago, to be exact – I spent most of my life at a dead run
across a tennis court in Nikes, ankle socks, shorts, and a
T-shirt, clutching a racket, not an evening bag. Even when
I was the number three player on the women's tour, where
events like awards dinners, fund-raisers, charity benefits,
and testimonials were part of the schedule, for the most
part my focus was on my training. When I had to show
up at an event, I fell back on my uniform – biannual
variations on a black synthetic dress that packed well,

could be de-wrinkled in shower steam, rinsed out in a bathroom sink, hung up to drip-dry, and worn that night, if necessary. As any woman who's ever played on the tour can attest, it's not your opponent that's your worst nightmare – it's your laundry.

But tonight was different. Everyone in the world of sports, which meant a major percentage of my old friends, not to mention my current and potential clients, was going to be at the Sports Network Awards, an event they accurately refer to in the press as 'star-studded' and 'glittering,' so I did make a particular and extensive effort – well, extensive for me, anyway. Before I flew to New York from Palm Springs for the awards, I bought a simple navy blue cocktail dress with an interesting backless look, and tonight I spent some time attacking my short, curly black hair with its natural enemy, the blowdryer. I never use much makeup, because frankly I do look better without it. My eyes are dark hazel, my color naturally high, my nose, which was once broken in a midcourt collision, beyond the ministrations of any over-the-counter beauty products. Things had looked promising until I had to deal with one critical issue women's evening wear has yet to address, which is where to put your beeper.

I'm a physical therapist at the Desert Springs Sports Science Clinic, and it's part of my job never to be unreachable. It's important to our clients that we are available at all times – many of them are high-profile celebrities who call in questions or problems from a mixed bag of time zones. In a crowd you can't hear a beeper in your purse, so I compromised by putting on a jacket and clipping the beeper to the pocket. The jacket covered up 90 percent of the dress, but what are you going to do?

Actually, who was going to care? Certainly not my escort – he had the proper perspective, having first met me in a hospital gown in traction, with pins and staples piecing my leg together after the mountain-climbing mishap that didn't kill me but managed to abruptly end my career in professional tennis when I was twenty-two. Officially, Gus is Dr. Augustus Laidlaw, director and cofounder of the Springs, my associate on the staff and one of the most brilliant, if controversial, sports psychologists in the world. Unofficially – very unofficially – he's a friend I'm involved with, and have been in varying degrees since he helped me get back on my feet, in more ways than one, after the accident. It's a complicated relationship, something you can't really label. Occasionally, when she thinks enough time has elapsed since the last time she shook the trees in hopes that some information would fall out, my mother will ask the usual discreet questions all mothers of single daughters ask. I never have the answers. What is Gus to me? A friend, a mentor, an associate, a lover, a role model, a doctor, a teacher, a conscience, a nemesis, a jerk. At any given moment, one or more of the above may apply.

I always tell myself things are as good as they were when I was playing tennis – in some ways, better. I have a stable life, a predictable if not astronomical income, a home of my own, friends, a profession I believe in that helps others. I'm a founding staff member of the Springs, an exciting new sports medicine clinic that helps athletes from every sport make the best of their minds and bodies. My failed marriage was in the past, if you can call something that only lasted six months, and which was therefore history almost the minute it began, a marriage. And there's Gus. In other words, I've gotten on with my life.

Which brought me to the Paramount Theater at Madison Square Garden for this convergence of the best and brightest in sports. It's sort of ironic, because, for so many years, the Garden was a regular part of my life – an every-November stopover for the Virginia Slims

Championships, the punctuation at the year's end of the women's tour. I don't know if I will ever get over feeling disconnected about being in New York and putting on a fancy outfit instead of baggy sweats and a T-shirt. Or drop the habit of feeling guilty when I eat a giant slice of tiramisù at Contrapunto. Or stop feeling strange about pulling out a business card that says *Jordan Myles, Physical Therapist* – or about having a business card, period. I have to keep reminding myself that things are different now.

All the big names were slated to be here tonight. I scanned the crowd milling through the vast entrance to Madison Square Garden, up the escalators and into the Paramount Theater, for Gus, who was flying in from a corporate speech in Detroit. At the top of the escalators, there is an Art Decoish lobby; here the entering crowd merged with the people spilling out from the glass-enclosed Play-by-Play Lounge, where a VIP dinner had been held for tonight's honorees and their guests. Through the glass, I could see the flicker of candles and white tablecloths and garlands of balloons and ribbons hanging from the ceiling. I spotted Ollie Cedars, the heavyweight title contender, his huge bulk and orbiting entourage parting the crowd. Ollie waved, revealing a massive diamond-studded watch. Behind us, cries of 'Mi-chael! Mi-chael!' signaled that Michael Jordan had arrived. Smiling to the bank of photographers, who obliged with a blinding flash of lights, was Linsey Marks, blond, in a white beaded gown, living up to her reputation as the glamour girl of golf. Billie Jean King walked in, and just behind her were country-music star Allie Trask and rapper Mr. Huge. A famous football star rode up the escalator with a gorgeous woman clinging to each arm. His public appearances and macho press coverage are always designed to mask the fact that he's known in sports circles to be gay.

Barricaded behind another storm of camera flashes,

her back pressed to the wall, was Mariska Storrs, her hair slicked back and sleek as her tuxedo. I wondered if I should rescue her, but if there's anybody who knows how to handle the press it's Mariska. Mariska, who has won more Grand Slam titles than any woman in history, is one of those people who has achieved a pinnacle so rarefied that her last name is an unnecessary appendage. She has true charisma, but has sustained the public's interest for this long because of sheer talent and ability; if you have charisma without ability, nobody cares. Since her highly publicized escape from behind the Iron Curtain almost twenty years ago, she's probably racked up more sports coverage – and gossip items – than all her rivals combined. Her unbroken string of seven consecutive Wimbledon singles wins is countered by overblown reports of her affairs with, variously, a British rock star, a top fashion model, and a housewife. Every year for fifteen years she's re-earned her spot in the standings by winning at least one Grand Slam tournament, and last year *Sports Illustrated* named her 'Athlete of the Nineties'. She's known for being an aggressive, tough – even brutal – player, and her media personality somewhat reflects this. In interviews she can come across like a sharp stick in the eye, but the upside is, she's always been uncondescendingly honest. Needless to say, some of the players are intimidated by her. Tonight, typically, Mariska moved through the crowd, acknowledging the rest of the world with an unapproachable, practised smile, an expression engineered to get her through the evening and disguise the fact that her mind is somewhere else entirely. On the court she is laserlike in her intensity, but off the court she tends to be unfocused, with a short attention span, almost like a child. She wants what she wants when she wants it. Period. You can find yourself talking to Mariska one minute, then conversing with thin air the next, because when she's had enough of listening to what you have to say, she's finished – even if you're not. Many people here tonight had been the victims of her legendary temper, or cut off by her abruptness. There were probably a couple dozen others who had phone calls in to her that would never be returned. Then there were those who are just plain scared of her, petrified in her presence – not just fans, but players, press, and even officials. Of course, whether they like her or not, virtually everyone is in awe of Mariska's achievements, a fact that only magnifies her flaws, real or perceived. She is very much aware of this. 'Everybody always complains that I make all the decisions,' Mariska once said to me, 'but the fact is that everybody defers to me because they want to make sure I approve of what's happening, or they want to make sure that I'm having a good time. So it just ends up that way.'

But of all the women in tennis, Mariska is the one who helped me the most. When I was playing, she took the time to give me tips on rackets and grips – attention many top players won't give to a lesser player on the tour. After my accident, she visited the hospital, sat by the bed, and talked me back from the despair that can only come from losing a career you can't imagine not having. Not that she was Florence Nightingale – she wasn't. Mariska's bedside manner consisted of about twenty sympathetic seconds followed by a barrage of orders: 'Get moving – oh, you can't move? Well, wiggle! Get off your butt! Stop feeling sorry for yourself! Stop whining! Grow up!' I was trapped in a bed with bars – I had to listen.

Then two years ago when Gus opened the Springs, Mariska became his charter client, thereby triggering an avalanche of business and landing us a feature story in *Time* magazine. Tonight, Mariska was being honored with a Lifetime Achievement Award, and there's no one who deserved it more. 'I've been in the twilight of my career for longer than most people have careers,' she often joked, and with no sign of retirement on the horizon, it's the truth. All comers continue to find themselves staring uncomfortably across the net at a demolition machine. If I'd gone to a Gypsy fortune-teller ten years ago, I'd have laughed her out of business if she'd peered into her crystal ball and predicted that I would leave tennis long before Mariska, who was even then, in her mid-twenties, the grand old lady.

'Jordan!' That voice. Smooth as café au lait and equally capable of scalding you to death. It is a deep, professionally honed voice I'd heard say my name many times, with many emotions, starting with a fascination that led to the altar and ending when he said goodbye and walked out on me once and for all. Yes, lunging through the sea of sequins, trailed by a videocam crew and a big-haired ex-Miss America with a microphone, was its possessor, Tim Tulley, cable network sportscaster, commentator, and my ex-husband. He still looked the same – better, actually. Wavy blond hair, green eyes, cleft chin like the kind usually reserved for statues, body only slightly less perfect than his tan. I almost felt sorry for Miss America. It must be devastating to win the pageant and then a few scant years later end up working with a man who was better-looking than you.

I certainly could see what I saw in Tim, but in retrospect I had been insane to marry him. Being competitive myself, I had liked his ambition, his aggressiveness. But there was a downside I hadn't counted on. A man like Tim is perpetually on the Stairmaster of Life – always stepping up to the next, better thing in any category, including job, home, apparel, and women. When I was a rising player, we shared a reasonable number of interests. We were both on the way up, we both liked sports obsessively, we both tended to travel a lot, although usually in different directions. There was also a certain element of opposites attracting, because in many ways we had absolutely nothing in common. For instance, for all his chiseled muscles and sports mania, Tim was totally uncoordinated. In the gym, his trainer had to hand him his weights or he would have dropped them on his foot. Still, things worked out fine for a while. But when I had some really big decisions to make, like would I stay on the tour and go for it or give it up and have another kind of career and possibly think about a family, I had to discuss it with Tim by fax. He'd gotten a promotion, he was unreachable on the road, and he just wasn't there for me. And in fairness, I suppose he could say the same about me. We probably should have had a date, not a marriage. Tim told me he wanted a divorce when I was in the hospital. Bad timing, he said, but he'd wanted to tell me about Ashley for some time. Ashley was his co-reporter at the station at the time. Apparently she was a co-many things at the time. Well, at least he didn't fax me the news.

I wondered whatever had happened to Ashley. Now it appeared that Tim had moved on to beauty queens, climbing to the top of the hairspray hierarchy. God, I hoped he wasn't involved with this one. I couldn't imagine having been married to a man who went on to date a woman who wore a crown and a sash.

They were coming closer. I found myself raising my eyebrows and waving my fingertips, as if to a cocktail-party acquaintance. Like such acquaintances, we are always cordial. But Tim was in a hurry. The crowd was no match for his flying wedge of equipment, and mouthing 'Catch you later,' his hand cupping Miss America's elbow as if she were a vessel that required steering, Tim passed me in the tidal wave of media racing to catch up with Shaquille O'Neal.

A sudden surge propelled me into the theater lobby, where I found myself standing next to XuXu Martin Lopez, who is ranked number four in women's tennis, and her mother. Maria Lopez straightened the shoulders of her daughter's dress as if she were preparing her gown for her wedding procession. The Lopezes, mother and daughter, always travel together.

'Hi, Jordan,' XuXu beamed at me. Her English is heavily accented but fluent. 'You are looking very good. Strong! Soon maybe you play again?'

We both laughed, knowing that wasn't going to happen, but I appreciated the encouragement. In a match she could be a pit bull. She had a typical clay-courter style. Small and pugilistic, she was a retriever and a counterpuncher rather than a creator, covering the court on bandy legs so tenacious you had to pry the points from her. XuXu would have made a wonderful heat-seeking missile. If she had an opportunity, she'd try to smash the ball right in your face, or go for your body instead of the open court. This would cost her points when you ducked and the ball went long, but she didn't seem to care. Next time you played XuXu you'd look across the net and she'd be gunning for you again. Privately, however, XuXu was always warm and friendly. I thought that had a lot to do with her stable home life. Tennis was a family tradition – her father had been one of the top players on the men's tour – but Mrs. Lopez, or Mama, as everyone calls her, was just that: a mother-in-residence. Somehow, without ever speaking a word of English, Mama Lopez always made her point unmistakably clear, which was that she was there to aid and protect her daughter, and she did that job very well. As a teenager on the tour, I'd envied girls like XuXu, whose parents traveled with them. Sometimes my mother made it to the big matches, but after my father died when I was fifteen, more often than not she stayed home in Pasadena with my sister, and except for my coach I was pretty much on my own.

Suddenly Mama Lopez waved excitedly and started chattering in Spanish, and I looked in the direction of her beckoning fingertips to see Marion Stryker, the venerable general manager of the Women's Tennis Association, a fixture on the circuit. Elegant and serene, Marion glided through the crowd like a queen, trailed by the assistant manager, Kanga Cheyne. Marion nodded and smiled to the Lopezes, relegating me to a slight lift of an eyebrow, as though she couldn't quite place me, although of course she could. No one involved with tennis will ever forget the huge buildup she orchestrated for me as the next phenom, the girl who was supposed to follow in the footsteps of Kelly Kendall, America's sweetheart, and become the challenger to Mariska's throne. I was a major disappointment to Marion. I turned out to be neither cute nor all-American, and after a while I started losing my matches, and then I fell off a mountain and never played again. These events had their tragic aspects, but from Marion's point of view, I suppose, it was a lot of time and money invested in building a crowd draw and nothing to show for it. In retrospect, however, she should thank me. My abrupt departure from the scene, my literal fall from grace, left the door wide open for somebody not only more talented but more eminently promotable, somebody the media could latch on to and the crowds would clamor for – specifically, Audrey Armat, the dazzling sixteen-year-old who was currently the number four woman player in the world, and rising fast.

'There you are!' Mariska, having escaped the photographers, now made her way against the tide of the crush to give me a quick hug. 'So how's it going out there in the desert?' Her Russian accent was faint, diluted by many years of Americanization.

'Our new golf course is great. Come out and we'll play,' I said, grinning. 'We'll play from the blue tees.'

'The pro tees? When did you take up golf?'

'Just. But I'll still beat you.' The competitive urge never dies. I would play tiddleywinks for blood. Of course, so would she.

'Please. You have more pins in that leg than there are in that fancy new course of yours.'

'I'll limp through it.' Actually, I was running a couple of miles a week and I felt amazingly good, better than I had ever imagined I could.

'You're on,' said Mariska.

'Where's Audrey?' A young woman in a black minidress with a silver plastic Sports Network badge dangling from a chain around her neck appeared beside us. She wore a high-tech remote headset and a small black nylon fanny pack, carried a clipboard, and was accompanied by a distinguished-looking white-haired gentleman I recognized as Milton Bevins, a tour regular. Milt – Uncle Miltie, as the girls called him – had spent years rotating his attentions from player to player, playing fairy godfather, showering various ones in turn with expensive gifts. These days he was attached to Audrey's entourage. Mariska had told me that he once tried to give her a car, and one of the stars of the men's tour had reportedly framed an uncashed $100,000 gift check from Milt, which he swore the bank verified as good. It was rumored that Uncle Miltie had a multimillion-dollar trust fund and a $6-million-a-year annuity with which to facilitate his largesse.

'The producer is looking for Audrey. She missed the rehearsal,' said the fanny pack woman, clearly disgruntled.

'I haven't seen her tonight.' Mariska shrugged. She didn't look around the room or devote a fragment of energy to wondering where anybody else might or might not be. Having burned the shoelaces off virtually every up-and-coming young woman player in the past decade, including myself, she seemed to view the never-ending roster of challengers as simply a passing parade. History had yet to prove her wrong, although to my mind her seeming disinterest signaled that, underneath the veneer, she was very aware of her vulnerability. How can you not be, I wondered, when there's no place to go but down?

The fanny pack woman and Uncle Miltie took off in another direction in search of Audrey. When she made her appearance, Audrey was bound to garner a lot of attention. She always did. The promotions for tonight's event had all prominently featured the fact that she would accept an award as 'Most Promising Young Female Tennis Player.' That was an understatement. This was a girl who by her fifteenth birthday had won ten tournament titles in two years, and this year, at sixteen, nailed the Australian Open for her first Grand Slam victory, setting her up against Mariska for what the media publicized as the Duel of the Grand Slams. The fact that she was strikingly pretty, with strawberry-blond hair and an aloof yet dynamic presence, drew the media like a magnet. Audrey's skills went beyond the basics of playing a brilliant game. She didn't just play matches, she gave performances, feeding the hungry crowd with carefully measured doses of virtuosity combined with a sweetness that was irresistible to fans and the media alike. I'd heard she had a sportswear line, a racket endorsement, and a soft-drink endorsement contract in the works. And she wasn't even out of high school.

I didn't know Audrey beyond a nodding acquaintance, but admittedly all the fuss made me a bit curious. 'Do you think Audrey's going to live up to everybody's expectations?' I asked Mariska. I'd seen Audrey play, but of course I'd never played her. Mariska had, many times, and once or twice she'd even lost to her, so she certainly had a basis for comparison.

Mariska frowned slightly. 'I don't know. She's good. She can beat me.' She paused. 'But I feel sorry for her.'

'Sorry?' I wanted to understand what Mariska meant, because she had a well-known ability to psych out her opponents, on and off court. It was one of the secrets to her game, how she consistently 'routined' – managed to routinely rout – younger, potentially stronger and faster players. Did she mean she felt sorry for what she, better than anyone, knew must lie ahead in a tennis career? A career that is rewarding and terrifying at the same time – the punishing effort, the unending hours of practice, the hotel-room existence, the sacrifice of a social life, the litany of injuries, the expense, the unavoidable zigzags of ecstasy and heartbreak cloaked in the tantalizing promise of glamour that only occasionally, and for the very few, materializes for any duration. Was she responding to expectations that the media were putting on Audrey before the young girl had a real chance to grow up? Or was this just professional competitiveness seeping through? I didn't find out then, because the crowd moved into the theater and Gus was there.

'I changed into my tux in the airport men's room,' he said, running a hand through his shaggy, sandy hair. He leafed through a glossy program of the night's events. 'But at least I'm here. God knows if I'll ever see my bag again. I tipped the taxi driver to take it to the hotel, but I'm not sure he spoke English. Mariska, if I'd known you looked so much better than me in a tux, I wouldn't have bothered.'

'Maybe you should have cleared your outfit with me beforehand, Dr. Gus,' she admonished. 'But I like the cowboy boots.'

Although Gus looked pretty good to me, with his

six-foot-three thin frame, angular face, and hazel eyes that at the moment seemed gray behind his glasses, he was right. She did look better in a tux. It was part of Mariska's androgynous appeal, an element of her charisma. Gus, like me, was in his natural element outdoors, in denim and khakis, with his sleeves short or rolled up, without a tie. He claimed he had medical evidence that neckties cut off circulation to the brain and shaved several points off your IQ. Even when he was appearing at industry gatherings or giving speeches, his tie was usually in his pocket, and more than once at a fancy restaurant I'd seen the maître d' slip Gus the house tie so that he could be seated. Gus's love of the outdoors was one reason he chose to apply his psychology specialty to sports. When he entered the field, it had not been a field as such – just a handful of experimenters. He had grown up with the profession, molded elements, made discoveries, accepted challenges, built a practice.

His work in helping Mariska intensify her game and escalate her performance level by monitoring her mental and emotional attitude had brought him to national prominence. After they worked together, Mariska rallied for an incredible midcareer resurgence to win yet another string of Grand Slam titles. Of course, as he always stressed, and was absolutely adamant about, Mariska had done it herself, but there's no doubt Gus was a factor.

'How'd it go in Detroit?' I asked.

'Car people,' he said. 'They're into golf. I made the Arnold Palmer analogy.' A firm nod indicated that it had been a satisfactory speech.

The link between Arnold Palmer and cars was not immediately obvious, even to me, but you can be certain that Gus made it and the audience loved it. He has an amazing talent for linking any activity, state of mind, or business situation to a sports scenario, a knack that resulted in his best-selling book, *Play to Win*, and a constant demand for him to appear on the corporate speaking podium.

Moving into the huge auditorium toward our seats was slow going. Every couple of feet someone reached out to shake Mariska's hand or congratulate her on her award, and several Springs clients, including Jake Stoppard, the Forty-Niners' quarterback, blocked the aisle to greet Gus and me.

'Do you have your acceptance speech written?' I asked Mariska as we finally took our seats.

'Oh God,' she said, shuddering. 'They just told me today that I had to say something, can you believe it? I wrote down a few notes on some cards, but . . .' She shook her head nervously. Mariska could face any opponent across the net, but facing a microphone was something else.

'Maybe you should make the tennis-automotive link,' I said, jabbing Gus with my elbow. 'Works every time.'

'Will everyone please take their seats,' a voice announced over the loudspeaker. A band on a riser to the right of the stage began a crashing overture. I showed an usher our tickets: Section 100, Center Aisle A. He pointed us to the area just in front of the stage, where the stars who were going to receive awards were taking their seats. Ours were in the third row.

'They have to start on time,' said the woman in the seat next to me to nobody in particular. 'It's live TV.'

An entertainer I didn't recognize came out on the stage and introduced himself as the warm-up act. Brandishing a cigar, he told the audience the ground rules: 'No leaving, no flash photography, no waving to the camera if it points at you, 'cause you'll look like a putz.' The stage was set up in a quasi-Greek-classic look, with three giant video monitors, each encased in a massive column. A long table held the awards, several dozen shimmering Lucite obelisks guarded by a man in a black jumpsuit and white gloves.

There was an especially vibrant rendition of 'New York, New York' and an announcer boomed, 'Welcome to the fifth annual Sports Network Awards, with special guest, Bill Murray.' Bill bounded on stage in a Chicago Cubs cap, a baseball shirt under his tuxedo.

Then I felt it. A familiar vibration, this time inside my jacket, on my thigh. The beeper. Simultaneously, Gus motioned to his tuxedo pocket. His beeper. The two of us rose in unison.

Instantly, a producer in black tie and headphones crouched in front of us and yanked us down. 'You can't leave now,' he hissed. 'You're in the front section. It won't look good on camera.'

'Sorry,' I said. 'It's an emergency.'

He probably wished he could get Ollie Cedars, who was on Gus's left, to throw himself in front of us and block our path, but we edged past him and headed toward the aisle. As we left, I heard the producer whisper frantically, 'Get some fillers in here!' A man and woman in evening dress materialized from thin air and stepped in front of us, taking our seats almost before we'd left them.

'I wonder what they're serving at the party afterward,' I whispered.

'Probably just your basic McSmoked salmon, pâté de foie gras, Dom Pérignon,' said Gus wistfully.

'Ugh,' I pronounced. 'Foie gras. Do you know where that comes from? They take these geese and force-feed them with tubes . . .'

'Spare me the lecture. Then again, it could be a wrong number. Or something that can wait till tomorrow. There's always that possibility.'

'Maybe two hundred grams of solid goose fat is good for you. There's always that possibility, too.' I leaned against the lobby wall as we both pulled out our cellular phones. 'If this isn't life-or-death, I'm going to kill Tony.'

I got through first. Tony, my administrative assistant, was breathless. 'Jordan, I hope you're packed,' he said. 'You and Gus have to get back to the Springs right away, tonight.' There was a dramatic pause.

'Why? What's the crisis?' Tony's flair for the theatrical could not be underestimated.

'A VIP client is arriving tonight on an emergency basis. Strictly hush-hush.' I could hear the computer keys clicking furiously in the background as Tony typed. He is one of those fast-motion people who are always doing two things at once, which makes him a particularly valuable assistant. 'It's an unusual circumstance, I admit,' Tony continued, lowering his voice conspiratorially as if he were worried that the line might be tapped, 'and I don't have all the details, but the client is insisting on immediate attention from Dr. Laidlaw, and Mr. Stokes thinks it would be best if you were available, too.'

Bill Stokes, a former Olympic gold medal-winning marathoner who once had his face on a cereal box, is the co-founder of the Springs and Gus's partner. Ten years ago they teamed up to develop and patent Pro-Aide, an electrolyte and nutrient energy replacement drink for athletes which they sold to a soft-drink company for millions of dollars. They then used the money as seed capital to found the Springs.

'Who is the client?'

'Frankly, I don't know. They wouldn't tell me – it's that secret. Dr. Laidlaw will probably have the details.'

'But, Tony, how are we going to get out tonight? We don't have plane reservations and Gus doesn't even know where his suitcase is.'

'The client has sent a private jet to the Marine Terminal at La Guardia. It's waiting on the tarmac with orders to take off as soon as you arrive. Your car is in front of the theater right now to take you straight to the airport. Obviously, it's a matter of utmost urgency. Let me worry about the luggage. I'll call your hotel. The Intercontinental, wasn't it? The concierge will arrange to have your bags packed and then FedEx your stuff back here. There wasn't any medicine in there that you needed or anything, was there?'

'No. But I'm not exactly in my travel clothes.'

'No time to change. Happy trails.'

'Till we meet again.' I pushed the END and CLEAR buttons, turned the phone off, and returned it to my purse.

Gus was still talking, and I could make out snatches of conversation. 'Right. Right. Are you sure? Actually, I'd prefer a one-on-one situation, Bill. I see. I suppose so, Bill. Yes.' He paused to search his pockets, pull out a wadded paper cocktail napkin from some event long past, and scribble a note on it. 'Fine. We're leaving now.'

We retraced our steps out of the lobby and down the escalators.

'I can't stand the suspense,' I said. 'Who's the mystery client?'

'Audrey Armat.'

'Audrey!' That explained why they wanted me. I was the point person for women's tennis. 'But she's supposed to be getting an award on live television in fifteen minutes.'

'Global Sport will handle the situation. They've got plenty of coverage here tonight. They'll arrange for somebody to accept for Audrey.' Global Sport, the biggest and most powerful sports talent agency in the world, was capable of handling any situation, from a press conference to Desert Storm.

'And what's the emergency? Audrey has a pimple?'

A Town Car was waiting at the curb on Sixth Avenue. A light summer rain had started, and the driver got out with an umbrella and held it over us as we climbed into the backseat.

'Her game is slipping.'

'Well, that's not a good thing. I'm sure it's a serious problem, and we can probably help. But we're supposed to rush out in the dead of night, fly across the country, and put her in serve-and-volley ICU?'

'Something like that.' The car turned and headed for the Midtown Tunnel. In the darkness I could see Gus's jaw clenching and unclenching, something he did when he was trying to figure things out. 'It's bizarre. I don't get it, either, but we won't know much till we get there. Bill shorthanded the explanation. I don't think even he has the story.' Gus squinted at the scribbles on the cocktail napkin, as if they contained the answer. 'What do you know about Audrey?'

'Well, I remember seeing pictures of her in *People* magazine when she was a little kid, four or five years old, whacking at tennis balls with a sawed-off racket. By the time she was nine, they had 'star' written all over her. By the time she was ten, she had a clothing deal.'

'What about her game?' Gus asked.

'Her game is incredible. A hundred-plus-mile-an-hour serve. Best second serve in women's tennis, and a running forehand down the line that most pros only dream about. A real power game. She was just coming onto the tour when I was leaving – but I've watched her play. Totally consistent, and what she can't put away, she runs down. Lots of endorsements, even before she turned pro. Off the court, she sort of keeps apart from the other players, but that's to be expected. She's young. Travels with her family. Her father's her coach, and she has a twin brother who's her hitting partner. I've never met him. Anyhow, she pulled a hamstring muscle a few months ago. Then, in February, she played a terrible final at the Lipton, and had just lost in the first round at Amelia Island. I assumed the leg was bothering her. Maybe it's worse, and they're worried about Wimbledon. But why can't this hold till morning? Or at least until we eat dinner and change clothes?'

'Apparently her family is very concerned that she get immediate attention.'

In other words, the mother was hysterical. Corinne Armat's tantrums were legendary. I had personally witnessed one. Three years ago, when I was on the staff of the Women's Tennis Association, I was what they call a primary health-care provider for the women's circuit, one of the people who travel from tournament to tournament giving on-premises physical therapy. I was working Wimbledon when Audrey made the semis. It was one of those rain-soaked Wimbledons, and I'd taken a break to dash to the players' lounge for some of the legendary strawberries and cream and a cup of hot tea. I was dripping wet, standing with my tray in the cafeteria checkout line. Mrs. Armat was in front of me – God, I'll never forget her outfit. Two prints that didn't match and a huge gold lamé Chanel purse with handles, like a shopping bag – anyway, she was complaining that the carrots and peas were not organic, that she refused to put pesticides in her daughter's system, and I remember standing there as the dampness seeped down to my skin while she kept up this tirade.

Somehow, heading back to the airport at nine o'clock at night, dinnerless, for a six-hour flight in a cocktail dress and heels that suddenly had taken on the ability to strangle feet where they stood, I had a premonition that I might soon be able to empathize all too well with those unfortunate vegetables.

'Gus,' I said, kicking off my shoes, 'this mother is one step from the edge. A major prima donna.'

Gus laughed softly in the darkness. 'Nothing we can't handle, I'm sure. Haven't we seen our share of prima donnas in this business?'

'The golfer who wanted me to baby-sit her pet monkey . . .'

'Now, there's a real nut case.' Gus burst out laughing, and so did I, because my own dog has gotten more than her fair share of star treatment – but then, she is a dog, and not your average dog. And now that I'm on the other side of the fence, a lot of things that I used to take for granted seem pretty ridiculous to me. 'How about the baseball player who complained about the mixed nuts on the Learjet that we sent for him?'

'The coach who wanted us to install a special bathtub for his three-day stay at the clinic?'

'And his girlfriend, who was on the lemon diet?'

'Maybe we could make a board game of this.'

'How about, roll the dice: if you like Monopoly, you'll love Idiosyncrasy?'

We laughed again, but we were both on the alert. Knowing Corinne Armat, I was actually very uneasy. I had the feeling that we were about to take off straight into a whirlwind that could turn into a full-fledged hurricane.

GEOFF NICHOLSON

Short story taken from Telling Stories 4

Some Metal Buildings

Geoff Nicholson's latest novel in paperback, *Still Life with Volkswagens*, is available now at your local Dillons store priced £5.99.

Bring this voucher with you to obtain £1.00 off the publisher's prices at all Dillons stores.

ſ

Some Metal Buildings

ONE

Ralph and Irena were looking for affordable luxury and they liked to think they'd found it. They lived in a flexible-plan single-storey house built around a small, decorative courtyard. And even though they hadn't been blessed with children, they were happy.

Ralph, moving with surprising grace for a large man, gathered up the post as it spilled through the letter box and took it into the kitchen where his wife Irena was weaving her breakfast culinary magic.

'Letter for you,' he said casually. 'Looks like junk.'

But he was wrong. It was a catalogue for maintenance-free, steel garden sheds with zinc coating and baked-on coloured finish.

Irena tore open the envelope and riffled through the pages of the catalogue. She observed the solid construction and careful engineering of the sheds. She read that they were easy to erect and came flat-packed for convenience.

She admired the way they were designed to harmonise with almost any environment.

Ralph saw what his wife was reading, and asked, 'Do we need a steel shed in our lives?'

'Everyone needs a steel shed in their lives,' said Irena, noticing that the French toast was about to burn.

TWO

Next day Irena should have been at work but instead she went to the Museum of Mankind to see an exhibition called 'Paradise: Change and Continuity in the New Guinea Highlands'.

It was a show about the life of the Wahgi, a race that had never encountered outsiders until about sixty years ago. It showed their customs, their ceremonies, their crafts; but most of this was of only passing interest to Irena. What really grabbed her attention was the exhibition's replica of a Wahgi 'trade-store'.

This was a chunky, sturdy structure, about the size of a single garage. It resembled an old-fashioned newspaper kiosk, with a sloping roof and a door and an open counter in the front. On the wall was a sign that said, 'No ken askim long dinan', which translates as 'Don't ask for credit'. Irena wouldn't dream of it.

Inside the trade-store, displayed on shelves, were scarfs, shirts, toys, balls of wool, and tins of meat loaf, dripping and 'banana-flavoured roll'.

Irena looked and learned. There's at least one of these trade-stores per Wahgi community and, as well as selling goods, they're used as places to store 'men's love magic', which injures the health of women and children if kept at home.

Irena found all this interesting enough but it still wasn't

what really fascinated her. What really fired her imagination was the fact this store was made out of unpainted corrugated iron. How come? Because, an explanatory label said, if someone tries to break into the store it makes a helluva lot of noise.

Irena smiled blissfully to herself and wondered to what extent the use of corrugated iron in architecture is a touchstone of human civilisation.

THREE

A day or two later they were enjoying an extremely quaffable bottle of Don Zolio luxury sherry and Irena said to Ralph, 'Corrugated iron was invented in the late 1820s and was to revolutionise building techniques. From the late 1830s prefabricated buildings made of corrugated iron were being shipped from this country to all parts of the globe; to California and Australia, to Africa and India; all kinds of buildings; bungalows, shooting lodges, hospitals, chapels, churches.'

'I see,' said Ralph savouring the deep velvety fino. 'And I suppose you want to spend the rest of your life going round the world looking at them.'

'At last,' thought Irena, 'a man, who understands.'

But she thought wrong.

FOUR

Ralph didn't mind too much when, later that same year, they went away for a long weekend to the Peak District, and visited the village of Youlgreave. It was the wrong season for well-dressing, nevertheless they found much to admire: the air, the limestone hills, the river, the old Co-op now converted into a Youth Hostel. But Irena was there for quite other reasons.

At the top of a lane that led down into the valley, she stopped to admire the scout hut, a two-storey building made of green corrugated iron. It had a black corrugated roof, smart red curtains at the windows, and a simple but effective portico, also made of corrugated iron.

'Gosh,' she said, not entirely to herself.

She stood in quiet admiration. It was a good half hour before poor Ralph could persuade her to come to the tea room with him.

FIVE

She discovered a metal church in Kilburn, next to the RSPCA, now used as a headquarters by some sort of youth project.

It had Gothic doorways and lancet windows, a tower, and the base to which a spire might be attached. It was painted in two shades of institutional blue, and across one metal wall someone, perhaps a well-wisher, had sprayed the slogan 'Toys not Guns'. In Kilburn this felt like progress.

SIX

Irena thought of Mary Kingsley. Wasn't it she who, in *Travels in West Africa*, wrote:

Corrugated iron is my abomination. I do not attack it from an aesthetic viewpoint (just as well, thinks Irena). There is, close to Christianborg Castle, at Acara, Gold Coast, a patch of bungalows and offices . . . that . . . in the hard, bright sunshine look like an encampment of snow white tents among the cocoa palms. But the heat inside . . .

Irena had never given much thought to the thermal properties of corrugated iron, but she now realised this was good advice and resolved never to live in a metal building in West Africa.

SEVEN

That night she and Ralph made love. He nuzzled his head against her ample breasts and said, 'What is it with you and metal buildings?'

She stroked his dense biceps and said girlishly, 'I think it's about morality or rather its absence. One hears so much about architecture as a force for social good, as something holy with an agenda and a philosophy. But a metal building has none of that. It has no architect, no pretension. It is morally blank.'

'Now hold your horses,' Ralph said as he drew her close to him. 'You yourself have described metal churches to me.'

'Yes, and they're morally blank too,' she said, her body crackling with coiled, sexual energy.

'A morally blank church,' he said with a gush. 'Now I've heard everything.'

But he hadn't.

EIGHT

Irena's work attendance record got worse and worse. Sometimes she took days from her holiday entitlement, but more often she simply called in sick. She spent a lot of time following her special interest.

She visited allotments to look at more sheds. She went in search of lock-up garages, lean-tos, Nissen huts, aircraft hangars, barns, warehouses, factories.

She visited a number of gas holders and she went to Paris in order to climb the Eiffel Tower, though she realised there were those who would argue that both gas holders and towers were structures rather than buildings.

She got particularly excited about a polyhedral metal construction adjacent to the Newport Pagnell Services on the M1 which was used to store road salt.

Ralph, who liked to think of himself as an understanding man, increasingly failed to understand.

NINE

She swung it so that she could get to go to a conference in California. Once there she skived off the lectures and seminars and went out in her rented car admiring car washes, body shops, the colourful metal shacks of dispossessed indigenous peoples. She picked up a cute hitchhiker and took him back to her room at the Motel 6.

When she got home she told Ralph it had been the trip of a lifetime.

TEN

And then one day, for no reason she could think of, she got in her Ford Mondeo, found herself driving up the A12, and before long was in Saxmundham. She looked for a place to stop, found the car park behind the Gateway supermarket, and as she brought her car to a halt, a wonderful sight loomed up in front of her.

She saw a large imposing metal building, two storeys

high, some sixty feet by forty, probably agricultural in origin, painted burnt ochre, and most importantly of all, with an estate agent's board attached to the side. The building was to let.

A few swift negotiations and the building was hers. She took possession. She moved in. Then she bought a small Yamaha electronic keyboard and installed it in a corner of her building. At various times of the day or night, though never at offensive volume, Irena could be heard playing standards on her new instrument, old favourites such as 'Autumn Leaves', 'These Foolish Things', 'In the Wee Small Hours of the Morning', and 'The Night We Called It A Day', to name only four.

ELEVEN

A distressed Ralph, wanting Irena more than ever in her absence, came to visit.

'Does our love count for nothing?' he asked.

'Consider this,' Irena replied. 'You are married to a woman who only has eyes for metal buildings. Ask yourself, "Is there iron in my soul?" If the answer is no, you can draw your own conclusions.'

'Poor Irena,' he thought. 'This will not bring her happiness and the love of a good man.'

But he was wrong again.

TWELVE

Then, early one June morning, she heard the snivel of an approaching diesel engine. She threw back one of the sliding metal doors and saw that a lightweight Land Rover had pulled up outside her building. A man got out, a real man. He was tough, wiry, suntanned, hirsute, part poet, part adventurer. His face was supremely strong and rugged, though not insensitive.

'Allow me to introduce myself,' he said. 'The name's Dan. Just plain Dan. I'm an engineer. I specialise in building multi-million gallon tanks and towers for rural water developments, mostly in South America. And I'd just like to say, that's some metal building you've got there.'

'Ah,' she said, 'my knight in shining armour.'

FRANK RONAN

Short story taken from Handsome
Men are Slightly Sunburnt *which will
be published in Sceptre hardback in
February 1996*

Kilbride

Frank Ronan's new novel, *Dixie Chicken*, is available now in paperback at your local Dillons store priced £5.99.

Bring this voucher with you to obtain £1.00 off the publisher's prices at all Dillons stores.

KILBRIDE ∫

While Michelle Kelly chopped vegetables in the kitchen, and Michelle Kelly's mother chain-smoked before the noon soap opera at the end of the kitchen table, Helen Flood stood outside, at the foot of the ladder which supported Michael Hanlon in espadrilles and loose shorts.

He said, 'It's bloody amazing. I never believed it. I've been in love before, but I thought that love like this only existed in books: when you wake up in the night and spend four hours just watching someone's face. I didn't think it could happen to me. Did you know that this could happen?'

Helen Flood said, 'I suppose I did. I suppose I believed in overwhelming love. But I've never believed that it could last. In the same way that you can believe in God, without necessarily thinking he's that intelligent.'

By looking up, as she spoke, among the shadows up the leg of his shorts she could distinguish his balls knocking against his thigh when he moved.

'I can see your balls from here,' she said.

'Oh shut up,' he said. But she could see that he had been amused by her observation. She didn't know how to interpret that. She would have liked to think that it meant his new love was not so overwhelmingly pure that it excluded his old enjoyment of ribaldry. But she feared, and it was more likely to be the truth, that he now regarded her more as an old friend than as an ex-lover, and saw no danger in foul talk between them.

She had driven here in anger and loneliness, with a confrontation in mind. She had arrived at this house in Kilbride determined to know if she was still loved, in any way, by Michael Hanlon, or whether she had ever been loved by him at all. When her car drew up she looked at the small, slovenly house and the haggard scratched by chickens of poverty and the row of blown modern roses, planted with no attempt to mitigate their vulgarity; when she saw all this she heard her grandmother's voice asking what else you could expect of a girl of that class; a girl out of a cottage by the side of the road?

Her grandmother had never approved of Michael Hanlon. 'None of his family were any good, and there's no reason why he should be.' If granny had a reason for disliking him it may have been because she seemed to know everyone's secrets, by instinct, by the tone of people's voices. She had always suspected that there was something going on between Helen and Michael. She had greeted every scrap of gossip about him, including the latest story that he had run away with Michelle Kelly, by saying with a triumphal snort, 'It wasn't off the grass he licked it.'

Helen got out of the car, leaving her thoughts of her grandmother behind her and, looking at the house again, wondered with intentional unkindness whether the place had a bathroom in it.

She slammed the car door, unnecessarily, and Michael's voice called to her from the other side of the haggard, 'Helen! I'm over here.'

She walked towards the voice, away from the house, relieved that she wouldn't have to knock at the door and explain herself to whatever might answer it.

'Where?' she said, as she pushed her way through the ash plants and the ragwort. 'I can't see you.'

He was up to his thighs in a stream, wearing only shorts, shaded from the August sun by the leaves of the ash trees which, in that light, were reflecting the undulations of the water like the roof of a cave. He looked thinner and flutter than she had ever seen him and, she thought, handsome. In all the years they had been lovers she had never considered him worth looking at. He had had other qualities. The irony of him seeming handsome to her now was more than she could bear to think about.

He had been lifting rocks to dam the river where it narrowed, and now he was scooping mud from the bottom with a bucket and dumping it beyond the dam.

'What do you think of the new swimming pool?' he said.

She didn't say anything, because the anger she had come with had gone away and she was in a state of deflation. But she was aware that she was smiling at him and pleased to see him.

'Roll your skirt up,' he said, 'and give us a hand.'

She declined. She hadn't come prepared for such innocent friendliness. She sat on the bank and talked to him.

By the time Michelle Kelly came along they were both laughing hard. He was recounting some new scandal from the town and Michelle Kelly, who had already heard the story, began to laugh with them as soon as she was within earshot: she did not laugh as they did; it was as though she were laughing at their amusement rather than the story itself.

Helen got to her feet and kissed the other woman on the cheek. If there was awkwardness in it, it probably had to do with the fact that Michelle Kelly came from a background where women did not normally kiss each other in greeting.

It was hard to know whether to call her Michelle, or Kelly. When she had first launched herself on a career as a Country & Western singer she had called herself Michelle, but after six months of failure someone had suggested to her that she use her surname and call herself Kelly. The name change had been followed by moderate success and, although no one of Helen's acquaintance had ever heard of her before the liaison with Michael, it was said that you could find her records in one or two shops in Waterford. On the covers of these she looked rather more like herself than she managed in real life: a sort of culchie sex kitten, as Helen would have put it. Her band was known as Kelly and the Ploughboys.

Helen decided in favour of calling her Michelle. She knew that she would have to meet the mother. She thought she might laugh out loud if she was in the same room as both of them and had to call one Kelly and the other Mrs Kelly.

Helen wondered if Michael had told Michelle about her; about her years of adulterous lovemaking with him: whether this overwhelming love of his had brought an overwhelming honesty with it. But, watching Michelle, she could see no sign of suspicion or jealousy. And, knowing Michael, his idea of honourable behaviour was to say anything that caused least trouble and embarrassment to himself. The closest he ever got to truth was silence.

He climbed out of the river and put his wet feet in the espadrilles on the bank.

'Why has your nipple turned grey?' she said.

He looked at her and down at his nipple with something like alarm. She knew that she shouldn't be watching his body so closely. It was like visiting a house you had once lived in, and looking for changes and faults; looking for reasons to hate the new owner. She wished he had more clothes on; that his body could be hidden from her memories of it.

'It's mud,' he said, wiping it away with the ball of his thumb. And it was only dried mud: the blemish fell as dust, leaving his left nipple identical to his right.

In the house there were photographs of family weddings; of young men looking uncomfortable and pleased with themselves in hired bow ties; of girls in peach sateen and of Michelle standing among them in scarlet, with the slightly superior air of a Country & Western star consorting with her origins. Helen asked for the bathroom, mostly to vex them because she was convinced that there wouldn't be one, and was shown to a room that was covered in mauve tiles; where the mauve handbasin was shaped like a scallop shell. She collapsed on the lavatory seat and her shoulders shook with silent laughter as she imagined Michael sitting in the mauve and gold bath every morning.

When she emerged Michael was no longer to be seen. She found herself trying to make conversation with Mrs Kelly, who had nicotine-stained hair and wore a tight denim skirt.

'It must be nice and quiet for you out here,' she said, and just at that moment an articulated lorry went past ten yards away on the road and the house shook.

Mrs Kelly seemed not to have noticed. 'I'd rather be in the town,' she said. 'But the Council won't give me a house.'

She dealt Helen an importunate glare as she spoke, knowing that Helen had a brother-in-law who was on the Urban District Council. Helen, not realising this, took the glare as natural animosity and asked where Michael had gone. Michelle said that he was fixing the window at the gable end, and Helen edged in the direction of the door, trying to look as though she was wandering across the room with no purpose. Not that anyone was taking any notice of her: Mrs Kelly had switched on the television set at the end of the table, and Michelle was peeling carrots with unwarranted concentration, taking half the flesh away with the skin. Watching Michelle handle and disfigure such phallic objects was more than Helen could bear and she left the house without excusing herself.

She thought she was going mad and when she got to the foot of Michael's ladder and looked up and saw his pink bollocks swinging in his shorts she had to think of something banal to say to contain herself.

She wanted to say that this was all very well, this simple idyll, and that he was looking very well on it too, but where did it leave her? She wanted to ask him whether they were still to consider themselves lovers or not.

But she knew the answer already, and she knew that to ask the question would make things awkward between them, so, instead, she said, 'What's wrong with the window?'

He was smearing putty into the cracks in the wood.

'Home improvements,' he said. 'I'm doing the place up for them. The mother-in-law thinks I'm the bees' knees.'

'Mother-in-law?' Helen said it in genuine puzzlement, then realised it was Mrs Kelly he meant, and laughed, derisively.

She noticed that he was not laughing with her. He was concentrating on the putty. She knew him well enough to be alarmed.

She said, 'You aren't serious?'

'About what?'

'You want to marry Michelle?'

He looked at her as though she had asked something preposterous: not as though the question was preposterous in itself, but as though it was something she need not have asked.

'Don't you know?' he said. 'Can't you see it?'

'Marriage?' she said. 'You?'

'I suppose,' he said, with an understanding tone, with a hint of condescension. 'I suppose a lot has happened since I saw you last. A lot has changed. We want to get married: children, the lot. It's like a whole new life since I left Loretta. When I first told Michelle that I loved her and that I was going to leave Loretta for her, she just looked at me with tears streaming down her face. Not crying. You can't imagine the intensity of it.'

'Good God,' Helen said.

'I know,' he said, interpreting her horror as amazement. 'It's wonderful. And we have you to thank for it. If it wasn't for you we might never have met.'

Helen could say nothing to this. She winced at his pluralization of the personal pronoun, a thing he had never done while he lived with Loretta. But she had no need to say anything. He was away on a monologue: a banal, feverous eulogy of his and Michelle's love for each other, while she held the ladder and gazed at his testicles.

Helen declined the offer to stay and have some of the stew that the carrots had been destined for. She drove away feeling impotent, and alarmed to be feeling that way, since a sensation of that sort was not one to which she was accustomed. What impinged on her most was his gratitude to her for putting him in the way of meeting Michelle Kelly. This situation had not been her intention and she resented being held responsible for an accident, even if the victims were grateful to her.

When, as he saw her to the car, he had thanked her for coming out to visit; he had said to her, 'Thank God you're not a snob. I've a feeling I might be losing a few friends over this one.'

She had smiled complacently, but now, alone in the car,

at the beginning of a torrent of *esprit de l'escalier*, she said, 'I wasn't, until I met that slut of yours, but I am now.'

A gap-toothed child, standing by the side of the road, saw her talking to herself in the car, and laughed at her, but she didn't see him.

'You bastard,' she said. 'You weak-minded little shit.'

She knew, all the same, that it had been clever of him to make her culpable for his happiness: that it avoided scenes; it allowed him to continue a cosy friendship with her; it prevented her from marring his bliss.

'You're the only person I know,' she said, 'who believes his own lies.'

She counted how many days it had been since he had first clapped his gobshit eyes on Michelle Kelly. Fifteen days: Saturday night to Sunday week.

'Marriage!' she said. 'Marriage?'

It was true that it had been her idea to go to the Starlite Lounge. She didn't know what had possessed her. That Saturday afternoon Fergal, her husband, was watching a soccer match on the television. He was hunched over, fixed on the set, clenching his fists and making little jerks at moments of excitement, muttering encouragement at the players. If she'd had a brick she would have hurled it through the screen.

When Michael phoned he sounded so distraught. He didn't say anything much, but she could hear the desperation in his voice. Loretta had gone to Dublin for the weekend and, although normally he would have been happy to be rid of her for a couple of days, things had been so bad between them lately that he couldn't escape her even when she was a hundred miles away, complaining about him to her friends in Blackrock.

Helen had often told him, with perfect disinterest, that she couldn't understand why he stayed with Loretta. A hen-pecked husband was understandable, in a way, but a hen-pecked boyfriend was a mystery. She often thought that he might have a masochistic streak in him. She had realised, too, that her best interest was served by his staying with Loretta. It was the misery of that relationship which had caused him to need Helen as a lover.

The hunted tone in his voice on the telephone bent her with pity, 'Why don't you come over?' she said. 'And have a bit of supper? No. I have a better idea. We should all go out. The house is driving me mad and we haven't been on the tear for a long while. The paper's here. There must something on.'

She reached for the local paper and rustled through it until she came to the entertainments page, and found the advertisement which said that Kelly and the Ploughboys would be appearing at the Starlite Lounge. She read it out loud to him as a joke, and it made him laugh, and then they discussed the other places, but those were all so dreary that they kept coming back to the Starlite Lounge, until it had made the subtle transition from running gag to possibility.

'I've never been there,' she said. 'We could go there for a drink and see what it's like. It might be a laugh. If it's awful we can crawl on somewhere else.'

By the time they had finished talking he was sounding more cheerful. Then she had work to do: persuading Fergal that he wanted to go out, and finding a babysitter.

The Starlite Lounge was a vast, flat-roofed, concrete building. Inside, there were acres of mock-Victorian furnishings and etched glass. In the summer night and the throng of young farmers the atmosphere was palpable. Helen, Fergal and Michael stood inside the door and made faces at each other, and would have left straightaway, but Helen said that she wanted to go to the ladies', and disappeared in the direction suggested by the signs. When she returned she said that she had found the original pub that the Starlite had been built onto, hidden at the back of the building, and that they could go and have a drink there.

They had been in the pub for less than half an hour when the band began to play next door, and Michael said he wanted to take a look at it. He hadn't been gone more than three or four minutes when he came back looking flushed and startled.

'I've just seen the girl I'm going to marry,' he said.

Of course, they thought it was a joke. They went to the door to catch a glimpse of Kelly on the bandstand. It was true that she was rather extraordinary-looking, but she had a fixed smile, and an odd way of flicking her head to every third bar of the music.

Even though she thought he was joking, Helen still felt a prick of jealousy at the possibility that Michael was admiring another woman. Being very careful of the degree of nonchalance she employed, in case Fergal should break the habit of a lifetime and be paying attention to the nuances of her voice, she said, 'You can't be serious. That girl has a mouth like a fertilizer sack.'

But Michael was serious. He went and spoke to the object of his new fixation during the band's break, and even managed to bring her back to where they were sitting, and introduced her. Neither Helen nor Fergal said much to her. Fergal assumed that their taciturnity was out of some sort of loyalty to Loretta. Helen was wondering whether or not it was a good idea to get drunk.

When the singing began again, Michael took the slip of paper on which she had written her name and looked at it, reverentially, for a long time. When, at the end of the evening, they were pulling out of the car park, their headlights shone on the back of the Ployghboys' transit van. Kelly was standing there. Michael shouted, as if in panic, 'I have to say goodbye to her,' and jumped out of the car while it was still moving.

When they began to snog, still standing in the glare of the headlights, it was too much for Helen. She reached across and flicked the dimmer switch on and off.

Fergal laughed. 'Michael's a fast worker,' he said.

'I'm tired,' she said. 'I want to get home.'

All the way back from Kilbride, Helen went over the events at the Starlite Lounge fifteen days before, wondering at what point she could have intervened: whether she could have prevented it from happening. Michael had made her culpable, so culpable she must be. She was still muttering to herself when she parked outside her house and looked at the quiet tastefulness of it; the outward signs that it was the house of someone who was secure, mature and intelligent. She scanned the front of the house for clues as, in a similar frame of mind, one might scan one's face in the mirror.

'He never offered to fix my fucking windows,' she said.

Inside, the house was quiet. The children had been playing in the sitting-room and had left their débris scattered across the floor. Irritably, automatically, she began to pick things up. She winced at her offspring's choice in playthings. There were the coy ponies with pink manes and the Steroid Avengers from the planet Grunt. There was Barbie and there was Ken. Barbie and Ken irritated her more than anything. Barbie looked complacent and Ken looked smug.

Holding Barbie in her left hand, Helen unhooked one of her earrings and straightened the hook so that it was like a long, blunt pin. She was about to stick the pin into Barbie when she changed her mind and picked up Ken instead. She turned him over and thrust the pin in him, straight up his backside.

She had not noticed Fergal, slippershod, come into the room.

'What's the matter?' he said. His expression bordered on the interested.

'Nothing,' she said. 'I'm tired. I need a holiday.'

HELEN STEVENSON

Extract taken from

Pierrot Lunaire

Pierrot Lunaire is available now at your local Dillons store priced £5.99.

Bring this voucher with you to obtain £1.00 off the publisher's prices at all Dillons stores.

At seventy-eight Ludmilla Pike was no longer exactly obese. Somehow it seemed, though, that each bit of body was rather too big for the next one. Her nose was too big for her face; her head too big for her neck; her shoulders were broad as a man's; but her bosom, ah her bosom, biggest of all, brooded huge and matriarchal, untapped and unmistakably female. With the onset of cold old age, the whole vast edifice had contracted a good deal, and cracks had appeared in the veneer. But despite a certain reduction in surface area, she was still one of those rather masculine women who are forever condemned to carry their womanhood all before them. In the case of Ludmilla Pike this condition was so acute that she might often be spotted coming round a corner long before her body's centre of gravity had even contemplated such a move. She would have made a poor private detective. Stealth did not come easily to a woman who, for at least the first fifty years of her life, had been accustomed to being so very large in build – and it seemed as though she had indeed been built, quite possibly on some sort of site, or in a shipyard. But despite the flagrance of her physical presence, she possessed a manipulative art which was so contorted and folded in upon itself that it must have occupied no more than the space of a walnut in what once had been the vast universe of her frame. Imaginatively cast she might have sold antiques.

Instead she taught people to play the piano, a vocation, certainly, but not one in which she had much opportunity to exercise her special gift. Except perhaps when, on occasions, she stood behind her little pupils, and pulled their arms and fingers about, dancing with them up and down on the keyboard. It was difficult to tell whether it was her fingers which were too big for her hands or vice versa. Her fingers had been crushed at one point in her childhood by the descent of a loose sash window. For six sickening hours she had sat there like a dummy at a keyboard, hands outstretched in mock five-finger exercises, pinned to the woodwork, fingernails blackening out of sight. For six terrible hours Ludmilla waited in silence until a window cleaner turned up and released her. His first encounter with the dark side of his work. Years later, he recognised Miss Pike in the street by the shape of her fingers. She offered him six free piano lessons. An hour each. It was her way of saying thank you.

It was difficult to imagine a time when Ludmilla's fingers had not been mangled and misshapen like distorted sausage off-cuts. Even as a young girl (never a little one), when exhorted to display her clever, piano-playing hands, as baby ballerinas show off their exquisite little feet, the horror of their deformity must have seemed to lend a sinister aspect to her talent. It was as though her gift had been acquired through some ghastly Faustian pact. With the passing years the deformity had matured, and, like the branches of an ancient, deviant oak, her fingers had taken on an almost old-world charm. They felt soft now, and towards the end of life the bones had found a comfortable position to lie in. The accident had never been an impediment to her performing even the trickiest Bach with complete dexterity.

She lived alone in an Edwardian house in the middle of England. There was no room for a companion in her life. Her outward face was stately, open to the public for seven hours a day, weekends excepted, but her private life was kept upstairs, above board, in a tight-fitting drawing room with bedroom attached.

It was her habit to go to the piano each morning once the kettle was on, before her first cup of tea. In her man-size dressing gown, with its slack-mouthed pockets and twizzled cord, she would solemnly crack her fingers, a bad but ineradicable habit, and shoot the rapids of some treacherous cadenza. In the case of concertos she would sing along a version of the orchestral part, but her voice could only hope to hit the notes by approaching each one with a hectic glissando, like some kind of vocal long jump. This brought a rather baleful quality to her singing, which began to sound more like some kind of protest or lament. At the moment, however, she was working on the cadenza to Rachmaninov III, and the orchestra was sitting quietly in the pit eating polo mints. After the final chord she rose from the piano, which she referred to in front of her pupils as the piano*forte*, pronounced with a distinct *marcato* over the word, pulled together the front of her dressing-gown and lowered the lid. The kettle would be well boiled.

She collected her little tray from the kitchen and paused on her way back upstairs to pick up the post. A weekly magazine by means of which, she said, she kept abreast of the world (men blushed and children giggled to hear her use of the idiom) was dangling through the letter box like a fish hook. She settled herself upstairs with her feet comfortably propped on a bar underneath her dining room table. 'If women spent more time looking after their feet,' she had read in a magazine at the dentist's, 'we beauticians would spend less time looking after their faces.' Ludmilla had pondered that one for some time, and having dismissed it as twaddle, now took pleasure in spending as much time as possible with her feet up, simply in order to disprove the theory empirically through the evidence of her catastrophic face.

She always read the classified advertisements first. The print was very fine, and she found it difficult not to cast shadows. The headings were relatively easy. SITUATIONS WANTED. No interest there. ACCOMMODATION WANTED. No *thank* you. She needed all the square footage she inhabited, and it was tight at that. SERVICES. The memorial service of a long lost friend? A new hat? No, services to the living, as always, to writers baffled by their home computers, to speakerless dining clubs, to city cottagers whose thatch was falling in tufts about their investment. Your needs supplied. She skimmed without interest. Life had supplied her with quite enough needs at the outset. It was too late to start fostering new ones, even with twenty-eight days only for delivery.

She poured her tea, three fluid ounces, a drop in the ocean. Ludmilla carried well over the standard seven pints within. The tiny Japanese cup with its detail of chintzy flowers was brimming over. An escapee leaf of jasmine clung to the spout of the pot.

Ludmilla pinched the end of her nose with a pigmy handkerchief. Nothing there. But at her age you had to be vigilant in the face of unsuspected seepage. In such respects caution had become a habit with her. She turned the page, wetting finger and thumb with a tongue hot from the tea. And there it was, tucked into a left hand column, cornered by an article about Gibraltar. WANTED.

Wanted. Each week she fondly fancied to read of million dollar rewards for the recapture of violent criminals, perhaps with a shoddily reproduced illustration, disturbingly reminiscent of the man next door. But people's wants were predictably meagre. Anyone wanting anything important would bill it under SITUATIONS or ACCOMMODATION, or PARTNERS. What more *could* you want. Ludmilla had always wanted fame, but third-rate notoriety had put paid to that. At her London solo debut in 1940, an occasion when a freshly broken heart should have lifted her performance nicely into something more than merely competent, she had been just distraught enough to make sure no one ever engaged her to work again. Since then, she sometimes said, it had been strictly children and animals.

But what was wanted here was information. Information was wanting. WRITER SEEKS INFORMATION CONCERNING CHÂTEAU MONVANITÉ, SOUTH WEST FRANCE, 1930s, PIERROT LUNAIRE. CONTACT TALBOT HARDY, CHÂTEAU MONVANITÉ. She was struck by the phrasing and immediately doubted 'writer'. 'Seeks', 'concerning'? What about 'wants', 'about'? The sparsity of the code words. There was no doubting it. Little pieces of festering bait. *Monvanité. Pierrot Lunaire.* The cartilage in Ludmilla's formidable nose clicked in her head. A treacherous eighteenth-century mirror, clustered about with gold-spray laurel leaves, caught her in a profile at once beaky and bulbous, the dressing-gown grizzling about her neck where it concertina-ed into chest. She caught it full face with a grimace, stopped short of shouting boo and turned regretfully away. Then with her thousand year old hands, brown stains flecked like tea leaves on the upper side, riddled palms a cartographer's life work on the lower, she reached towards her destiny and the spotless mobile phone.

Talbot Hardy was separated from his amiable but middle-aging wife, Posy, who, rather beyond the call of amiability, had arranged for him to spend a year away from it all in a magnificent French property she had recently inherited from her Aunt Isa.

Isa Fontaine, before English respectability and, later, a title had hit her, had seen herself as a rather clever amateur impresario. A slight woman of many accomplishments, taught to dance by Isadora Duncan, with Rodin limbs and an accent of unfamiliarity in all her many languages, she had held court for those three pre-war summers in a house in South West France bequeathed to her by a distant relative, short of ideas on his death bed. Monvanité's proximity to the Spanish border and the langorous look in Isa's opium eyes had spiced the allure of the place for a generation of dancers, writers and artists. In the summers of pre-war Europe, though, the heat was intense, weighing down the dancers' feet, bleaching the artists' colours, dragging back each allegro to andante. Few works of great merit could still be traced back to that particular cradle. Full marks then, to Talbot Hardy, who was sitting on the original manuscript of *Pierrot Lunaire*, a novel by Thomas Hanley Flynn.

Pierrot Lunaire had not found favour with Isa Gresham. Shortly after her marriage, she became editor-in-chief of Gresham's publishing house. When the manuscript arrived on her desk in June 1939 with an accompanying note describing the circumstances of its discovery amongst the effects of Thomas Hanley Flynn, one of her own former guests, killed in action at Salamanca in 1938, she simply cursed once more the proximity of Château Monvanité to the Spanish border and deleted a name from her address book.

On Isa's death the parcel passed to Posy, along with the deeds of Monvanité, to which Isa had never returned after her marriage. The book was typed on fine onion-skin paper, the pages so delicate that as you turned each one it refused to sink down quietly and seemed to hover slightly under your fingers.

Posy was used to reading manuscripts. It was part of her job. She called the time she spent, as consultant editor for Gresham Publishers, her Marigold hours, after the rubber gloves which stop you getting your hands dirty. She worked as little or as often as she chose, and attended some of the more interesting parties.

Pierrot Lunaire was different. Her Aunt Isa had written her a letter, describing how it had been recovered from the effects of T.H. Flynn, who had died fighting in Spain. He had spent the summer months before his death at Monvanité, where the three-year-long *fête galante* had drawn to a mournful close.

Uncle John and I were married early that summer, Isa wrote, and had honeymooned sensibly in Paris. We didn't bother with chantilly-topped extravaganzas in remote corners of the empire in those days. They tended to come after the honeymoon. Most of the artists had left by then. The party spirit had died. Or perhaps it just went to live somewhere more dangerous. The men seemed to favour Berlin. The musicians all went back to London, but they are always the most sober. Flynn rather missed out, I think. It must have been late spring when I was introduced to him. He'd had a couple of poems published in *Horizon* which showed promise. (It was quite possible to be thought promising in your mid-thirties in those days.) He'd met Ludmilla Pike at a concert in Dublin. She and I were living in London in the winter, but otherwise spent as much time as we could in Monvanité planning and running the house parties. She introduced him to me in London and we invited him out. As far as I remember he looked a bit like Orwell, but perhaps I only think that because of him dying like that. As I say, that was the last summer and by late June I'd had enough, so I married Uncle John who liked Kipling and drop scones and had a lot of money. Of course we had quite a lot too, but it was always so difficult to find. John's was always in the right place just when you wanted it, and you always knew how much of it there was, at least someone who was paid to, did. I don't think I was actually there when Flynn arrived.

The book, as you will see, is a journal intime, which always sounds like two people kissing behind a newspaper. It's written retrospectively – a recollection from not very tranquil Spain. The entries are daily and, eccentrically, in the third person, though from his own clear point of view. They describe how the place gradually emptied as summer reached its height and people began to think of war. By August, according to his account, Flynn was the only one left. Plus the girl, Chloe, who he's in love with, though we don't learn much about her.

Posy was tickled by the poignancy of this relic. She was collecting a bottom drawer for when she divorced. The manuscript almost went in, next to the single person's passport form and a voucher for a weekend at a health farm. But in the end, distracted by the prospect of a safari in Zimbabwe with an old schoolfriend, and with a hint of mischief in her mind, she passed it to her husband. Talbot was a disenchanted television journalist, whose experience had been largely in the area of fly on the wall documentaries. A year's sabbatical was planned, in which he would write and direct the feature film which would allow his long submerged creative flair to prove and rise. Posy kneaded gently, and off Talbot shot with the book to Château Monvanité. Where better to find inspiration for his script than Château Monvanité itself, the scene both of the drama and the writing of the story. For a wronged husband, Talbot was easily righted. What a year it would be. What a figure he would cut in that feature which would no doubt follow in a Sunday magazine, where separated couples display the generous seams in the weightless garment of their marriage; estrangement makes the heart grow larger, warmer, in every way; celebrities both, he a little wayward, artistic, newly fulfilled, bachelor boy again; she a little preoccupied with her career, perhaps even slightly down at heel these days, but loyally supportive down to the latest introduction to an attractive new friend – just your type I think, darling, and oh – she's vegetarian.

Two months on, work wasn't going well. Sure, the material was perfect. Perfection, Talbot wrote to the backers, whom Posy, a powerful lady, or at least well enough connected to carry a hefty current, had lined up on the touchline of Talbot's territory. In Brussels, in Venice, in London and Barcelona, they waited with impatience for Talbot's script. It would be one of those wistful, thoughtful, utterly ravishing pastoral films which would play and play, from St Martin's Lane to the Grand Spa Deluxe in Scarborough. A classic, a drama in watercolour, poignant, elegant, eternally true, a film to remind you of student days in a private cinema, where you queued each time it came to town, and for once, afterwards, somehow didn't feel like chips and a hamburger. Someone would mention Visconti, but no, they would say, it's this chap Hardy, English believe it or not. Incredible. A love story like that, Englishman, Englishwoman – English *director*. The hero's own story. Before I die (head blown off near Salamanca, 1938), know this . . .

Talbot was not above cultivating a bit of mystique before the event. He was incommunicado, or rather, he was communicating with things a little higher than contractual details. They would have to wait. As time went on he staved them off with postcards of the area, written in apparent haste with an elegant ink pen. The time devoted to the composition of these cunningly effete dispatches was not wasted. A meeting was planned for early July, when all would be revealed. Talbot was holding back on copies of the novel. A masterpiece it was. Airplane reading it wasn't. By the time of the meeting, the script would be well nigh complete. That would be what they wanted to see.

Unlike his wife's wealthy business contacts, whom she had largely chosen in order of pocket, Talbot was a well-educated, widely read man. Appetite and discernment in all things. He had not been embittered when, after a hugely enjoyable and stimulating year at Oxford, he had succumbed to glandular fever and eventually judged best not to return to sit mods but to go straight into the newspaper business. But his active and successful career had only been a deferment. All he had ever really wanted was this – the chance to create something living, real, his own – well, the author was dead, naturally – or rather not so naturally (the mine in Salamanca). France, the château, solitude, food, sun, wine, books, money, he had it all. What bitterness, not in him, but in the taste of things, when somehow it wouldn't come alive.

On the telephone, responding to his rather desperate appeal, Miss Pike had sounded nothing if not alive. Indeed she sounded as though someone, a retired colonel perhaps, might have told her at an impressionable age, and one at which one promises oneself never to change, that she was quite a live wire. She possessed, it was said, a very thick skin, but her curiosity lay surprisingly near its surface, and came out like a rash at the prick of the unexpected.

'I'm sorry, what did you say your name was?'

'Pike. Ludmilla. *Miss*.'

Talbot wrote it out backwards on the blotter, feeling already like a detective.

'You have some information about *Pierrot Lunaire*?' he asked gently. He was quite a pro, still.

'That will depend on what you would like to know.' Ludmilla narrowed her eyes in the glass.

'Let me fill you in,' offered Talbot. (Oh yes, it would be wonderful, just wonderful, to be filled in, she thought, mindful of all those cracks across her surface.) So Talbot filled her in, a little indiscreetly, he later thought. There was no trace of the author's family. Unless, of course . . .

'No,' said Ludmilla firmly. Not family. He needed detail, a hint of period atmosphere. Ludmilla was a positive crematorium of period atmosphere, she told him. Talbot did wonder whether that was necessarily a recommendation.

'I could tell you,' she said breathily, 'what really happened.'

With her head tilted at forty-five degrees to the receiver she sounded as frail as any laced and scented gentlewoman who ever received grace and favour.

'Let's separate fact from fiction here,' Talbot replied with professional ease and, for the record, Ludmilla agreed. She would be with him next week.

Talbot, who liked to think he was a dreamer, had always

dreamed that Chloe might still be living. Of course the biographical aspect of the novel, the existence of the source material, as he called it, in the first place, could not help but slightly compromise his determination to work, for once, in the realm of the imagination. He recalled a phrase of Oscar Wilde: 'The true artist is known by the use he makes of what he annexes, and he annexes everything.' Talbot didn't entirely go along with it, but it legitimised, without allowing for formal recognition of, his lack of talent for invention. Had he been aware in advance of the somewhat monumental character of Ludmilla he would perhaps have thought twice about what he meant by annex. Arrogate. Appropriate. Abduct?

But Talbot, who was careless, and already half in love with his heroine, was faint with anticipation. It was late May in Monvanité. Already the heat was rising, with lilac and blackthorn well passed. He cancelled a dinner party and took some long walks.

ANDREW TAYLOR

Previously unpublished short story

Nibble-Nibble

Andrew Taylor's new novel, *An Air that Kills*, is available now in paperback at your local Dillons store priced £5.99

Bring this voucher with you to obtain £1.00 off the publisher's prices at all Dillons stores.

NIBBLE-NIBBLE

All of them say that ghosts aren't real. Ask any grown-up. Ask my granny.

I used to think that ghosts wore white sheets and clanked when they moved and groaned like the wind in the chimney. That's kids' stuff. Real ghosts are like John. You don't see them, and you don't hear them very often either, or not as you hear you or me. Instead they slip silently inside your head, and just as silently they leave. John says ghosts are the same as people: some you like, some you don't.

He usually comes at night-time. I can never be certain he will be there. When he's there, we talk. He doesn't say words out loud. Sometimes I do, but sometimes not. It depends how I feel and what I want to say.

This house was built before Granny was born. I came to live here when I was a kid, after my parents died. John lived here too when he was alive. He told me that he slept more or less where I sleep, except his head was where my feet are, and the room was much larger because in those days it included what's now our bathroom. The partition wall between my bedroom and the bathroom is very thin. I hear what's being said in the bathroom even when I don't want to.

I heard Aunt and Uncle talking about Granny coming. 'It'll only be for a few nights,' said Uncle.

Aunt sniffed. 'I've heard that before.'

When Granny came to stay she usually brought one suitcase and a small handbag. This time she brought three suitcases and a large handbag as well as the small one.

The first thing she said to me was: 'Still talking to your little pretend friend?' And she scratched my cheek with a finger like a talon. 'You'll grow out of it, dear.'

Granny was shorter than Aunt and Uncle, and taller than me. Her skin was grey and powdery like the dust under my bed. She smelled too, partly of very old perfume and partly of stale, sick-making things. She had white, shiny teeth which she took out of her mouth every night. I wouldn't have minded that if she didn't leave them on the bathroom windowsill. She put them in a glass jar and covered them with a clear liquid. Through the curved glass you could see the teeth looking larger than life and ready to slip out and bite you. I tried to shut my eyes in the bathroom when she was staying with us but sometimes I forgot.

I've left the worst thing till last – something even worse than the teeth because there was nothing you could do about it. Granny talked. She started talking when she woke up and she went on talking until she fell asleep. Sometimes I even heard her talking *in* her sleep. She talked with her mouth full, she talked when the television was on, she talked when I was reading, and she talked in the lavatory. If you were too far away to hear the words she was saying, they all sounded the same: like 'Nibble-nibble, nibble-nibble, nibble-nibble,' repeated over and over again.

On the third night of her stay John and I were having a chat about relations. John said they were people too, so you could like or dislike them just as you chose. You didn't *have* to like them because they were related to you. While we were chatting Granny was in the bathroom. 'Nibble-nibble,' she murmured to herself. 'Nibble-nibble.'

'She's talking to her teeth,' I said to John, and we laughed.

On her way to bed she put her head inside my room. Just her head. It floated five feet above the floor. It as as if she'd unscrewed it from her body. She had her wiry hair in curlers and a hairnet on top.

'Still awake, are we?' She was mumbling because she'd left her teeth in the bathroom. The lower half of her skull had shrunk, and she looked different – more like an owl than a person. 'I could hear you chatting away to your little friend. Naughty. You won't be able to do that at school, will you?'

'I don't sleep at school,' I said.

She chuckled. 'Nightie-nightie, and no more talking. Sleepie-tightie.' She blew me a wet kiss that sounded like a balloon losing its air. The head vanished. The nibble-nibbles grew fainter. Her door closed.

'What did she mean?' I asked John.

How do I know?

'I wish she'd go away.'

She's a wicked grandmother. Like a wicked stepmother but worse.

Granny's visit dragged on into the second week. I spent as much time as I could in my bedroom. But I couldn't get away from the sound of her talking for long. 'Nibble-nibble, nibble-nibble.'

One night John and I were upstairs, playing quietly in the darkness. Neither of us needs much sleep. We heard Granny nibble-nibbling in the bathroom. At last she came out.

Her head floated into my room. 'Nightie nightie,' it said. 'Sleepie-tightie.'

Afterwards Uncle and Aunt went into the bathroom. There was a rushing of waters as the bath filled.

'. . . it's a very generous offer,' Uncle was saying. 'You have to admit that.'

Aunt hissed back: 'But money isn't everything.'

'Well, yes – but anyway she's got nowhere else to go.'

'She could stay where she is, with all her friends. She'd be lonely here.'

'She wants to be with family, not friends. Of course she finds children very tiring. Natural enough, at her age.' There was an interruption filled with a great deal of splashing. Then Uncle went on, 'We could never afford a boarding school on our own, let alone a decent one like that. Do you know what the fees are?'

Before Aunt answered, the splashing started once more. Aunt and Uncle were still talking. John went away. I didn't notice his going because I was listening so hard. When the splashing stopped, Aunt was saying, '. . . the most important thing – a good education.'

'You won't find that around here. So you agree it would be best for them both?'

There was a pause. While it lasted, I bit my lower lip until I tasted blood.

'I'll have a think about it,' Aunt said, which was one of her ways of saying yes.

Later I snuggled down in bed. I hoped John would come back so we could talk. But he didn't. Before I slept, I grew colder and colder. I don't mind admitting I cried a little. Tears are warm when they come out but they soon cool on your skin.

I woke before dawn. John was there.

Been crying?

'Yes.'

Bad. Why?

'Granny's going to give them money so she can live here.'

Nibble-nibble. Yuk.

'She's going to pay them to send me away to boarding school.'

John screamed. I'd never heard him scream before. Then he was gone, leaving me with a headache where the scream had been.

In the morning I was the first downstairs. I liked breakfast because it was the quietest meal in the day. Granny didn't get up until afterwards. On the other hand it wasn't a good time for trying to discuss anything with Uncle and Aunt. They both go out to work. I go to school. There's always too many things to do in the time before we leave.

'Aunt,' I said when I'd finished my second slice of toast, 'I don't want to go to boarding school.'

She looked startled. 'How did you gather that was on the cards?'

I shrugged.

'Walls have ears,' said Uncle, and his eyes drifted back to the newspaper.

'Darling, nothing's settled. It's just an idea. You might like it.'

'I won't,' I told her. 'I know I won't. Really.'

Uncle looked up. 'How can you know until you've tried?'

'I just know.'

'The school would be much more fun than the one here,' Aunt said. 'You'd make lots of friends and you'd learn more, too.'

'No,' I said. 'No, no, no.'

I finished my breakfast and went upstairs to the bathroom and brushed my teeth without being told to. I kept my eyes screwed shut. Normally grannies were meant to be nice, and ghosts were meant to be scary. Why did it have to be the other way round for me? Why couldn't I be like everyone else? Still, I thought, it could be worse: think how horrible it would be if I didn't have a friend like John, if I just had Granny.

As I was rinsing the toothbrush I foolishly opened my eyes. I glimpsed Granny's teeth. I thought I saw a tongue peeping between the two rows. I ran out of the room.

We were putting on our coats when Granny came downstairs in her dressing gown.

'Hello, Mother,' my uncle said. 'You're early.'

'Sleep well?' Aunt asked.

'Not quite as well as usual,' Granny mumbled. 'Never mind.'

In the evening we were watching television while Granny nibble-nibbled.

Uncle glanced at her during the adverts. 'What did you say? The pipes?'

'Yes, dear,' Granny said. 'Central heating, would it be? They make the most extraordinary noises. They gurgle. More like mutter, actually. Kept me awake all night.'

'I never noticed it,' Aunt said. 'Did you know we slept in that room for a while?'

'But that was in summer,' Uncle pointed out. 'So the central heating wouldn't have been on. The pipes contract and expand in the cold weather.'

'Then I wish the pipes would do it more quietly,' Granny said.

When I got back from school in the afternoon, Aunt and Uncle were still at work. I saw Granny through the sitting-room window. She was talking to the television.

The first thing she said when she saw me was, 'Something wrong with that television.'

'Looks all right to me.'

'It's the sound that's the problem, you silly child. Listen.'

I listened for a few seconds. 'What's wrong with it?'

'Can't you hear the interference? Like someone talking in the background?'

'No.'

'Then you need to have your ears tested.'

Granny told Uncle about it as soon as he came in. He wasn't sure if he could hear it or not. Maybe the TV was picking up the soundtrack from another station. They tried the little portable in the kitchen, and Granny said that was just as bad. Uncle looked relieved. In that case, he said, it must be a problem with the transmitter. Granny suggested he write to his Member of Parliament and complain.

'It's not right,' she said, 'not with the licence fee they charge.'

When I went to bed, I told John about it. While we talked we heard Granny grumbling to herself in the bathroom.

Nibble-Nibble.

'She's going round the bend,' I said.

So far round the bend she won't come back.

Next day Granny said the interference was worse. The muttering voice seemed to be everywhere, in the wind, in the hissing of the kettle, in the rustle of leaves. Aunt and I couldn't hear it. Uncle wasn't sure.

The day after that Granny didn't mention it, or not in my hearing. But John and I heard Uncle and Aunt talking in the bathroom.

'I'm having second thoughts about her living with us,' Aunt said. 'To be frank, she's getting a bit past it.'

Uncle cleared his throat. 'Just a phase.'

'She'll be saying the place is haunted next.'

'No, she won't. She doesn't believe in ghosts.'

In the night John woke me.

Listen.

Granny's slippered feet shuffled along the landing. 'Nibble-nibble, nibble-nibble,' she muttered. She went into the bedroom and closed the door. I felt John slipping away from me. I waited.

'Nibble-nibble, nibble-nibble . . .'

Granny flushed the lavatory. She turned on the tap to wash her hands.

'Nibble-nibble, nibble-nibble . . .'

There was an echo tonight. The nibble-nibbles bounced back on one another. It was as if they were having a conversation.

'Help!' Her voice was loud, clear and surprised. 'Help!'

I jumped out of bed and ran onto the landing.

'Help!'

The bathroom door was shut. I tried the handle. The door opened. Granny was standing in front of the basin looking at the windowsill. She didn't turn to look at me. Her face was mottled and faded, like an old newspaper stained with damp.

'Nibble-nibble, nibble-nibble . . .'

But Granny's mouth was closed. Her face was absolutely still, even her lips. Especially her lips. I looked at what was on the windowsill.

'Nibble-nibble, nibble-nibble . . .'

It wasn't possible. The liquid in the jar was swaying. The teeth were moving up and down. A tongue flickered behind them.

'Nibble-nibble,' the teeth were saying, 'Nibble-nibble, nibble-nibble . . .'

A door opened behind me. Uncle and Aunt rushed down the landing.

'Mother? Is that you? What's wrong?'

'Oh,' Granny said. 'Did I wake you? So sorry.'

Her eyes moved from the three of us in the doorway to the glass jar. The teeth were still. Perhaps the liquid was trembling slightly. I wasn't sure.

'Mother, are you all right?'

'I think I'll go home tomorrow,' Granny said. 'I'm not sleeping well here.'

My aunt nodded. 'You're used to a town. It's so quiet in the country.'

'Yes, too quiet.' Granny frowned at her teeth in the jar. 'That's it. I just can't get used to the silence. Not surprising, really, is it?'

We stood aside. She shuffled along the landing to her room. At her doorway she glanced back.

'Nightie-nightie,' she said. 'Sleepie-tightie.'

When I was alone again, John came back.

'Did Granny mean it? Will she go?'

She'll go. Has to.

'Why?'

Because she doesn't believe in ghosts.

'It was you, wasn't it?'

John laughed. *Nibble-nibble.*

D M THOMAS

Extract taken from

Eating Pavlova

Eating Pavlova is available now at your local Dillons store priced £5.99.

Bring this voucher with you to obtain £1.00 off the publisher's prices at all Dillons stores.

And again it's Anna, bending over me in the dark. It seems I've been moaning. She bathes my forehead with a flannel. Her touch so gentle. I grasp her other hand. 'Tomorrow,' I say thickly. 'It's become pointless, my dear.'

'No, Papa, please. Not tomorrow. The day after.'

'Well, we'll see. Perhaps I can bear one more day.'

She lays her face against my hand and I feel her tears.

In the morning light, when Schur comes, I tell him Not yet; and he nods. As he prepares the injection I whisper, 'Not too much.'

With him is the woman called Martha. Her sad eyes, the grey hair and sunken features. I can recognise Anna in her, only Anna's hair is black and her eyes still glow with a fire that might have appealed to men. I have wronged Martha. I called her our maid, but that is incorrect; she is of course my wife. Once upon a time I wrote passionate letters to her, pleaded with her to be faithful.

Mistakes will inevitably creep into this memoir. I believe I called my father Joseph, whereas his real name was Jacob. It is I who always, as his eldest son by Amalie, have identified with Joseph. Perhaps I find it hard to see my mild father, who once stepped into the gutter to retrieve his hat after a Gentile had insulted him, wrestling with an angel.

A more extraordinary error in this narrative was my changing our faithful maid Paula to Pauli. Though Pauli was born in Vienna in the same year as my *Intrepretation of Dreams*, the year 1900, I am not aware of ever having met him; but Einstein recommended to me an essay of his, for an encyclopedia, as the clearest explanation for a layman of the Theory of Relativity. I made a small effort to get hold of the encyclopedia, however it proved difficult and life rolled on. But his name has occurred several times since. I recall being told about Pauli's conflict with Bohr at a public lecture in Denmark. Pauli had expounded some new idea in quantum physics – I believe in fact it was the concept of multiple, universal coitus first touched upon by the Kabbalists – and Bohr leapt to his feet exclaiming: 'It's not crazy enough! It can't be right!' And Pauli snarled in reply: 'It *is* crazy enough!'

And surely he was right. The imagination faints before the concept of millions of godlike creatures wrestling sexually together, sustaining life thereby. It is a crazy idea, yet also with a certain aesthetic grandeur and simplicity.

It may have been the association with dreams, my book of dreaming, that sent Paulo across the mare's field to bring my daughter Francesca a glass of cool lemonade in this Indian summer.

I am fondling Venus. A gift from my Parisian friend Marie Bonaparte on her last visit, she is nude to her hips, where drapery hides her sex; she is holding a mirror.

The sudden wail of a banshee, her shrill note rising and falling. Anna, who has been squatting at my feet reading, rises in a panic and runs into the house. She returns with two Egyptian masks in her arms and makes to put one on me; but I wave it away. What more should I have to do with masks? She concedes, bowing her head; lays both masks on the ground. She sits on the grass, drawing her broad brown skirt around her legs, and resumes her reading.

Let the banshees wail, let the demons appear in the cloudlessly blue sky.

The wailing stops. Silence falls. Only the humming of insects. Ants scurry along the arm of a garden seat. They too have their Adam and Eve, their Moses, their Jacob, their sacred book, their exile, their Red Sea, their literature, their Shakespeare. Their Freud.

The banshee wails again, but this time on a prolonged monotonous note. Anna relaxes. 'Another false alarm,' she says. 'You were right, Papa. You are always right.' Her words, half respectful half annoyed, remind me of one of my sisters left behind. The aunts are attracted by a speck of jam. '*Stwawbewy jam*! *Stwawbewy jam*!' Anna pipes up, an infant; her first dream.

My father came to Freiberg in the middle of the last century to join his grandfather, a merchant. After a while his two sons, Emanuel and Philipp, came to Freiberg also; and with them was my father's second wife, Rebecca of the burning eyes. They lived in one second-storey room of a house of a street whose name escapes me. My father was then about forty. Within three years he had married my mother Amalie, aged nineteen. She was of an age with my half-brothers. When I was born I was cauled and covered in black hairs from head to toe. Julius, who came next, fortunately died within a few months. Then followed five girls, Anna, Rosa, Mitzi, Dolfi and Pauline; finally a second brother, Alexander. In my infancy my two playmates were my nephew and niece, children of Emanuel and his bride Marie; their names were John and Pauline. One day, playing in a meadow, John and I fell upon Pauline and robbed her of her golden flowers.

My half-brothers could have been my fathers; my father could have been my grandfather; my nephew and niece could have been my brother and sister; my mother could have been my wife as my shaggy-haired face buried into her oily, sweating teats. I also had another mother, an old and ugly maid called Monika. Although she could not have been so very old, since one day her bath water became the Red Sea. She allowed my chubby little hairy hands to explore its source. She laughed as I urinated into the Red Sea.

We could have been Germans or we could have been Jews. My father, an unbeliever, studied the Talmud constantly, and my mother was all-Jewish. It did not matter who we were: the Czechs not much caring for either Germans or Jews.

We shared the one big room. And my mother, my mothers, my sisters, showed me the forest. They led me into its depths, where I smelled the divinely secret fragrances of flowers.

I recall an afforested *cabinet* in a train. My mother let go of my hand and I saw the white flanks of the Carpathians, and a golden hissing cascade that went on and on. The train rumbles and jerks; I don't know where we are going.

Amalie, I think her name was. Or was it Anna. Anna baths me now; Anna at night lifts up her nightdress, crouching, unashamed. She holds the chamber for me; her head turns aside, but at the end she sees it, unashamed, the organ that conceived her. Shrunken now. Anna is Mama. Well, it's natural. I'm her helpless child, and the forests spin around us. Forests of wolves and banshees, spirits and flowers. I have swallowed my Mama, I wear her nightcap. Anna enters with her basket of strawberries. *Stwawbewies*!

The world only exists because of seemingly trivial, random rules. I know little of physics but I know that two electrons cannot occupy the same position. If they share the same position momentarily, one will have a different velocity; if they share the same velocity they will not be together in space. It's as arbitrary and crazy as the rules of chess, yet otherwise the universe would collapse into a soup. This, as I understand it, is the law Paula discovered.

A dream that my daughter Anna brings a letter. It is from France, and enclosed is a photo of Eva. Eva is my favourite grand-daughter. What lovely eyes she has, and what a fresh look of hope for the miserable world! How it stretches out – life – beyond me. She will marry and have children, and be a little old lady receiving photos of her grandson; who will marry, have children, etc. . . . It stretches out further than the line of stars from the Hunter to Andromeda. I should see the stars for the last time; and yet it doesn't seem necessary. As we were born from the stars, so we carry them with us, on into death. In the dust of my body the constellations will glow.

But I would like to have seen Eva one more time. We don't carry young children on into death. Eva is fifteen, I think. She means more to me than Oliver her father. My sons have become very vague creatures. Martin fancies himself as a bit of a Romeo, but his wife dies at least every day. My third son is called . . . I have forgotten for the moment. In dull middle age. Mediocrities, I fear.

Ernst!

It's very easy to forget the name of one's son, not the eldest.

I named them after heroes. Cromwell. Luther. My old teacher. But alas . . . *Martin* Luther would not have allowed his wife to find a photograph album of his girlfriends, standing on street corners. And Martin a banker! *This* apple hasn't fallen under the tree. Ah, well . . .

Late in the morning, cumulus builds up on the horizon; yet most of the sky remains bright blue. The cumulus is pure white, and looks in contrast as the first sight of Antarctica must appear to the southward-sailing mariner. There is a hint of chill in the air today, and I sit hunched in overcoat and cap. When our chow Lün appears and rushes up to me, I bend to stroke her but she retreats, she cowers. Only Anna now, and Schur, steadfastly come close without betraying their disgust at the smell coming from my jaw.

Faithful Schur arrives again to give me a top-up injection. The pain eases slightly.

The long, quiet afternoon is made eventful by the appearance of three guests – Lou Andreas-Salomé, Isaac Newton and Charles Darwin. Stout, bosomy Lou is particularly welcome, since I had thought she was dead. No one could be more alive than Lou, her clear blue eyes sparkling, her generous mouth curved in a smile, the sunlight glinting on her rich wheaten hair. Her radiant personality completely outshines that of the dour Englishmen, in their dark frock-coats. Her fur coat, glistening, seems to embody all Russia's forests; the philosopher Plato and the poet Goethe loved to vanish into their depths. She visited her native land with Goethe after the Revolution – which paled in face of Lou.

I am at first embarrassed because Darwin, Newton and I are all Fellows of the Royal Society, whereas Lou is not. However, she quickly makes us feel at ease. Conversation flows among us all; for a while I feel free of the years and of pain. Darwin discourses on his great discovery that Love binds together everything in the universe. I ask him how he made the discovery and he tells me it was when a sparrow fell into his lap.

'For us women,' Lou reflects, 'love and existence are one. We have no need of a seam – ' she lifts her fur coat slightly, turning on her chair to show the back of a leg – 'we are all of a piece. Similarly with our bodies: the cloaca is only taken from our vagina on lease.'

'My friend Darwin,' Newton murmurs, 'was referring to spiritual love.'

'Yes, but for a woman there is no difference. The spiritual

and the erotic are one and the same. That's why we women make such good analysts – am I right?' She glances at me for confirmation, and I nod. 'We don't find anything shocking, you see. For example, masturbation . . .'

She slips out of her fur. Soon she is stark naked. She squats, one heel digging into the region of her anus. Her face wears a seraphic look, the eyes closed. After a few minutes she starts to shiver, to shudder; throws her head back in a scream.

She lifts her heavy, white buttocks from her heel; lies on the lawn, an arm flung out. And slowly from her anus emerges a green snake. When its tail appears I see the snake is about five feet long. A green mamba. It winds itself around Darwin's dark-trousered leg and continues up. Its head enters his long white beard; eventually the whole mamba disappears into it.

'Don't worry, it's poisonous,' I say. 'It's because they're killing the snakes.'

At this moment I have an impression of Anna bending over me tenderly, asking if I want anything. I shake my head.

Lou quotes a line from a book of Russian poetry she gave me once. *'When Psyche-Life descends into the shadows . . .'* we hear, in her resonant, husky tones. A Russian poem by the geneticist Mendel. She bought the book on a return visit to Petersburg after the Revolution. She was with her husband Andreas and her lover Rilke.

I speak of the difficulty of finding a safe haven in the tall unbroken white cliffs. With the seas mountainous. 'But you will make it; you were always a conquistador, Freud,' says the sombre-eyed Newton.

'Yes.' I sigh.

Monika, hobbling, ungainly, brings us tea. We sprawl, Lou naked, like that famous picture by Manet. Perfectly at ease.

My vigorous mood ebbing fast, I drowse; and dream of pain, and of Paula and Ernst carrying me into the house. Paula echoes Paul, the Jewish Gentile; and Ernst brings back my good-hearted teacher, Brücke. A bridge between two worlds.

I drowse on the threshold of waking, and half-see, half-create, newspaper comments adrift between sense and absurdity. One of them is 'A common interest in the meat haulage industry links Mussolini and Mrs Virginia Woolf.'

I remember the Woolfs visited me. He with the face of an English garden, she with the face of a constipated horse.

When I force myself to go over the threshold, I find Anna making me comfortable. 'Sophie called in to see how you were,' she says.

A confused joy overcomes me. 'Sophie!' So radiant on her wedding day; though it was taking her away from us.

She nods. 'She's growing into a lovely girl. In her teens she's becoming much more like Martin.'

'Ah! Yes. Sophie.' Martin's daughter.

There's still that slight resentment about the living, on Sophie's behalf, on Heinele's, her dear son.

Picnics in the Woods, as Mathilde and Anna tried to make him forget the loss of his Mama . . . 'Picnic on the Grass.' Or it may have been Renoir. Anyway, the exhibition I saw with the Charcots. Jean-Martin: '*Mon cher*, these so-called painters are crazier than our patients!' His bright, laughing eyes; hand on my shoulder.

Life resplendently open to me. No Sophie yet, even as a dream; no Heinele, playing with flowers or closing his eyes in death.

ROSE TREMAIN

Short story taken from her collection
The Garden of the Villa Mollini

The Garden of the Villa Mollini

Rose Tremain's award-winning novel, *Restoration*, soon to be a major film, is available now in paperback at your local Dillons store priced at £5.99.

Bring this voucher with you to obtain £1.00 off the publisher's prices at all Dillons stores.

RESTORATION
by Rose Tremain

This voucher entitles you to **£1** OFF *Restoration* by *Rose Tremain*

CONDITIONS

- *This voucher is only redeemable at Dillons Bookstores.*
- *Only one voucher may be redeemed per transaction.*
- *This voucher may not be used in conjunction with any other offer and is not exchangeable for cash.*

Promoter: Dillons Bookstore, Berwick House, 35 Livery Street, Birmingham, B3 2PB
Offer closes 31st October 1995

BEFORE THE ARRIVAL of Antonio Mollini in 1877, the villa had been called, simply, the Villa Bianca, the White House. It came to be known as the Villa Mollini, not through the vanity of Antonio Mollini himself, but through the pride of the people of the village. They wanted to be able to say – to travellers who passed that way, to relations who journeyed there from Arezzo or Rapolano or Assisi – 'We have in our midst the great Mollini, the world's most renowned opera singer. He knows us and even remembers the names of our children.'

In fact, Antonio Mollini was seldom there. He was forty-one when he bought the villa and his voice had entered what the critics later termed its 'decade of magnificence'. His life was passed in the musical capitals of Europe — Milan, Paris, Vienna. He came to the Villa Mollini only to rest, to visit his wife and to plan his garden.

He wanted, in the design of this garden, to express a simple and optimistic philosophy. He believed that his life was a journey of discovery, revelation and surprise and that it led forward perpetually, never back. In it, there was not merely one goal, one destination, but many, each one leading forwards from the next. All were different. Repetition seldom, if ever, occurred. He would not allow it to occur. And even at life's close, he thought there would be new landscapes and new visions of hope. The garden he was going to create would thus be infinitely varied, intricate and above all beautiful.

It was fortunate, then, that the terrain on which he would realise the garden wasn't flat, but sloped gently upwards away from the house to a cypress grove, and then descended, equally gently, towards a river. On the other side of the river, there were clover fields and, beyond these, a forest. The far edge of the forest was the boundary of Mollini's land.

His head gardener, Paulo Pappavincente, was the illegitimate son of a priest. Pappavincente's mother had died at his birth and he'd been brought up by aged and devout grandparents unable to conceal their shame at his existence. Though Mollini explained his philosophy carefully to Pappavincente, using simple terms, baby language almost, the gardener was unable to see life as his master saw it. To him, it led, repetitively and inevitably, to dark and deep abysses of guilt. But he didn't want to bore Mollini or anger him with chatter about his own sufferings; he wanted to design the most beautiful garden in Tuscany, so that one day he could say to his own legitimate grandchildren, 'I made it. I made the garden of the Villa Mollini.' He did suggest, however, that a well be sunk at a certain place, not far from the house, where Mollini had thought a statue of the goddess Diana would draw the eye forward. 'I think a well also beckons, Sir,' he said. To his surprise and also to his relief, Mollini agreed. That night, as he knelt to say his prayers, Pappavincente began to feel that good fortune was stealing into his life.

The same night, Antonio Mollini's wife, Rosa, stared by candlelight at the half-completed sketches of the box aisles and the fountains, the herbarium and the rose trellises, the steps and terraces leading up to the cypress grove and down to the river, and said aloud, 'I think he must contrive a lake.'

Mollini was asleep. He lay on his back, snoring, with his legs apart. From his magnificent lungs came an unmelodious kind of squealing. Rosa pulled aside the curtains of the bed and leaned over him, holding her candle.

'Antonio,' she whispered, 'please, Antonio.'

He opened his eyes. This thin white face of Rosa's on its

pale neck sometimes reminded him of a sad mask on a stick.

'What, Rosa?'

'When the river leaves our land, westwards, where does it arrive, Antonio?'

'In the village.'

'Then I expect we may have to move the village.'

Mollini stared up. He chose his mistresses for their roundness, for their bright colour. Rosa was his little ghostly possession.

'We cannot move the village, Rosa.'

Tears sparkled in her eyes.

'Please, Antonio. You must make a lake.'

Pappavincente was consulted. When he heard of the plan to dam up the river, he descended once more into his habitual pessimism. Politely, he informed his master of the life-sustaining properties of the village water supply. Antonio Mollini felt ashamed. He loved the village people. He'd made a list of all their names and the names of their children so that he wouldn't forget them, and now, in the night, he'd allowed his wife to suggest something that would impoverish and destroy them. 'Rosa is mad', he said to Pappavincente, 'but forgive her. Since the death of Pietro, her mind often wanders astray.'

The death of Pietro had occurred in the same year that Mollini's fame was born. Consumption thus played a role in both events. As Mollini sang Alfredo in Verdi's *La Traviata*, his son Pietro was dying of Violetta's disease. He refused to mourn. He looked at the little coffin. He would have more sons. He would replace Pietro. He would christen all his sons 'Pietro', so that if another one died, he, too, could be replaced. Rosa accused him of callousness. 'No,' he said, 'but I will not let death win.'

Rosa didn't conceive. She knew that loss, like starvation, can make a woman barren. She would be barren for ever, mourning Pietro. She longed, at that time, for a garden. She thought it would make her feel more kindly towards the world if she could bury seeds in the earth and see leaves emerge, bright green. But Mollini wasn't yet rich. They lived in Milan in a narrow house on a dark courtyard. The Villa Mollini was six years away.

In those six years, Pappavincente fathered four sons, one of whom he christened Pietro.

Mollini fathered none. His fame grew. 'There is no adequate epithet to describe Mollini's voice,' one French critic wrote. 'To say it is like honey, or like velvet, or like silver is merely to debase it. It is like no other voice we have ever heard.'

On its gentle hillside, the Villa Mollini, still known as the Villa Bianca and occupied by a professor of medicine, waited for the great man's arrival.

In the week following Rosa's dreadful request for a lake, Mollini left for Milan. On his forty-second birthday, the day he began rehearsals for La Scala's new production of Wagner's *Tristan und Isolde*, he met for the first time the internationally known soprano, Verena Dusa, and fell in love with her.

La Dusa was thirty-four. Her elbows were dimpled and her belly and breasts round and firm and fat. She was the mistress of the impresario, Riccardo Levi, from whose bed Mollini quickly wooed her.

Riccardo Levi demanded a duel and was refused. He threatened to ruin La Dusa's career, but his threats were ignored. La Dusa moved her dresses and her fan collection from Levi's apartment to Mollini's town house. In despair, Riccardo Levi wrote a letter to Rosa, telling Mollini's wife that she had been betrayed.

Rosa examined the letter. She held it near to her face because her eyesight was getting bad and Riccardo Levi had small, mean handwriting. As she read the word 'betrayed', she felt a pain shoot down from her knees to the soles of her feet, as if in seconds she'd become an old crone, unable to walk. She put the letter down and stood up, clinging first to the writing table, then to the wall. She went to the window. A team of surveyors had arrived. Pappavincente was describing to them an imaginary circle, the site of his well. Rosa tapped on the window, to summon Pappavincente to help her, but her tap was too feeble and he couldn't hear her. Her maid came in a while later and found her lying on the floor. She was unable to speak. Her maid called for help. Rosa was put to bed and a doctor sent for. With the arrival of the doctor, word spread to Pappavincente and the other gardeners that the Signora was ill. Retribution, thought Pappavincente.

The doctor examined Rosa. She was in shock, he told the servants. Something must have frightened her – something she'd seen from the window, perhaps? The servants shrugged their choulders. Rosa's maid stroked her mistress's cold white forehead. Keep her warm, said the doctor and went away. Coverlets were piled on the bed, one on top of another, so that the shape of Rosa's body disappeared completely beneath them and only her small head stuck out like a tiny sprout on a desirée potato.

She lay without speaking for a week. Her maid propped her up and spooned vermicelli broth into her narrow mouth. Outside her window, she could hear men talking and tried to turn her head to listen. 'Drains,' her maid explained gently, 'they're here to re-route the drains and lay conduits to the fountains.'

The doctor returned. His own wife quite often irritated him by succumbing to illnesses he was unable to cure except by cradling her in his arms like a baby. He looked at Rosa's blank face. He refused to cradle *her* in his arms. There were dark hairs on her top lip and creases in her eyelids. 'Where is Signor Mollini?' he snapped. 'He must be sent for.'

So the servants sent for the priest. He, too, came and stared at Rosa and placed a palm leaf cross on her coverlet mountain and then sat down, in the silence of her room, and wrote in exquisite calligraphy to Antonio Mollini, informing him that his wife appeared to be dying.

When the letter arrived in Milan, on an early morning of grey mist, Mollini's voice – that same voice that had caused thousands of Society women to weep with wonder behind their opera glasses – was whispering playful obscenities in La Dusa's ear. She squirmed and giggled and pouted and the pout of her wide lips was so delicious and irresistible that Mollini was unable to stop himself from kissing them again and murmuring through his nose, 'I love you, Verena. I love you beyond everything.'

His servant knocked at his door. He rolled over and covered La Dusa's breasts with the sheet. The servant excused himself and came forward to the bed and offered Mollini the priest's letter on a silver salver. It was written on fine parchment, like a communion wafer. Mollini snatched it up and told the servant not to disturb him again that morning. The servant bowed and retreated. Mollini glanced at the letter, tossed it onto the marble bedside cabinet and turned back to La Dusa who lay with her arms above her head, waiting for his embrace.

The letter was forgotten. He remembered it at last towards six o'clock that evening, as he was preparing to leave for the opera house. He opened it as he was gargling with blackcurrant cordial. When he read the word 'dying', he choked on the gargle and spat it all over the bathroom floor. He wiped his mouth, read the letter again and sat down on a stool. For the first time in several months, he remembered Pietro, and at once he saw, clearly and beautifully, where fate had led and where indeed it was leading. It was leading to La Dusa. Rosa was dying because she was unable to bear him more sons. It was fitting. Rosa was dried up, barren, old before her time. But here, right here in his bed, was Verena Dusa with her succulent round hips that would accommodate his future children. All he had to do was to marry her. It was gloriously simple. It was like stepping from a dark, shaded laurel walk onto a sunny terrace and finding at your feet pots of scented jasmine.

That same evening, Rosa spoke for the first time in seven days. She asked her maid to help her into the garden. When she crept out from under the coverlets, she seemed to have shrunk. Her long white nightgown was tangled round her feet. She looked like a chrysalis.

She was wrapped up in a cloak. Her hair was brushed and pinned up. She went hesitantly down the stairs, clinging to her maid's arm.

Pappavincente was standing in the garden in the twilight, looking at the well shafts. The water table was low.

The construction workers had sunk the shafts almost fifty feet. He looked up and saw Rosa totter out with her maid. 'Forgive her', Mollini had said. Pappavincente left the well and started to walk towards her. Her maid sat her down on a little stone seat. She stared about her in bewilderment. Deep trenches had been dug in the terraces. Mounds of red earth and lengths of lead piping lay all around.

'Signora,' said Pappavincente, bowing, 'for your recovery we are making all these waterworks.' But she only stared at him in bewilderment too, as if he were a lunatic, as if he were the village idiot. 'I want,' she said, looking at the devastation round her, 'my husband back.' Up above the chimneys of the house and above the garden several bats were circling. Rosa liked bats. 'Pipistrelli,' she'd call, 'pipi, pipi . . .'

Unaware that the priest had written to Mollini, Rosa that night had the lamp lit on her writing desk and sat down with her pen. She told Mollini that she had been ill and that she had imagined she was lying in a grave with Pietro. Over her body, the earth had been piled higher and higher in a colossal mound, with only her head sticking out. She could not, she said, endure such imaginings and only his love could save her from them. She would forgive him his sin of the flesh if he would just return to her. She signed the letter *Your Wife Until Death, Rosa Mollini*. Her writing, unlike the priest's hand, was cramped and ugly and her spelling not terribly good.

Rosa's letter reached Milan four days later. Mollini and La Dusa had triumphed in *Tristan und Isolde* and had been invited each night to elegant suppers by the likes of the Duke of Milan and the Count of Piedmont and had revelled together in their glory. At one of these suppers Mollini had become tottering drunk on a surfeit of champagne and pleasure and had rested his head on La Dusa's bosom and proposed marriage to her. The other guests had gasped, remembering the small, elegant wife he used to bring to evenings such as these, but La Dusa had only laughed and stroked his burning cheek and told him she was his till she died.

When he read Rosa's letter (he had a hangover when it

was brought to him and his head was throbbing) he knew that he wouldn't, *couldn't* go back to her. When he thought about his life with Rosa, he was amazed he'd been able to endure it for so many years. Because it seemed full of shadow. Only at Pietro's birth had the sun shone on it and after his death it had become colourless and ghostly.

But Mollini knew also that he couldn't abandon his plans for the garden to Rosa and Pappavincente, both of whose natures were pessimistic and depressive. So he decided he would take La Dusa back with him to the Villa Mollini. He was a great man, revered in the village. He could do as he liked. He was beyond criticism. And he wouldn't hide La Dusa away. Oh, no. He would move out of the rooms he'd shared with Rosa and into other rooms which he'd share with La Dusa. When they were invited out, both women would accompany him, wife and mistress. Tuscan society would be given the chance to exclaim upon La Dusa's gorgeous beauty. And Rosa? Rosa was a religious, reserved woman. She would behave piously, with dignity, staying away from him most of the time, reading or sewing in her rooms or going to communion.

Having obtained La Dusa's willing agreement to these arrangements, Mollini wrote to tell Rosa that he was returning home, but that he was unable to live without Verena Dusa and that she would therefore be coming with him.

Five days later, they arrived at the Villa Mollini to be told by the servants that Rosa was dead. She had been found with a burned scrap of paper in her hand, which they thought might have been a letter. She had shot herself with one of Mollini's duelling pistols.

Summer was coming. The re-routing of the drains wasn't entirely successful. As Mollini and his love sat with their fingers entwined on the first of the terraces to be completed, they fancied they could smell something decidedly unsavoury.

It had been a dry spring and the river was low. Verena Dusa went down and looked at the river and said, as she strolled along with her plump little hand fondling

Mollini's velvet–clad buttocks, 'You know what I would like here, my darling? A lake.'

Pappavincente was summoned. 'I am going to dam up the river,' Mollini informed him. 'Water will be taken to the village in metal containers. Every villager will have his rightful share.'

Pappavincente went down to the village, informed the people what was happening and told them to march shoulder to shoulder up to the Villa and break down the gates and threaten to kill Signor Mollini if he went ahead with his dam. 'We will!' said a few voices. 'We won't let our river be taken away!' And some of the men got out their pitchforks and their scythes. But nearly all the women of the village folded their arms and shrugged their shoulders. 'As long as we have water,' they said, 'we're really perfectly happy. Perhaps it will be less trouble to get water from the containers than from the river. And anyway, we mustn't forget how lucky we are to have Signor Mollini right here in our valley . . .'

They could see, however, that Pappavincente was in despair. They comforted him. 'You're adding to the fame of this region with your wonderful garden,' they told him, 'and a lake will make it even better. You must put swans on it, Pappavincente, and graceful boats.'

So Pappavincente walked back up to the Villa with not one villager standing with him, shoulder to shoulder. He thought he would sell his cottage and take his wife and sons and leave Mollini for ever. But then he let himself into the garden by a side gate and stood and stared at one of the new fountains and at the water lilies he'd planted at its base and thought of all the work still to be done, and he knew that, if he left the garden, he'd regret it till he died. It was his one work of art.

Mollini had understood the look of agony on Pappavincente's face. He was relieved he'd thought up the idea of taking water to the villagers in containers, because he knew that if La Dusa wanted a lake, he would have to give her a lake. He was much too afraid of losing her to deny her anything. Indeed, he begged her, begged her on his knees with his arms round her thighs to ask of him whatever she wanted, no matter how costly, no matter how perverse. All he longed to do was to give, to give.

She laughed at him. He adored her laugh, It made him tremble with delight. 'You can give me a wedding ring, Antonio!' she giggled.

He'd thought, after burying Rosa, that he would wait six months before marrying Verena. It seemed right to wait. But it was clear to him as the summer advanced that La Dusa would insist on being married before new opera commitments began for them both in September. Hardly a day went by now without her asking, 'Will it be August, Antonio?'

So he decided he wouldn't wait six months. He set a date: August 17th. He wanted the dam completed by then and a chapel built at the lake's edge, where the wedding would take place. More builders were hired. The same priest who had written to Mollini on Rosa's behalf was now given money to consecrate the ground on which the chapel was going to stand. An order was sent to Lake Trasimeno for forty-two swans. A fat ruby, encircled with diamonds, was placed on La Dusa's finger. Invitations went out to all the important people in the opera world – patrons and practitioners, both – and rooms booked for them in every inn and hostelry for miles around.

Then in July, as the dam was finished and the river went dry and the first containers of water rolled in on carts to the village, Mollini fell ill. He started vomiting. Pain in his bowel made him curse in agony. He had a terrible fever.

The doctor came. He took off his tail coat and rolled up his shirtsleeves and gave Mollini an enema. The contents of the bowel were putrified, he noticed, greenish and foul. 'Advanced colonic infection,' he diagnosed and arranged for Mollini to be taken that night to a hospital in Siena.

La Dusa travelled in the carriage with him. His face, normally ruddy and healthy, looked grey. He was suffering. La Dusa wiped his forehead with a little lace handkerchief. She was petrified. Supposing he died before the wedding?

When they reached the hospital, Mollini appeared to be delirious, not knowing where he was. As they went in through a heavy, iron-studded door, La Dusa held her lace handkerchief to her nostrils. The stench of the place was appalling. Every breath she breathed seemed to her to be full of poison. And though it was night-time, it was a stupidly rowdy place. Doors slammed, nurses marched up and down the echoing corridors in stalwart shoes, patients cried out, gas lamps hissed, cleaning women in filthy aprons pushed iron slop buckets forward on the stone floors with their mops

La Dusa felt sick. How could anyone be made well in such a place? As Mollini was carried in, they passed a flight of stairs leading downwards. TO THE MORGUE, said a sign. The sign was accompanied by a drawing of a hand with a pointing finger. La Dusa couldn't help noticing that the drawing of the hand was very fine, like a drawing by da Vinci or Michelangelo. This must be where their talents lie, she thought – in the direction of death.

Mollini was put into an iron bed in the middle of a long ward. La Dusa protested, but no one listened and they were left quite alone. All along the row, men were groaning and sighing. A nurse came in. She passed briskly down the line of groaning patients, barely glancing at any of them. La Dusa stood up. She took her handkerchief away from her nose, drew in a breath and then let out a high F Sharp with extraordinary force.

The nurse stopped in her tracks and stared at her with a look of utter incredulity. Several of the patients woke from sleep and raised their heads.

La Dusa heard herself shout at the nurse, 'Do you know who this is? This is Antonio Mollini! Why has he been put here?'

'This is the Men's Ward, Signora.'

'And why is there no surgeon? Is this what you do to your patients – put them in a line and forget them?'

'Of course we don't forget them.'

'I want Signor Mollini moved to a quiet room and I want a surgeon called now!'

The nurse gave La Dusa a dirty look and stomped out of the ward. La Dusa returned to Mollini's bed and stared at him. His eyes were closed and his breathing shallow. She was glad, in a way, that he couldn't see the terrible ward or hear or smell the sufferings of the other men. She stroked his hand. 'I will fight for you, my love,' she said.

After half an hour, the nurse returned. 'There is no surgeon here at the moment,' she said sourly. 'Surgeons need rest, you know. But if you can pay, we can have Signor Mollini moved to a more secluded room.'

'Pay?' said La Dusa, 'Of course we can pay!'

Mollini was lifted onto a stretcher and carried out of the ward. He was put into another iron bed in a tiny room, like a cell. A chair was brought to La Dusa and she sat down. They told her that one of the surgeons had woken up and would come and look at Mollini as soon as he had cleaned his teeth.

The door of the little cell was shut. Alone with Mollini's sufferings, La Dusa felt so frightened that she began to cry. Her tears were very bright and copious and the little lace handkerchief was soon saturated with them.

When the surgeon arrived, she was still weeping. The surgeon wore a silk cravat. He shook her hand, that was wet from holding the handkerchief. She gave him a scribbled note from Mollini's doctor. When he'd read it, he lifted up the covers and began to prod Mollini's belly.

The surgeon's hand on his bowel caused terrible pain. Mollini's eyes opened and rolled about and he choked in agony. The face of the surgeon became grave. La Dusa wiped her wet hand on her skirt and knelt by Mollini, holding him and kissing his face as the surgeon's fingers probed.

The surgeon replaced Mollini's covers and put his hands together in a kind of steeple under his chin. 'We must open him up,' he said.

He was taken away. La Dusa was told to wait in the tiny room. She lay on the bed and tried to doze, but her own anxiety and the unceasing noise of the hospital prevented sleep. The short night passed and a grey light seeped in through the tiny window.

At seven, Mollini was brought in on a stretcher and put back into the bed. He was unconscious and pale as death. The surgeon, too, looked pale and there was sweat on his top lip. 'I'm afraid,' he said, 'the decay of the large intestine was far advanced. We have done the only thing possible to save his life: we have cut the putrified section and joined the bowel together where the tissue was healthy. We believe he will survive.'

La Dusa knew that Mollini's convalescence would be long. She rented a house in a nearby street, so that she could come at any hour of the day or night to visit her love.

In the days following the operation, Mollini seemed, very slowly, to be getting well and La Dusa was full of praise for the surgeon who had saved his life. But then, on the fifth day, the wound became infected. Mollini's temperature soared and pain returned. For the first time, the nurses became attentive and La Dusa thought again of the beautiful hand pointing downwards to the morgue and became convinced that Mollini was going to die.

She had dreams of her lost wedding. In them, the forty-two swans Mollini had ordered were black. She made a decision. She would not let Mollini die before they were joined in marriage. She asked for the priest to be sent. He arrived with his candle and his holy water, thinking he was needed to administer the last rites. But no, La Dusa told him, she wanted him to marry them. The priest looked at Mollini and shook his head. He couldn't marry them if the groom was too ill to speak, he told her, and went away, giving La Dusa a strange and suspicious look.

She was in despair. She sat and watched her lover's life ebb.

But Mollini didn't die. His body's own magnificent healing powers surprised even the surgeon by fighting the infection till it was finally vanquished. He sat up. He began to eat, to laugh, to hold Verena's hand in a strong grip.

They returned to the Villa Mollini. The chapel was finished. Rain had come and the lake was brimming. In September, Verena Dusa and Antonio Mollini were married. The bride wore white satin and swans' feathers in her hair.

In the years that followed, all the original plans made by

Mollini and Pappavincente for the garden were implemented. Every statue, every shrub, every rockery and fountain was in place. 'All we can do now, Master,' said Pappavincente, 'is to wait for everything to grow.' But Mollini, whose fame and wealth had already grown to giant proportions, began to conceive the idea of buying land beyond the forest, of making pathways through the forest in order to extend his garden to the other side of it. He liked what had been achieved so far. He was especially proud of the winding maze that led down to the lake, but there were no surprises for him in the garden any more. As he turned each corner, he knew exactly what he was going to see.

The land on the other side of the wood was common land, used by the villagers as pasture for their animals. Pappavincente was told to go down to the village and inform the farmers that ten hectares of pastureland were going to be fenced off. He refused to go. He was ageing and growing stubborn as he aged. 'Very well,' said Mollini, 'I shall go myself.'

He didn't often visit the village now. He had long ago stopped making his list of the names of the villagers' children and he couldn't, in fact, remember the surnames of many of the villagers themselves. He knew, however, that the oldest man of the village, Emilio Verri, had recently died. So Mollini decided to go straight to the house of his widow, allegedly to offer his condolences.

Signora Verri was an old, old woman. 'I lost a husband, and you, Signor Mollini, you lost your beloved wife,' she said as the great man bent over her and put his hand on her bony shoulders. Mollini straightened up. He couldn't stand it when anyone mentioned Rosa's death. 'That was long ago, Signora,' he said, 'and anyway, I have some good news to cheer you up. My wife, Verena, is expecting a child.'

The old crone lifted her face.

'A child, Signor Mollini?'

'Yes. In the spring.'

Signora Verri's eyes were wet. To her, a new child was still a miracle of God.

'God bless the child, Sir.'

'Yes. He will be blessed, I'm sure. And I wanted to tell you something else. I am going to buy from the village – at a price that will keep you all in clover for many months – a little land, about twelve hectares north of my forest. And on this land, do you know what I'm going to make?'

'No, Signor.'

'A child's garden.'

'Ah. A child's garden?'

'Yes. It will be full of wonders. There will be peacocks and guinea fowl and rabbits and doves and goldfish and little houses in the trees and an aviary and a secret cave and hundreds of thousands of flowers.'

Signora Verri went to the door of her house and called her sons. There were three of them. Their handshakes were hard and their teeth yellowed from pipe tobacco. They demanded at once to know what price Mollini would pay for the land, explaining that a loss of twelve hectares would mean a reduction in livestock.

'A fair price,' said Mollini. 'What's more, I will buy all the livestock you have to slaughter and put the carcasses in my ice house till my son is born, and then there will be a huge feast and everyone in the village will be invited.'

He got away as quickly as he could. He looked back and saw the men of the village standing about in little groups, talking anxiously. But he wasn't worried. They'd get used to the idea of the loss of their pasture just as they'd got used to getting their water supply from containers and not from the river. They know, he told himself, that the only thing, apart from their children, which brings honour into their miserable lives is my fame. People of this calibre will sacrifice a lot to keep their dignity.

He was able to tell Pappavincente that the fencing of the land could begin straight away. 'No, Master,' said Pappavincente, 'the ground is much too hard. We shall have to wait till the frosts are over.'

Mollini agreed reluctantly. It was a very cold winter. Parts of the lake were frozen. Irritatingly, quite a few of the evergreens in the garden had died and the camellias were showing signs of winter damage. All of these would have to be torn out and replaced.

Mollini walked in the forest with his wife and showed her which ways the paths would go. They would zig-zag and cross each other, he explained. Then, little Pietro would be able to play games of tracking and hide-and-seek.

Although she tried not to show it, it saddened Verena that she was going to have to call her son Pietro. She liked the name Giuseppe, which was her father's name. But she was relieved to be pregnant at last. She was thirty-nine. Mollini had been nagging her for four years, ever since their first passionate year of love was over, to conceive. She'd tried very hard. She'd pampered herself with mounds of nutritious food. She'd even turned down an engagement to sing *Lucia di Lammermoor* in London, in order to follow Mollini to Vienna, so that he could make love to her at the right time of the month. She'd begun to fear that she would never conceive and she thought that if she didn't, it was possible that Mollini would leave her. My love is unquenchable, his is not, she told herself.

When her breasts began to swell and the time for her period had passed, she sent for the doctor. It was the same doctor who had given Mollini his enema and seen the slime in his bowel. He rolled up his sleeves. He inserted two icy fingers into Verena's vagina and pressed on her belly with the palm of the other hand. 'Well,' he said at last, as he disinfected his hands, 'your husband's wish has been granted.'

She decked herself in fussy, voluptuous gowns. Her bosom became gargantuan and she liked to show it off with lace frills and little cheeky ribbons. She didn't mind that she was getting ridiculously fat. She revelled in it. And Mollini too, from the moment he knew she was expecting his child, seemed to fall in love with her all over again. Even in public, he often couldn't refrain from fondling her breasts and whispering deliciously dirty suggestions in her ear. She giggled and screeched. She was delirious with happiness.

Several rooms in the Villa Mollini were being prepared for the baby. Nurses were interviewed and two engaged for the end of April. In March, the weather grew warmer. The fencing off of the twelve hectares was completed. Nine bullocks were slaughtered and stored in the ice house. In the forest, trees were felled to make way for the paths, wire for the aviary was ordered from Florence and a million bulbs came by cart from Holland.

Then, on the night of April 1st, a cold, relentless wind began to blow from the north. This wind terrified Verena. She liked Nature to be quiet. She put her head under her coverlet and encircled her unborn baby with her hands. An hour later, her waters broke.

The midwife came stumbling through the wind, holding her shawl round her chin. In the Villa Mollini, all the lamps were lit and the servants woken from sleep. Mollini stared at the midwife scuttling about with her towels and her basins and thought of all the births that had occurred in the village since he'd built his dam. Children were alive in the village who had never seen the river.

He went, feeling anxious, and sat on his own in his music room. Upstairs, Verena was behaving like a courageous rower, pushing with the tides. The seas were stormy. The pain tore at Verena's body and the wind tore at the garden, disturbing its order.

At dawn, the baby was born. It was a boy. It weighed less than two kilogrammes. Its first cry was feeble because, despite its magnificent parentage, its lungs were not properly formed. It gasped and gasped, like a little slithery eel, for air, and died within two hours.

Verena screamed till she was sick. The wind, blowing in the direction of the village, carried her screams to the ears of the villagers as the women made coffee and the men put on their working clothes.

It was strange. A few days after the baby died, Mollini sent for Pappavincente to tell him to redesign the child's garden, and then he changed his mind. Although there was now no son to inhabit the garden, Mollini realised that he still wanted it made, exactly as he'd planned it.

'Master,' said Pappavincente, 'you will never bear to walk in it.'

'Then someone else will.'

'Who, Sir?'

'We shall see.'

Verena, huge in the bed, her breasts full of milk, announced: 'I never want to sing again. I'm going to cancel all my contracts.'

In May, Mollini left for Paris, where he was to sing Lensky in *Eugene Onegin*. Before leaving, he looked at his fat wife. She nourished herself, he decided, her own greedy flesh, not the baby's. She was still ridiculously gross and the baby, his poor little Pietro, was a tiny, sickly fish.

Verena didn't want Mollini to go to Paris. 'This world,' she said, 'this world we inhabit of roles and costumes and competition and money isn't worth a thing.' And she held Mollini so tightly to her that he felt himself suffocating. For the first time since he met her, he longed to be away from her, miles and miles away.

On the morning of his departure, Pappavincente came to see Mollini. He told him that wire for the aviary had arrived and asked him whether he should employ builders to start work on it. 'Of course,' said Mollini, 'of course.'

As the summer was coming, Mollini had decided to rent a house rather than an apartment in Paris. It wasn't far from the Bois de Boulogne. It had a pretty courtyard with a fountain.

In this house, a long way from Verena, he felt his sadness begin to ebb and his energy return. He gave a party on a warm June evening. A string quartet played Mozart. Sitting by his fountain, he saw bats circling over the city and remembered Rosa. He shuddered. He took the white wrist of his young co-star, Clara Buig, and held it to his lips. I will amuse myself, he decided, by making love to Clara.

La Buig was twenty-two. She was French. Paris

thought her enchanting. Her career was at its beginning. She wasn't known outside her country yet, but to be singing Tatiana to Mollini's Lensky would soon ensure her international status.

When Mollini's party was over, La Buig stayed behind. Mollini undressed her tenderly, as he would have undressed a child. She was slim and pale. 'Do you like gardens, Clara?' he asked.

Mollini was now forty-eight. Clara Buig was young enough to be his daughter. When he touched her, her eyes watched him gravely.

The next morning, he woke alone. He sent a servant with a note inviting Clara to lunch. But Mademoiselle Buig was not at home, she was working with her voice coach. Mollini went early to the Opéra. When La Buig arrived, she was wearing a pale lemon-coloured dress. She moved very gracefully, Mollini noted, like a dancer.

After the rehearsal, he invited her to supper. They would dine in the Bois after going for a stroll under the chestnut trees. But she refused. She was very tired, she said. To sing well, she needed a lot of rest.

Mollini went back to his house and sat by his fountain. He loved Paris. No other city satisfied the eye so agreeably. I shall stay here till autumn, he decided. It's so hot in Tuscany in the summer and here, it's cool. But he knew that if he stayed till autumn, Verena would arrive, with her trunks full of dresses and jewellery and her fan collection and her maids and her boxes of sweets. The thought of this arrival dismayed him. Hastily, he sat down and wrote to his wife. He informed her that there was a typhoid epidemic in Paris. 'I implore you, do not come near the city,' he wrote. 'For my sake, my love.'

And every time he saw Clara Buig, her sweet neck, her shy smile, her expressive hands, it was as if he was seeing a corner of his garden that he'd never noticed, never expected to be there, but which, given his care and his talents, would one day be the most beautiful place of all. As the days passed, he became more and more convinced that Clara Buig could not be absent from his future.

He waited. He had to wait patiently. His invitations to supper were, night after night, refused. 'Why?' he asked eventually. 'Why, Clara?'

She took his hand, noticing as she did so that several of his nails were bitten. 'The night of your party, I was so excited,' she said, 'so flattered. I just let myself go. I couldn't help it.'

'And was that wrong, my adorable Clara?'

'Oh yes. But I won't let it happen again.'

So, only on stage did she look at him adoringly. Outside the Opéra, she refused ever to be alone with him.

Verena wrote to him almost every day. Her fortieth birthday was approaching. She was depressed. She begged Mollini to let her know the moment the typhoid epidemic was over so that she could come to Paris and be with him. She told him that the loss of their child had only deepened her love for him.

What she didn't say in her letters, because at first she didn't notice it, was that since the second week of April no rain had fallen and that the level of the lake was going down fast as the villagers pumped out more and more water for their potato crop, for their vines, for their thirsty animals.

Pappavincente was worried about all the new shrubs he'd planted in the child's garden. Water containers were driven through the new paths in the forest. He and the other gardeners spent two hours every evening going round with watering cans.

One evening, Pappavincente took a walk up the valley. He saw that the river was dangerously low and he remembered with dread the terrible drought of 1856, when all the villages along the valley began desperately trying to sink new wells and when his grandmother had wondered aloud whether Pappavincente's existence wasn't to blame for all the anxiety and suffering.

As he walked back towards the lake, he saw La Dusa standing by it, holding a parasol. He bowed to her. She was dressed in grey satin with a high lace collar and, with her feet tucked into red shoes, Pappavincente thought she looked like a fat pigeon. Her once beautiful eyes were now just two dark pleats in the flesh of her face.

'I'm so sorry, Signora,' said Pappavincente, 'about the baby . . .'

'Yes,' said La Dusa and waddled away up the path to the forest, carrying her weight, as she carried her sorrow, awkwardly.

The forest was cool. A hundred times, Verena had rehearsed in her mind the day when she would push the ornate baby carriage under the magnificent fans of oak and beech and watch the dappling of sunlight on her son, Giuseppe. Now, she was there alone. And it was her birthday. She stopped and folded her parasol and examined her hands for signs of age. Mollini's wedding ring was wedged so tightly onto her finger, she was unable, these days, to take it off. 'Look at these fat hands!' she said aloud and recalled with a strange kind of fascination the beautifully drawn thin hand pointing downwards to the hospital morgue.

She'd intended to visit the child's garden. Mollini had refused to discuss with her his decision to carry on with the project and the thought of this garden being designed and planted for someone who would never see it filled her with sadness. She found, as she neared it and caught sight of the half-completed aviary that she really didn't want to go there, and anyway she was out of breath.

She returned to the house. On the first terrace she noticed that the drains were stinking again. The smell was disgusting, but she lingered near it for a moment. It reminded her of happier times.

On the opening night of *Eugene Onegin*, La Dusa arrived, uninvited, in Paris.

Mollini's house was filled with servants preparing for a party. Lanterns had been lit all round the courtyard and tables set up near the fountain.

Mollini wasn't there. La Dusa dressed herself in a white gown and put feathers in her hair. She didn't go to the Opéra, but sat in the cool garden sipping champagne and questioning the servants about the typhoid epidemic. 'What typhoid epidemic?' they inquired politely.

When Mollini returned, Clara Buig was with him, holding on to his arm. La Dusa looked at them. Mollini had grown a beard, put on weight. He looked like an English king. When he saw his wife, he bowed – just as Pappavincente had bowed to her beside the lake – and led Clara Buig forward and introduced her formally. La Dusa didn't get up. She ignored Clara's outstretched hand, but reached up and pulled Mollini towards her, so that he stumbled and fell into her lap. She bit his ear. 'If you lie to me again, Antonio, I shall kill you,' she said.

Two weeks later, they returned together to the Villa Mollini. On the journey, Mollini feigned illness, a return of the pain in his bowel. And it was true, he was suffering. He was now madly, dementedly, obsessively in love with Clara Buig. He couldn't look at his wife, let alone touch her. All he could remember was the one beautiful night when Clara had let him love her, a night he had so carefully planned to repeat by giving a party in her honour.

He couldn't close his eyes without dreaming of Clara. Thoughts of her never left his mind. By the time he arrived at the Villa, he felt so troubled he had to sit down and write to her straight away and in the letter he found that he was telling her that he loved her more than he'd ever loved anyone, that his love for La Dusa had been pale in comparison. *Pale?* As he wrote this word, he couldn't help remembering certain nights, certain delectable afternoons he'd spent with Verena, but of course these had been long ago and she'd been beautiful then. And things pass, he said to himself. We move. The horizon changes. We turn a corner and a new sight greets us. This is how it has to be.

And to reassure himself, he went out into the garden. He was shocked at what he saw. The earth was parched. The smell near the house was terrible. Everywhere, as he strolled from path to path, from terrace to terrace, there were gaps in the borders and beds where plants had withered. The fountains had been turned off. The water in the fountain pools was bright green and foul-smelling. Mollini stood still and stared up at the sky. It was a deep, relentless blue. The sun on his face was fierce and all he could hear and feel was the buzzing and shimmering of the heat.

At that moment, he remembered the nine bullock carcasses. His stomach turned. Sorrow for his little dead child compounded his sickness. He sat down on a stone seat and put his head in his hands. The salt sweat from his brow stung his eyes.

He prayed the nausea would pass. It seemed like the nausea of death, when the appetite for the world drains, leaving the mind filled with loathing.

To soothe himself, he thought of his music. 'Mollini's voice is not simply a voice,' a Paris critic had declared, 'it is an instrument. I have never before heard such an astonishing sound come out of a man.' And the sickness did, after a while, begin to pass. So Mollini stood up. Instead of returning to the house – to Verena's tears and entreaties which only repelled him and were utterly in vain – he walked on down to the lake. It was no longer blue, but brownish and full of silt. He skirted it and went up into the forest. Here, it was cool. In the shade of the big trees, nettles and sweet briars were green.

He followed one of the winding paths. He began to feel better. If only, he thought, I could stroll here with Clara, with her little hand tucked into my arm.

As he neared the child's garden, he feared that all the new bushes and hedges planted in the spring would have died, but the moment he left the forest and came out again into the sunlight, he saw that everything here was living and healthy, that already roses were climbing up the trellises and that purple and white clematis were growing strongly up the sides of the aviary.

Mollini smiled. It was a smile of gratitude and a smile of hope renewed. As he looked at the faithful work of Pappavincente and the other gardeners, he knew why he had made them go on with the child's garden: he would give it to Clara.

In August, Mollini told Pappavincente that water to the village would have to be rationed. The ration was so meagre and insufficient that the young men led nightly raiding parties to the lake, carrying buckets and churns, but the water itself was becoming soupy and brackish and the villagers and their animals developed intestinal illnesses.

Then, the widow Verri died. Mollini attended the funeral. He sensed, for the first time, that his presence among the villagers no longer filled them with pride. As he held out his hand for them to shake, they let their fingers touch his, but wouldn't hold his hand in a firm grip. To cheer them up and win back their reverence, he invited them to come and see the child's garden and to drink wine with him on the site of the summer house he was planning to build there.

So they came one morning and stood about awkwardly. The garden was beautiful, lush and healthy. They touched the flowers. The scent of them was extraordinary. They'd forgotten how superb the world could seem. They drank the dry white wine, bottle after bottle, and staggered home in mid-afternoon to dream muddled dreams. Before they left, Mollini had embraced the men and kissed the women on the lips. 'I made them happy,' he told Verena.

Verena didn't move out of her room these days. She sat up in her bed and fed her sorrow with sweet wine and chocolate. Her feet began to swell and the doctor was called. Verena burst into tears. 'I know what would cure me,' she sobbed, 'if Antonio would only take me in his arms . . .' The doctor went away, disgusted.

'My wife is suffering,' Mollini wrote to Clara, 'and I cannot help but feel sorry for her. But her suffering is nothing to my own: I'm in love with a woman I cannot marry.'

In September, Mollini left for Vienna. He was to take on his most demanding and difficult role, in Verdi's *Otello*. He had signed the contract on one condition, that the part of Desdemona be given to Clara Buig. And in Vienna at last Clara became Mollini's mistress. She had been so moved, she said, by his letters, she knew she could no longer resist.

He was in heaven. La Buig wasn't a sensual woman like La Dusa. There were moments, even, when her grave face beneath his reminded Mollini of Rosa's face, long, long ago. 'You give our love nobility and dignity,' he told Clara, 'you turn the past into the future.'

He was determined, now, that there would be a future with Clara. He wrote to Pappavincente with new designs for the summer house. It would no longer be a summer house: it would have a sumptuous bedroom and bathroom and fires in all the rooms. It would be Clara's residence.

As rumours of the love affair of Antonio Mollini and the 23-year-old Clara Buig spread in whispers round the tea-rooms and the musical salons of Vienna, it began at last to rain in Tuscany. It rained for seventeen days and nights. The villagers came out of their hovels and stuck their tongues out and let the sweet rain trickle down their throats. Verena got out of bed, threw a shawl round her shoulders and walked out in the downpour to the lake side. The water had risen by several feet. Verena walked into the water, wearing her pink satin slippers. The slippers stuck in the mud, so she waded on without them, feeling her petticoats and her skirt become heavy.

She lay on her back. She expected to sink straight away, but her large body was buoyant and she found that she was floating. She stared at the grey sky and thought how astonishingly full of colour her life had been. It took her three hours to die. On the brink of death, it seemed to La Dusa that the grey cloud moved away and that the hot sun was shining on her round face. And for a second, she imagined the autumn to come and the wonderful vibrant reds and umbers of the leaves.

By the time the winter came, Clara's house was finished. Mollini, however, didn't bother to have the fires lit.

'Clara will live with me in the Villa Mollini,' he told

Pappavincente, so the shutters were closed and the place locked.

When Clara Buig at last arrived at the Villa Mollini, however, and was led by a maid to the very room La Dusa had occupied, she refused to sleep there. The house, in fact, gave her the creeps, she said. She couldn't possibly spend a night in it.

Mollini wrapped her in her velvet coat and walked with her, arm in arm, through the garden, round the lake and up into the forest. The great trees were silent. Winter had begun to bite early this year.

The pleasure Mollini took from seeing Clara's little gloved hand on his arm was acute, too precious and fleeting to mention. They walked on in silence, descending at last down the intricate paths of the child's garden to Clara's house. Golden pheasants in the aviary squawked and pecked at the wire as they passed.

Mollini opened the shutters of the house and got on his knees and lit a fire in one of the grates.

Clara walked on her own from room to room and then went outside again and walked all round the house. It was nicely set in the child's garden, surrounded by stone terraces and ornate balustrading and small cypresses. At the back of it, however, about forty yards away, Clara could see an ugly post-and-rails fence and beyond this a boring slope of empty pastureland.

'What is that?' she asked Mollini.

Mollini had followed her outside and now looked to where she was pointing.

'Common land,' said Mollini. 'The village people use it to graze their cattle.'

La Buig sniffed. Then she turned her stern child's face towards Mollini and said: 'You know what I would like to see there instead of that?'

'No, my love.'

'An English lawn. This whole garden is nothing but steps and piazzas and gazebos and mazes and borders and beds. If I'm going to live here, I really want a lawn.'

Mollini sent for Pappavincente. One of his sons arrived

instead and told him that Pappavincente was ill and couldn't come.

Mollini went at once to the village, not to tell the people that he was going to take away the rest of their pasture for Clara's lawn, but to see the old man and take him some of the strong red wine he knew he liked to drink.

'We believe he's dying,' said Signora Pappavincente. She was holding a rag to her nose, and when Mollini went into the room where Pappavincente lay, it seemed to him that the odour of death was indeed very strong.

'Listen, old friend,' he whispered to Pappavincente, 'remember all that you've achieved here. Dwell on that. Feel proud of it. You've made the most beautiful garden in Tuscany, perhaps the most beautiful garden in all Italy. And it's not finished yet. It lives on. It changes and grows. It will last for ever.'

Pappavincente's head rolled on the pillow and he turned his staring, angry eyes on Mollini. 'I have sinned, Master,' he said.

He died that night. Mollini wanted him buried in the garden, but the old man's family were stubborn and wouldn't allow it.

Mollini explained to Clara that the whole village would be in mourning for a while and that it would be impossible, just at the moment, to mention the land he was going to take for her lawn.

'I understand,' said Clara, 'but you will tell them in the spring?'

'Yes. In the spring.'

'Because I want to push my baby's bassinet on the lawn. Like an English duchess. You see?'

'Your baby's bassinet, Clara?'

'Yes, Antonio. I'm going to have your child.'

Mollini took Clara's serious little face in his hands and covered it with kisses. Three weeks later, he married her. Once again, the cream of the opera world was invited to the Villa Mollini. Among the cream was an extraordinarily beautiful English soprano called Marion Shepherd. Marion Shepherd told Mollini that she thought his garden was as unbelievable as his voice and smiled such a dazzling smile that Mollini was forced to reach out and caress her mouth with his finger.

On the wedding night, Clara Buig was very restless. The baby inside her, little Pietro, as Mollini called him, kept kicking her and her head seemed to be full of strange visions and fears.

The dawn was icy cold, but as soon as the sky was light, Clara got up and dressed herself and went out into the garden. She didn't wake Mollini. He lay snoring on his back with his legs apart.

She walked towards the Villa Mollini itself, which seemed to beckon her. On the way, she came across an old stone well with delicate arching ironwork that she'd never noticed before. I expect it's just ornamental, she thought, like everything else in this garden. But she was curious about it, so she walked to the edge of it and peered in. Much to her surprise, she found that she was looking down into darkness.